THE DEMON GUNNER

THE DARKNESS GROWS WITHIN

ERIC BOWDEN

THE DEMON GUNNER: THE DARKNESS GROWS WITHIN

Published by Park City Publishing
Book Design by Lauren Nadler
Cover Illustration by Andrea Tentori Montalto
Cover Design by Lauren Nadler

The Demon Gunner: The Darkness Grows Within is a work of fiction.
ISBN: 978-1-7350749-6-2 Paperback

Printed in the USA

To my incredible parents,
you heard the story first.
Thank you for cheering me on to the finish line.

THE DARKNESS GROWS WITHIN

TABLE OF CONTENTS

PART ONE
THE DESERT

CHAPTER ONE

ROSE & THORN

The sun fell toward the veiled horizon, and the Darkness grew closer. A lone Demon Gunner named Wade sat atop a decaying horse with piercing blue eyes of fire. Its hollow body was draped in tattered, gray muslin, and smoke billowed from its nostrils, quickly being blown away by the prevailing wind. Fine particles of sand ripped across the Demon Gunner's scarred face, causing him to pull up his dusty kerchief onto his nose.

Shadowed by the brim of his leather hat, Wade's gaze fixed on a rock formation in the distance. It would provide shelter for the night, *if* he could get to it, but he could feel the Darkness growing stronger with each passing second.

There was no more time to waste.

Wade dug his heels into the ribs of the horse and yelled, "Get on, Quicksilver!"

The horse whinnied and broke out into a full gallop, bolting across the arid landscape, while the Veil of Darkness formed around him. Suddenly, the temperature dropped, raising goosebumps on his arms.

The arch-like formation grew larger as they approached, but they *weren't* moving fast enough. The Veil was getting so thick now that he could only barely make out the silhouette of his destination.

Wade shot nervous looks to either side of him, as the familiar sounds of the Demons that roamed in the Darkness echoed in his ears. He heard devilish laughs, ear-piercing screeches, labored groans, and cries for help, but he ignored them all, digging his heels in deeper and prodding the horse to run faster. The thick, metal chains that wrapped around his forearms clanged together as he rode, and on his waist, large revolvers gilded in silver and gold sat in leather holsters. They constantly bounced against his legs, waiting to rid Rhodahn of the monsters that lurked in the shadows.

Come on, Wade thought to himself, *we're almost there.*

The horse was flying now, hooves colliding with dirt, sand, and bones as it ebbed closer to the rock formation. Wade looked past it and saw that the sun had now fully dipped below the horizon. Then the Blood Moon appeared, casting a crimson hue over the land and signaling the true beginning of the Consumption.

A cave became visible within the formation–his home for the night–and the gaping entrance grew wider as they neared, like a mouth opening to scream. But suddenly, something tackled the Demon Gunner off his horse. He tumbled across the dirt, rolling and flipping over himself until he finally skidded to a halt. Without hesitation, he drew both revolvers, revealing a raised *R* on the left one and a *T* on the right one, etched into the glistening metal. Then the chains on his forearms magnetically snapped to the grips of the weapons, preventing them from being ripped from his hands.

Wade now saw what had thrown him from his horse: a Demon that was charging forward with hate and hunger in its glowing green eyes. It had a sleek, black body and moved on four pointed, slender limbs, which it used to dig into the dirt and propel itself across the ground as if it were flying. Its wide mouth held hundreds of jagged and razor-sharp teeth that chomped at him, patiently waiting to sink into the Demon Gunner's soft flesh.

Wade knew them as the hellspawn they were…

Bone Eaters.

The Demon, with its mouth hung open and black drool dripping from it, jumped forward toward Wade. A quick shot rang out, striking the Bone Eater right between the eyes. In a flash of dark green blood and fire, its head exploded, lighting up the desert. As its body crashed into the hardpack, more Bone Eaters became visible behind it, crawling out from the dirt. They were now racing toward him, trampling over each other, all trying to be the first one to get to him. But Wade wasn't going to wait to die.

He brought his fingers to his dry lips and whistled hard, calling his horse back to him, and in the distance, the great steed started to run in his direction. In a lightning-fast barrage, Wade unloaded eleven shots into the Bone Eaters in an attempt to thin out the horde, blowing their heads clean off, but just as they fell, *more* appeared, as if they were duplicating before his very eyes.

Bullets wouldn't cut it this time; he needed more *firepower.*

Wade casually reloaded his iron and dropped the revolvers back into their holsters before facing the approaching Demons once more. He drew in a deep breath, and as he exhaled, two small, blue flames ignited within his palms. He raised his hands, and just as the Bone Eaters leaped into the air to strike him down, he unleashed a great wave of fire upon them.

The Bone Eaters ignited instantly, like dry brush in a parched field. They screamed into the night, running madly and clawing at their melting flesh, which dripped from their bones like wax from a dying candle. The ones who hadn't been caught in the flames bolted at the sight of them, sprinting away from their burning brethren in fear. Wade used this distraction to mount Quicksilver who had finally appeared next to him. He whipped the reins twice and took off once more toward the cave. Once he was mere feet from it, Wade jumped from the horse, unlatched one of his saddlebags, and swiftly led his horse to the mouth of the cave.

After entering, Wade tossed the leather saddlebag onto the ground and opened it up, revealing a set of candles, a small water sack, and a rolled sleeping pad. He quickly set the candles up at the cave's entrance before lighting each one with his index finger and thumb, creating a small barrier of fire. Next, he uncorked the water sack and poured out dark green blood *in front* of the candles–a ritual he had grown all too accustomed to.

It would have to do for the night, it would have to... he thought to himself.

In the distance, Wade could faintly make out the Bone Eaters who had collapsed in the dirt, their bodies starting to smolder.

POP!
POP!
POP!
POP!

One by one, they exploded like firecrackers, spraying blood into the air like mini geysers. None of the other remaining Bone Eaters dared to come near him now, and they took off further into the Darkness–as far from the Demon Gunner as their legs would take them.

Wade then turned away from the scene in the desert and retreated past his undead horse deeper into the cave. A ring of ash covered, charred rocks sat before him, and it appeared that someone–perhaps long ago–had constructed a rough-hewn fire. Wade grabbed a fascine off the side of his horse and tossed the bundle into the center of the ring. He crouched down next to it and presented a small flame from his index finger that immediately ignited the dry tinder. The fire slowly began to grow, eventually burning brightly, which illuminated his tired face in the dark.

Lastly, Wade grabbed his rolled sleeping pad–which was nothing more than cotton and down stuffed in a burlap sack. He laid it flat across the redstone and smoothed it out with opened palms before finally sitting down and leaning against the wall of rock behind him.

Ahhhhh.

He took a deep breath and closed his eyes, basking in the unexpected comfort of the cave. It no doubt beat the tent he had been sleeping in the past few weeks while on the road.

Wade then began to undress himself, pulling off his thick leather boots which immediately sent a ghastly odor into the air that pinned his ears back. He rotated them upside down and dumped out the sand that resided in the toe box before tossing them aside. It had been *weeks* since he had last bathed, and he didn't expect to find a watering hole this far out in the desert anytime soon, so he surmised it would be a few more weeks before he could properly clean himself. Besides, there wasn't anyone around to complain–at least it didn't seem like Quicksilver minded all that much.

Next, he started to unbutton his shirt–his weathered and calloused hands plucking the buttons off one by one until he revealed a muscular body littered with scars, particularly a large one across his midsection. A gnarly gash now sat on his elbow where he had taken the fall from earlier, but it looked as if it were already starting to heal with the edges coming together–*slowly* at that.

Wade rummaged around in his saddle bag until he found *another* water sack and a small pouch of dried jerky. He dug his dirt-covered fingers into the pouch, pulled out a piece, and tossed it in his mouth. He followed this with a small sip of water, making sure to savor it before placing the sack back down on the cool stone.

The fire before him crackled and popped, and for the first time today, he felt warm. He almost fell asleep right then and there, but he still had one final task to complete before he could rest–arguably the *most* important task.

Wade unsheathed his left gun *Rose*, and flipped open the cylinder. He shook out the cartridges and began to swab the inside of the barrel and cylinder with a cloth and stick. He pulled out the extractor rod and cocked the hammer back before cleaning behind both. Finally, Wade rubbed lubricant in every nook and cranny he could find. Once he had replaced the rod and reloaded the cylinder, he flipped it close and began to do the same with his right revolver *Thorn*.

The cleaning of the weapons–his tools–was an essential task for any Gunner, and was something Wade had been taught many, *many* years ago when he was trained in the way of the gun. Break the gun, clean the gun, and build the gun, that was how it went after every shooting lesson. Wade would do this over and over again until he wasn't even thinking about it, just relying on muscle memory to get the job over with. His hands would move in a precise and fluid rhythm, going through the motions, much as he was now doing in this cave with his eyes closed. He thought back to the time when he had been tasked to do this while wearing a blindfold or face expulsion from the School, causing him to chuckle.

Back then, he hated it, but now there seemed to be something therapeutic about the process. It slowed the world down—made it feel smaller and *safer.* While he cleaned, he was only thinking about one thing: the iron in his hands and nothing else—especially not the dark, Demon-infested world that sat outside, just mere feet away from him.

Wade had been taught to respect his weapons—to love and care for them, as they would reciprocate that affection by never malfunctioning and always being there when he needed them to save his life. At least that was what he was told by his master, and he still lived by those words today, never doubting them for a second.

Now that the second gun was cleaned, it was time to reload them, as a true Gunner never goes to bed without both weapons ready to be fired. Especially being this deep into the Veil, Wade never knew when he would be woken up by a Nightwalker or Bone Eater creeping into his home, needing its brains painted on a wall. He loaded the cylinders with a total of twelve fresh cartridges before laying both guns down next to him on the mat. They were prepared for the day ahead, and he was ready for rest... but he almost forgot.

He still had one more thing to do.

"Wade…" the faint voice of a woman called out from outside the cave. "Come, Wade. Come home to me."

He recognized it instantly as the woman he once loved. But it wasn't her; Jess wasn't really out there, and she would *never* be out there. Only death waited for him with open arms, standing alone in the Darkness.

Instead of course, he knew it to be a trap, orchestrated by the Soul Stealers. They had the power to see inside one's mind, locate deep seeded memories, and use them against their victim, driving them mad. Wade didn't know how they were capable of such a feat, but then again, *nothing* made sense out here. Regardless, he wouldn't stand for it any longer. Wade fished around in his saddlebag for two tiny bundles of wax and cloth stuck together, no bigger than a thumb tack, which he placed into his ears to block out the singing of the Demons. Finally, he laid his head down on the sleeping pad, ready for rest.

But Wade would only rest as much as any Demon Gunner truly could, and in his slumber, he would dream of something that no longer existed–a place he once knew before the light of the world had gone out, before the Darkness grew at night.

CHAPTER TWO
THE DANCING DEMONS

Sunlight slowly filled the cave, causing the Demon Gunner to stir and wake up. His face was pressed hard into his sleeping pad, and the fabric he laid on stuck to his face as he pulled away from it to sit up. He rubbed his eyes with balled fists while yawning before scanning the interior of the cave, wall to wall.

Thankfully, the candles at the entrance had done their job, warding off the Demons that lurked in the Darkness. The ritual of the candles was something he had learned on his journey through the Veil, and thankfully, the night had turned out to be uneventful.

Although the fire that sat before him was now nothing more than a dying flame, he still felt warmer than he had the night before, indicating that the Consumption had finally receded.

Wade removed his makeshift earplugs and stretched his arms above his head. Cracks and pops echoed in the cave, which were promptly followed by a deep growl from his stomach. His body still ached from the blow he sustained the night before, and his mouth felt incredibly dry. He rolled up his sleeve and inspected the gash on his elbow once more and saw that it had mostly healed.

Thank Nor.

And after a few pieces of jerky and a hearty sip of water, he was ready to begin the teardown process to leave the cave and carry on his quest.

As he threw on his long-sleeve button-down shirt and thick leather jacket again, he felt the map he had tucked into his chest pocket poking through the fabric. He pulled it out, rolled it across the stone floor, and inspected it.

Within the expansive map of Rhodahn, a course for a small town was charted on it, and he knew he wasn't far from it now. Once he reached it, it would be a straight shot West to the Forest of Delfar, which would hopefully provide more answers as to where the light went. He had been following this course for months, and all signs indicated that he was going in the right direction. The Demons that lurked in the Darkness were growing stronger, and the singing of the Soul Stealers was getting louder and more powerful.

Wade had gotten lucky last night, and he knew he could not make the same mistake of setting up camp that late again.

Next to the Demon Gunner sat his revolvers that rested on a piece of cloth, and he tossed them into his rawhide holsters before making his way over to the candles that were positioned at the mouth of the cave. They were still burning–as they would *forever*–and he blew them out and rolled them up in his sleeping pad once more.

He grabbed Quicksilver by the reins and led her out of the cave and into the open air, which was as cool and crisp as it always was while the sun sat high in the sky, barely emitting any warmth. One would expect oppressive heat in a desert like this, but nothing was warm since the light of the world had gone out, not even Wade himself.

Wade climbed onto Quicksilver, whipped the reins twice, and set off across the arid, desolate land. The undead horse he rode upon could travel incredibly fast, never tire, and carry heavy loads that other horses wouldn't be able to. She was the only reason why Wade was even still alive. They had been able to outrun most of the Demons that chased them through the Darkness, but if last night was any indication of what was to come, that soon wouldn't be the case. The Demons were getting stronger, faster... *smarter.*

The Demon Gunner had been traveling for many months, *always* alone, and had rarely seen a soul. In his solitude, he thought about the world he left behind, before he journeyed into the Darkness, and what he might find at the source of the Consumption.

A Demon King? Nor himself? Nothing?

Wade knew not what, but it couldn't be nothing. *Something* had to be there, as the Consumption grew in the same direction every night, like waves crashing on a beach. It had a source, and therefore, it could be stopped—turned off, reversed, whatever it took to bring the light back—to bring the *world* back.

He didn't know why he continued this quest, but he knew he had to, not for himself, and perhaps not even for those who were slain... but perhaps to save a world that never knew him—or would *ever* know him, even if he did find what he was looking for. Nor put him on Rhodahn for a reason, and he wouldn't waste his life as long as he was still breathing.

A small pump house appeared in the distance, pulling Wade from his thoughts. He steered Quicksilver in the direction of it before digging into her ribs with his heels, sending the pair ripping across the desert toward it.

After a few short minutes, they were upon it, and Wade pulled back on the reins and brought the horse to a screeching halt right next to a small metal pump that jutted out from the ground. He slid off the side of the horse and retrieved the clean water sack from his pack before placing it below the spigot. He began to crank the handle, sending cold water from a well below his feet out into the sack. Once it was full, he placed his lips into the stream and drank a healthy amount before washing the dust off his face with a cupped hand.

Now that he was clean, he pulled his face from the water and dried it with his kerchief before looking back out into the desert. The town wasn't visible yet, but he knew he wasn't far from it now. With his water sack replenished, it was time to set off again. And just as he did, something caught his eye: a skeleton half-buried in the sand. Its broken jaw hung open, swaying with the wind, and atop its head sat a wide-brimmed hat. The Demon Gunner stared at it, then, he rode on.

• • •

The rest of the ride was uneventful, much as it *always* was when the Darkness wasn't present. To put it simply, it was empty, desolate, and *gray,* and the journey consisted of riding across a hard-packed desert that turned into sandy dunes and back into hardpack.

Luckily, Quicksilver made good time, taking Wade miles and miles across the arid landscape by the time the sun was nearing the horizon. He was right on schedule and would not stupidly be out in the open again as the

Darkness consumed the world.

The town he had marked on his map was now growing in size in the distance, and he continued to steer Quicksilver toward it. And once they finally approached the town square, Wade grabbed hold of the reins and pulled back as hard as he could. The horse skidded to a halt, sending dust up in front of them. Wade scanned his surroundings, inspecting the small, deserted town he now found himself in. He saw a bank, a saloon, a jail—relics of a time before the light of the world had gone out, now forgotten, ruinous, and covered in dust.

He climbed off of his horse and hitched it to a post outside the saloon. The sun had just touched the horizon, which meant that he had time for a drink, *if* he could find a bottle.

Wade unholstered Rose and Thorn from his side, hearing the engraved metal sliding across the worn leather holsters. He reached the double doors of the saloon and slowly pushed them open with the tips of the blades that jutted from the barrels of his guns. The doors creaked and dust fell from them as they swung open, revealing a dilapidated saloon with dust-covered chairs, tables, and a bar. No one had been inside in ages—no one *alive* that was, and he would need to check out the rest of the building to confirm that. He found a door next to the bar and pressed his ear against it, listening for anything groaning within.

Nothing.

He took a deep breath and kicked it open, immediately aiming his revolvers inside, only to see a small kitchen, a rocking chair, glass bottles, and tattered clothes thrown around, all covered in dust.

Empty, thank Nor.

But there was still another floor to check.

The stairs to the second floor creaked beneath his feet as he crept up them, and once he reached it, he placed his ear on the first door he came upon but heard nothing within. His hand wrapped around the brass knob of the door before twisting and pushing it open. His guns shot upward to face an empty room once again. Wade backed out and turned to the next door. He listened for sounds and *immediately* heard a faint groaning noise. His hand crept down to the knob and began to twist.

But suddenly, the door burst open, and an elderly man with glowing green eyes tackled him backward. Together, they smashed into the balcony railing and fell from the second floor, crashing hard onto a table below. The Nightwalker's face was mere inches from his own, and Wade could smell the rotten and pungent breath leaking from his mouth. Jagged and mangled teeth chomped and bit at his nose as black drool dripped from his lips and spilled onto Wade's shirt. The Nightwalker thrashed, trying to grab a delicious morsel of his flesh while Wade struggled against it, attempting to raise his revolver upward to his attacker's chin. The tip of Thorn's blade pierced the Nightwalker's skin before Wade pulled the trigger, sending a bullet through its head and out the back of it. Green blood sprayed across the room, painting the wall in it. The thrashing stopped, and the Nightwalker's body went limp.

Wade pushed it away from him, but before he could get up, more Nightwalkers emerged from the room, *diving* off the balcony toward him. Wade unleashed a barrage of shots, striking each one directly between the eyes with perfect accuracy, killing them instantly. He rolled to the side as their bodies crashed into the tables and chairs below, narrowly missing him. Wade breathed heavily, keeping his weapons raised before him, but no more came, and the dusty, deserted saloon fell silent again.

"Bastards," he muttered under his breath.

He was alone once more, and as Wade looked around at the carnage that had just unfolded, he knew it was time for a drink.

He lifted his back off the floor with a groan, spun his neck in a circle to get a few audible clicks and pops out of it, and finally stood up again. Wade made his way to the bar and rummaged through the shelves. To his dismay, most of the bottles he inspected were empty, only to be pulled out and tossed behind him, shattering across the floor next to the dead Nightwalkers.

Finally, he spotted one at the very top, unopened and untouched. Wade got up on his tiptoes and extended for it, wrapping his fingers around the cold glass. He pulled it from the shelf and popped the cork, immediately bringing his nose to it to take a long sniff. The eye-watering aroma filled his nostrils, and as he took his first sip of it, a warm hug wrapped around him. He looked back down at the whiskey bottle and admired it for a moment, remembering the memories he used to share with his friends over a drink like this.

Then, a cold sensation washed over him, and he saw through the large saloon windows that the sun was nearly hidden by the horizon. The short period of peace was gone yet again, and the Darkness would only continue to grow.

Wade took one last sip of the dark liquor before setting the bottle down and exiting the bar. He immediately saw

Quicksilver standing where he had last left her, waiting to be ridden once again. But they were done riding for the day, as they had gone as far as they could before the sun set.

Now, it was time for rest.

Wade carried the saddlebag that held his sleeping pad into the saloon and placed it on a table before kneeling down and refilling his jug of Nightwalker blood from a leaking corpse. He grabbed both items and hurried up the stairs to the first bedroom and set them down before unfurling the sleeping pad across the floor.

Next, he pulled out a small piece of cloth, dipped the tip in the Nightwalker's blood, and drew a circle on the floor around the sleeping pad. He did this over and over again until the lines of the circle were *thick*. The smell of the blood would help to hide his scent from the Demons that would soon surround the building.

While looking at the sleeping pad that lay before him, his body ached and yearned for rest, as the high winds and trek across the desert had tired him out, but there would be no rest–not yet at least. He had tasks to complete first to protect himself, then, and only then, could he potentially find sleep.

One by one, he placed the candles in a star formation around the circle of blood. As he did this, his breath turned visible, and goosebumps raised on his arms. The Darkness had consumed the town, and it wouldn't be long before the Demons would come out to play in the streets.

He needed to quickly light the candles and plug his ears before the singing picked up again. A small fire ignited from the tip of his index finger, and just as he lit the wick of the first candle, a *scream* echoed outside. But it wasn't the singing of the Soul Stealers, the moans and groans of

16

the Nightwalkers, or the screeches of the Bone Eaters, no, this was a real–unmistakably real–blood curdling *scream.*

The lone Demon Gunner couldn't remember the last time he had heard such a thing as he hadn't encountered anyone alive this deep into the Veil. At first, he thought he was hallucinating and tried to ignore it by jamming his fingers into his ears, but the screams persisted.

Wade quickly sat up and moved to the window that was covered in a rawhide, makeshift blind. His fingers pinched the edge of it, and he pulled it to the side. Immediately, he saw a woman and a young girl running through the middle of the town.

Wade did nothing, he only stood frozen in shock.

Further down the road sat an overturned carriage with a bleeding man laying next to it. Four Bone Eaters inched closer to him, drool spilling from their crooked smiles.

"Have mercy... Have m–"

The Bone Eaters lunged forward, each biting into a different part of him. He screamed in pain as they all pulled in opposite directions. The force of the attack lifted him into the air, his arms and legs fully extended outward like a star.

"Papa!" the girl cried out, clutching her mother in fear.

His stomach began to tear open, starting from the middle and growing outward. The wound gushed blood and threads of skin popped like violin strings. He was pulled further and further apart, screaming in agony, until his body *fully* ripped in two, sending blood and guts spraying across the Demons. They ran off into the shadows, each with their own piece of him, and his entrails dragged across the dirt, leaving a trail of blood behind him.

Wade drew the blind back and turned away as the

woman screamed once more.

Just stay here, he thought to himself. *Don't get in the middle of that, you fool.*

The screams grew louder, and he felt his hands reaching for his revolvers.

Stop.

But these were the first living people that he had seen in as long as he could remember. He couldn't let them die, not when he had the power to save them resting on his waist.

"Fuck…" Wade sighed as he shot up and bounded across the room.

Outside, Nightwalkers and Bone Eaters crept toward the woman and girl. The monsters shuddered and twitched, dying to get a taste of their sweet flesh. The pair held each other as they sobbed, and the mother pulled her daughter's head into her shoulder to cover her eyes.

"Don't look, Sarah, don't look," she said as she held her tightly, accepting their fate.

A Nightwalker lunged at them, mouth gaping open, and just before it reached them, a bullet tore through its face and exploded out the back of its head in a spray of bone, green blood, and fire. The woman quickly turned in shock and saw Wade standing on the porch with a smoking revolver outstretched before him.

All at once, shots began ringing out across the dusty road, dropping Nightwalkers and Bone Eaters like flies. His aim was true, and he hadn't missed a shot since he had started firing, not *once*, but he could see that the herd wasn't thinning, as more and more of them were approaching from the alleyways.

He unloaded his final shots before hearing the familiar

click that meant you were either out of ammo or fucked, usually *both*. With a flick of his wrist, he opened the cylinder, shook out the spent casings, and slid in a fresh set of bullets from his ammo pouch.

"Move!" he yelled, before he began firing again, blasting Demons backward while sending blood and guts flying in every direction.

The pair ran frantically toward Wade, but just before they got to the porch, a Bone Eater stabbed downward into the mother's calf with its pointed limb. She fell forward and yelled in agony before digging her fingernails into the dirt, attempting to resist the pull of the Demon behind her.

"Momma!" the young girl cried out as she grabbed her hand and tried to pull in the opposite direction.

A Nightwalker lunged forward and bit into her mother, tearing the flesh from the woman's leg. She screamed in pain as tears streamed down her face. Shots rang out, and Wade blasted the two monsters back, freeing her. Her body dropped into the dirt and blood gushed from her open wounds.

"Sarah, you need to go, get inside!" she cried out.

"I can't leave you!"

Wade looked down the road in the opposite direction. More Nightwalkers had begun to come out from the buildings, pouring into the town square.

"I'm bit, Sarah, you need to save yourself."

Demons ran toward them from every direction. Wade couldn't kill them all, and they would soon be overwhelmed.

"We can get you help!" the girl promised.

He had to make a choice, and without hesitating any longer, he ran down the saloon's front steps, grabbed hold of the girl, and swept her up.

"I'm sorry," Wade said as he took off.

"I love you, Sarah!"

The girl kicked and screamed as they ducked into the saloon.

"MOMMA!" she cried out.

Wade sprinted up the stairs to the second floor, carrying the girl in his arms. They burst through the first door and entered the make-shift camp he had just set up.

"LET GO OF ME!"

The Demon Gunner quickly covered her mouth, muffling her cries. He stuffed earplugs into his ears with his free hand and smothered her in green blood before aiming his pistol at the door.

Outside the thin wooden walls of the saloon, the screams of the mother were heard as she was torn apart, limb by limb, and eaten alive. Wade pressed the girl's ear into his shoulder, hoping to block out the noises.

And all at once, the screams *stopped*, the Bone Eaters screeched, and the Nightwalkers devoured her corpse. Wade sat there, listening to bones snapping and crunching, blood gushing, and ligaments and tendons being pulled apart. These noises filled his ears until the girl had finally tired herself out and went limp in Wade's arms.

That night, Wade prayed to Nor that the Demons wouldn't come upstairs–wouldn't find them sitting helplessly on the floor, waiting to be torn to shreds. His revolver hung in the air before him, aimed at the door, as the Demons feasted and danced in the streets outside, screeching endlessly into the Darkness.

DG

CHAPTER THREE

THE STRANGER'S DECISION

Sun light broke through the shutters of the room where the Demon Gunner and girl lay. Wade continued to aim Thorn at the door–a position he hadn't changed the *entire* night. The gun shook violently within his grip but never dropped.

Below him, the stranger in his arms stirred awake, only to immediately scream and push away from the unknown man who held her.

"Who are you!" she yelled, feet kicking and scraping across the floor until she slammed her back against the nearest wall. "Get away from me!"

"I'm not going to hurt you," Wade responded as he holstered his pistol and raised his hands in surrender. "You're safe now."

"Where's Momma! Where's my…" her voice trailed off as a look of realization grew on her face. "Last night, it was *real*, wasn't it?"

Wade nodded.

"My parents?" she asked with tears welling in her eyes.

"I'm sorry."

Her head dropped to her crossed arms, and she began

to sob.

Wade watched her for a moment before getting up from the floor and turning to his belongings. One by one, he gathered his candles and sleeping pad before crossing the room to the door.

When his calloused hand met the brass knob to open it, the girl looked up and said, "Where are you going?"

"Outside," he responded. "The sun's up."

"Aren't there more of them?"

"No, they should be gone now, but if they aren't, I'll make sure they are," and with that, he turned the knob and exited the room.

• • •

Wade stood on the street and inspected the horrific scene before him. The dirt road that cut the town in half was covered in a mixture of dark green and red blood, creating hints of brown where the two colors met. Bone fragments, guts, and hair littered the area, and the distinct trail of blood from her father curved behind the deserted jail and led off into the distance. Deep claw marks overlapped it.

Wade followed the trail until it led to an overturned wagon on the outskirts of the town. What was left of the girl's father lay in front of him, and he stepped over his bloody remains to inspect its contents.

His former master Ulysses used to say that within tragedy lay opportunity, and that was exactly what he found sitting before him. Rations of food, water, a repeater rifle, and a small revolver rested in a wooden crate under a canvas tarp. Wade gathered the items into his arms and made his way back toward Quicksilver, who, of course, had survived the night unscathed, as the Demons never seemed to bother her.

Can't kill what's already dead, he thought to himself.

He flipped open the leather saddlebags and began to pack in the items, but then, he stopped.

The girl.

Wade glanced over his shoulder at the saloon and remembered her sitting on the floor with her face down, *sobbing.* He brought his fingers to the bridge of his nose and scrunched his eyes in contemplation.

He could barely take care of himself, and now he was supposed to take care of another person, let alone a young girl? But in reality, who said he *had* to? Of course, he could just leave her. All he had to do was hop onto Quicksilver and *go,* ride off into the distance and leave her behind forever. No one would stop him; no one would even judge him for it—except perhaps Nor.

But if Nor was *truly* all-seeing, then he would know the treacherous road that lay ahead of the Demon Gunner. Leaving her here to starve to death could truly be better than what awaited her if she joined him on his journey. Wade would be the only one who would have to live with the guilt of leaving her behind... but that was nothing a bottle of whiskey couldn't fix.

Just then, the saloon doors creaked open.

"You shouldn't see this," Wade said without facing her.

"I need to," the girl responded. "To know that it's real— that it happened."

Wade sighed and relatched the saddlebag before turning around.

"Why the hell were you out at night anyways?" Wade asked.

"We were fleeing."

"From what?"

"I'm not sure? It felt cold, really, *really* cold."

The Consumption.

"The world became dark, as if someone had blocked out the sun. Everything looked gray, plants were dying, and there were things, horrible things. They started to attack our settlement."

"The same things you saw last night?" Wade asked. She nodded, and the Demon Gunner sighed. "That means it's still spreading."

"We thought we were running away from it, but we must've gotten turned around in a storm."

"That tracks. The storms have gotten worse out here," Wade said, looking across the town that appeared to be heavily damaged and dilapidated. "Another effect of the Darkness."

"The *Darkness?*"

"That's what I call it at least. It's where that chill you mentioned came from, it's what drifts across this land each night, and it's what took the light and the world with it."

"I don't understand?"

"Well neither do I," he responded.

Behind him, Wade could hear the soft, muffled cries of the girl as she sat on the front steps of the saloon.

Wade looked into the sky and saw that the sun was already directly overhead. He needed to get going *fast*, or tonight would be a terrible repeat of the last.

Wade grabbed the saddle of Quicksilver and hoisted himself up. He wanted to just dig his heels into the undead horse's ribs and take off. He didn't ask for this—he didn't ask for *any* of this, but as his heels lifted, the faint sobs of the lost and alone girl echoed in his ears.

She didn't ask for this either...

Wade looked up at the sky once more and pictured Nor staring down at him. It was a test, and he knew it.

Damn you.

He turned over his shoulder and said, "You have a choice. I'm not gonna to force you either way, but I'm heading West, far from this place. I don't know what lies ahead, but I know it ain't any better than this. I found the weapons and rations you packed for the trip. I can also give you what I can spare from my own, but I can't stay with you. I *need* to continue my search. You can stay here," Wade inhaled deeply and let out a long sigh, "or... you can come with me."

The crying girl pulled her face up from her wet hands and looked at Wade.

"How long do you think I'd last?" she asked.

"What?"

"If I don't come with you, be honest, how long do you think I'd last here?"

Wade thought about it for a moment before saying, "I can give you a gun and enough ammo to last an eternity, but you only got enough food to last a couple a weeks, *if* that. However, I can't promise you'd make it that long."

"So, I'm dead either way?" Wade didn't respond. "Well then, I'd rather be dead in good company."

Wade nodded and said, "Can't argue with that."

The girl composed herself once more and got off the steps. Wade reached down and held out a hand to help her up onto the back of the horse.

"What is your name?" she asked.

"Wade, Wade Russell. And yours?"

"Sarah Jane. Thank you, Wade."

Wade tipped his hat, dug into his horse, and set off once more across the desert.

CHAPTER FOUR
A PAINFUL LULLABY

Harsh desert winds tore across the rolling dunes that stretched as far as the eye could see. Wade and Sarah rode atop Quicksilver, whose deep hoofprints left an endless trail behind them.

Dust devils appeared on the horizon, and tumbleweeds blew by, flipping over and over themselves. What should've been a scorching hot landscape was instead incredibly brisk, as the sun above them provided almost no warmth, causing Wade to raise the collar of his jacket to his jaw. It was as if the Darkness had sucked any form of heat right out of the air.

As Wade continued to scan the horizon, he was constantly reminded of the sad reality that he had grown all too accustomed to. Everything around him had been consumed and was now left barren and desolate. The wonderful color that used to remind you of life in all forms was now *gone*, replaced with a stale, monochromatic gray. Wade looked down at his own arm and wondered if he too were slowly becoming the same color.

Wade's gaze shifted from the horizon and down toward the pale white arms that wrapped around his waist. He had almost forgotten she was there, and surprisingly, she even provided a small amount of warmth to his otherwise cold body.

When they first set out, Wade had given her food and water from the wagon rations. She thanked him, but since then, neither one of them had spoken another word.

What was there to talk about?

Although Wade had saved her life, he was still nothing more than a stranger. Everytime he tried speaking to her, no words came out, as if he *couldn't*. It had been so long since Wade had seen another living human in Rhodahn, and it seemed he had almost forgotten how to socialize and carry a conversation. Besides, there was nothing to talk about. Nor had brought them together, perhaps in a test of the Demon Gunner's goodwill, but besides that, they had no history and shared nothing in common.

Wade was on a mission to find the source of the Darkness and prevent it from consuming any more of his world. But now it seemed Nor had given him another task: protect the girl who rode behind him.

• • •

They had made good progress on the day, and as they continued to travel further West, chasing the setting sun, the temperature grew colder and colder. He could feel the subtle trembling and crying of the frail girl behind him. Wade pulled back on the reins and brought the horse to a halt in the middle of a barren valley.

"Would you like my jacket?" Wade asked over his shoulder.

"I'm… I'm fine," she said between chattering teeth.

Wade chuckled, released the reins, and began pulling his thick rawhide jacket off his back to give to her. Of course, she didn't refuse it, and soon after, the shaking ceased.

Surprisingly, even without the jacket, the Demon Gunner didn't find himself terribly cold. The fire within him seemed to be doing its job, and whenever he wanted to warm himself, he would stoke it by inhaling deeply with closed eyes. As he exhaled, smoke would billow from his nostrils as if he were puffing on a cigarette. Not only would this action warm himself, it would also warm the girl.

As they rode, the dunes returned to hardpack, and the trail they followed flowed into a deep wash between two rock edifices. But as they traveled down it, Wade felt a single rain droplet bounce off his wide-brimmed hat. He stopped Quicksilver and craned his head up. Immediately, they found themselves in a torrential downpour, and the wash quickly turned into a fast moving stream. They were too far down the trail to turn back, and Wade quickly kicked into the horse's ribs to get moving.

The stream rapidly became a small river, and an overwhelming amount of water began to rush past Quicksilver's legs. Wade dug hard into the horse again, picking up even *more* speed. Following the winding direction of the wash, he pulled on the reins each time it turned, flipping back and forth as the water climbed higher and higher. Wade could feel the horse's grip on the dirt loosening, and soon they would be floating if he didn't act fast.

Then, he saw it. A small ramp-like formation leading out of the wash.

"HANG ON!" Wade shouted as he yanked the reins hard to the right.

They burst out of the wash and narrowly escaped the newly formed river that violently rushed past them.

Wade and Sarah breathed heavily as the rain continued to come down, soaking their clothes. They needed to get somewhere safe and dry, *quickly*, as the sun was now setting on the horizon.

Without wasting any more time, Wade began to scan the desert for shelter, but then, he felt a light tap on his back.

"Up there," Sarah said, pointing to a rock formation in the distance.

Wade confirmed by pointing with the reins bundled in his hand, "There?" She nodded. "Good eyes."

The Demon Gunner whipped the reins twice, sending them on their way again.

• • •

As they approached the weathered formation, a deep cave revealed itself, marked by uneven and jagged walls of rock. The pair slid off the side of the horse, but before Wade could say anything, Sarah made a break for the opening, attempting to get out of the rain as quickly as possible.

"Hold it!" Wade shouted before she entered. "I gotta clear it first. Step back."

Wade strode forward and drew Rose and Thorn from the leather holsters they sat in. He raised the heavy iron into the air and carefully crept toward the opening of the cave. The inside was pitch black, like an infinite void of darkness that seemed to creep toward him the longer he stared at it, and as the Demon Gunner got closer, the air grew *colder.*

His heartbeat picked up, and his palms, firmly pressed

against the thick metal grips of the iron, began to sweat. A sound like the dull crunching of a bone echoed from the cave, causing him to stop in his tracks, but when he tried to focus on it, it was gone, replaced by silence. He carried on and entered the mouth of the cave, leaving Sarah behind.

The drumming of the rain on the rock above him now filled his ears, as if encouraging him to march onward. It was freezing inside, and his breath was visible like thick clouds of smoke. He paused, listened, and then continued further into the cave. Each one of his steps rattled the spurs of his boots, echoing deeper down into it.

Finally, the Demon Gunner stopped. He holstered Thorn, raised his hand, and snapped his fingers, causing a small blue flame to appear. The pathetic firelight barely illuminated the space, and sitting before him were *hundreds* of animal and human bones.

Plop.

Plop.

Plop.

Thick, viscous strands of green, mucus-like slime dripped from above and landed at Wade's feet. Without moving, he slowly craned his neck upward, revealing dozens of sleeping Bone Eaters attached to the ceiling by their feet. Their razor-sharp teeth remained hidden, their arms were pressed tightly to their sleek, slender chests, and their bodies were frozen and stiff–but most importantly, the menacing green glow of their eyes was absent.

The Demon Gunner immediately killed the flame and held his breath while softly pulling Thorn out from its holster. He stole backward, attempting to be as quiet as possible. One wrong move and...

Crunch.

A human skull was crushed beneath his boot and echoed loudly through the cave. A set of green eyes appeared, followed by another and another, and another. They stared at the Demon Gunner, motionless.

"Shit…"

All at once, the Bone Eaters released ear-piercing screeches before detaching from the ceiling. Wade fired his weapon as they fell, striking one between the eyes in midair and sending bone and blood out of the back of its skull. Immediately, he yelped and flinched in pain, as the sound of the Hellfire blowing out of his gun was so loud that it nearly bursted his eardrum.

"Wade!" Sarah cried out from the mouth of the cave.

"Stay back!" he yelled as he frantically backpedaled while sending out more shots.

The heads of the Bone Eaters exploded, momentarily halting their advance, but more and more appeared, climbing along the roof and walls of the cave like bats, using their sharp limbs to stab into the rock.

Wade quickly raised his weapons to fire again.

Click! Click!

He was out of ammo *and* in deep shit. Wade turned around and bolted, dumping out the casings from the revolvers and loading the empty cylinders with fresh ones. He flipped back and fired into the herd once more, thinning them out until his guns clicked empty.

As he went to reload again, a final one lunged at him, mouth agape. He thrust his iron forward and stabbed the blades of Rose and Thorn into its chest, keeping the chomping teeth from tearing his face off as he fell backward into the dirt, losing his hat in the process. He fought with all of his might, pushing the creature away from him until…

BANG!

Its head exploded, caking the Demon Gunner in green blood. Next to him, Sarah was knocked backward off her feet from the kick of the gun. She crashed into the dirt and landed flat on her back. The repeater rifle she used to shoot the monster lay a few feet away from her, covered in sand.

The Bone Eater's body went limp, and the Demon Gunner pushed it off of him and tossed it aside. Sarah gasped for air, and Wade shot off the ground and ran toward her, sliding down next to her. She was unharmed, but the air in her lungs had left her.

"You're alright, just breathe… *breathe…*" he said while holding her hand. Slowly, she seemed to regain her breath as she blinked wildly. "See? You're alright."

"Are *you* ok?" Sarah finally muttered.

"I'm fine." Wade looked over at the Demon's corpse that lay in the dirt. "Thanks for saving my skin, it won't happen again."

Wade grabbed his hat out of the muck and got to his feet.

"Give me the gun first next time, so I won't have to look for it," she said while dusting herself off.

Wade laughed and shook his head. "So you can be blown off your feet again?" A smile grew on her face as he held out a hand to help her up. "Was that the first time you've fired one of those?" She nodded. "Well then, I've got an idea for tomorrow."

"What is it?"

"Let's get our stuff inside and make a fire first. We don't want to be out here much longer."

Sarah didn't argue with that.

. . .

The sun had now set, the Blood Moon sat high in the sky, and the Consumption had begun. A cold chill filled the cave, and the screeches of the Bone Eaters and other Demons that waited for them outside their cavernous refuge echoed across the barren wasteland.

Wade formed a small fire pit in the center of the cave with a ring of rocks, stacked high with twigs, tumbleweeds, and branches that he had found laying near the entrance of the cave. He ignited the tinder with a burst of fire from his fingertip, and the flames helped to keep Sarah warm while also drying their soaked belongings. Of course, a small wall of lit candles had been erected at the mouth of the cave to ward off any Demons of the Darkness that dared come near.

As the night went on, Wade and Sarah sat across from each other, eating the jerky that Wade had packed. They passed the water sack back and forth a few times, gulping the cool liquid down until they were satiated, and then, they laid back and listened to the soft sounds of the drumming rain.

Although the smell from the rotting corpses of the Bone Eaters filled his nostrils and nearly made him gag, Wade knew it would do a good job of hiding their scent. Perhaps, he could even have a restful night's sleep. His eyes began to close...

"I have a question," Sarah said, looking at Wade between the dancing flames.

Wade sighed and then nodded, as if to say *go on.*

"Where'd you get those guns?" Thorn sat in Wade's lap,

glistening in the firelight as he disassembled and cleaned it. Rose sat propped up against the wall next to Wade, resting on the point of its blade. Whenever a Gunner cleaned his weapons, he always left one ready for use, never to be caught unarmed. "I've never seen guns like that. They look *fancy*."

Wade chuckled and ran his calloused index finger across the raised gold engravings. He followed them to the letter T in the center of the mighty weapon.

"These old things?" Wade said as he removed his finger and wiped the dust and dirt off of them with his palm. "They were given to me."

"By who?" Sarah asked.

"The Order, but they belonged to Shar, a Gunner before me."

"Did the Order take them from him?"

"Maybe, but he couldn't stop them."

"Why not?"

Wade chuckled as he fed a piece of cloth through the barrel of the weapon. "He was six feet under when that time came."

"Oh… Well, how'd he die?"

"He couldn't defeat the inescapable, unstoppable force that many great men have lost the battle to."

"And what's that?"

"Time."

Sarah's eyes grew wide.

"So why'd they pick you? I mean, not that you didn't deserve them, but I bet a lot of people wanted 'em."

Wade paused his cleaning, looked up, and said, "I guess I'm still trying to figure that part out," before beginning again.

They sat in silence once more.

"Are you an only child?" Wade finally asked.

Sarah shook her head and said, "I *had* a sister, but one day she got a cough and wasn't the same ever again. She didn't make it to her next birthday."

"I'm sorry," Wade said. "How old was she?"

"Ten, almost eleven."

Wade nodded. "And how old are you?"

"Sixteen. How old are you?"

"I stopped counting my birthdays around thirty-three."

"Why would you do that?"

"I guess once you reach a certain age, they lose meanin'. You don't get excited for 'em like you did when you were young."

"Why not?"

"Well when you're young, birthdays mean you're growing up. When you're old, they remind you that you're dying. So, I stopped counting 'em. I don't need a reminder. I know I am because I feel it all the time, that's why."

Sarah looked down and sadness grew on her face.

"Do you miss her?" Wade asked. "Your sister?"

"Yes…" Sarah responded. *"A lot."*

"What was her name?"

"Annie. I like to think she's up there," she looked up to the roof of the cave, "with my momma and papa, holding hands with Nor, smiling down on me."

"I think she is."

"What about you? You got any siblings?"

"No, not anymore."

"What happened to 'em?"

Wade stared at the fire and muttered, "He's been gone for a while."

"What happened—"

"Wade…" a familiar female voice called out from outside the cave.

Both of their heads shot to the exit, but Wade knew they heard *different* things.

"Momma?" Sarah said. "Momma!"

Just as she shot up, Wade grabbed her arm, still sitting down—still looking at the fire.

"They ain't real, Sarah," Wade said.

"She's out there! She's still alive, I can hear her!"

"She ain't." Wade held up earplugs. "It's the singing of the Demons. It's only the *singing.*"

Sarah wanted to protest and rip away from his grip, but Wade pulled her down and placed an earplug in her ear. Immediately, the trance seemed to be *partially* broken, and her distraught face relaxed. She turned toward him, and he placed the other in, fully breaking her from the spell.

"Wade… I'm right here, baby. Please come to me," Jess said from outside the cave, but Wade didn't move— he didn't even look. "Why do you hide from me! YOU KILLED ME, WADE! YOU BASTARD! I HATE YOU! YOU KILLED—"

Silence.

Another set of earplugs did their job, and Wade heard nothing. He signaled to Sarah that it was time for bed by pointing downward and laying flat hands against the side of his head. She nodded and laid out across his sleeping pad; Wade sat on the other end, leaning against the wall of rock.

Although the singing had stopped, the Demon's words still echoed in his mind.

YOU KILLED ME.

YOU KILLED ME.
YOU KILLED ME.

Until sleep finally swept over him like a wave, bringing the Demon Gunner a *much-needed* rest.

DG

CHAPTER FIVE

THE FINAL TEST

A bright light shone through an open window as Wade's eyes fluttered open. Drapes flapped softly from a gentle breeze, and graceful robins flew past, singing their morning tune.

As Wade lifted his head from his pillow, he wiped his eyes and rolled over, seeing the voluminous, soft brown hair of a beautiful girl laying gently on him, like a thousand small fingers reaching out to pull him in closer. She was still asleep, and Wade watched her for a moment, not daring to wake her. To Wade, there were few things in Rhodahn more peaceful than watching the girl he loved sleep, and he sure wouldn't find them by leaving his warm bed.

But, the morning sun had already begun to expel the night back to its hiding place beyond the reaches of sight, and he knew they would soon need to get moving. It was the day before Bestowment, and Master Ulysses would *not* accept tardiness.

A loud horn blew in the distance, causing the girl to wake up. Slowly, her head lifted from the pillow.

"Is it that time already?" she asked as she turned over, her piercing brown eyes looking deep into Wade's.

"It is," Wade responded. "Are you nervous?"

"A little. Are you?"

"A little."

They smiled, and she brought her fingers through Wade's hair, pulling him into a deep and passionate kiss before climbing on top of him. He couldn't help himself as his hands ran up her body until he was caressing her breasts.

"We're going to be late, Jess," but her hands were already under the sheet and feeling the stiff object that waited for her.

"I'll make it quick."

Then, a surge of warmth and wetness went over his throbbing appendage. His body felt weightless as blood rushed to his head.

"I love you, Wade."

"I love you too."

As she rode up and down, her soft moans filled his ears, like an angel singing a beautiful melody of affection to him, and as he looked out at the rising sun cracking through the drapes, bliss enveloped him like a warm blanket made from the softest fur.

• • •

After finally getting out of bed, Wade and Jess walked down the long corridors of stone that made up the School of the Gunners. Their revolvers hung by their sides, and the clinking of their boot spurs echoed down the cold and fusty hallways. It finally made sense to Wade why Master Ulysses always said it was impossible for a Gunner to sneak up on him, but he and his friends still tried anyway.

Around them, large archways ran across the ceilings, stained glass windows cast beautiful displays of multicolored light, and grand paintings of former Master Gunners–each holding their signature revolvers–hung on the walls, *judging* them. Passing by the paintings always gave Wade an uncomfortable feeling. As the saying went, if walls could talk, these walls would be yelling.

They made their way into a sprawling refectory, where dozens of other cadets sat at long wooden tables with dual revolvers strapped to their waists. At the far end of the room stood an elevated stage with a podium at its center and imposing, throne-like chairs arranged beside it.

Before they sat down, the pair removed their wide-brimmed hats and placed them on the table–a common courtesy in the refectory. Their friends–John, Westin, Elenor, and Colt–were already seated. They were dressed in the basic cadet attire: long, dark leather coats with brass buttons and the school's emblem–a revolver–stamped over the heart. Underneath the coats, they wore tan, fitted cotton shirts with high collars and rollable sleeves. Their hats sat in front of their plates, revealing the boy's buzz cuts and Elenor's long, blonde hair.

The friends all nodded as they took their seats at the table.

"Didn't think y'all were going to make it!" Westin said with a smirk. "You look like you just ran a damn mile, Wade."

Wade couldn't hide his smile, but before he could respond, Jess said, "We were busy, that's all," while squeezing his hand under the table.

"Oh for sure, just glad you made it," John said, giving Wade a nod of respect before turning to the rest of the group. "Ready for the final test?"

Everyone shrugged and shared worried looks.

"How am I supposed to be ready? We couldn't even prepare for it!" Wade finally said with a sour look.

"I heard they tie a weight to your ankle and make you bob up and down in the lake for 3 hours," Elenor joked, trying to lighten the mood again.

"I heard something else." Westin paused for dramatic effect and leaned in. "I heard they make you swallow a *bullet…* without any water."

The group laughed as Wade shook his head and said, "Bullshit."

"What do you think it's going to be then, marksman?" Colt said, nudging him in the ribs.

"I don't have a clue," Wade responded. "What could they even test us on that they haven't already, 'specially this close to Bestowment?"

"Well, if they make us shoot six bullseyes in a row, we all know Westin is screwed," Jess added, which drew another round of laughs.

He rolled his eyes and said, "Yeah, yeah, whatever. We can't all be like your boyfriend here."

Then, another horn blew, abruptly cutting off their conversation. All at once, the cadets shot up from the benches and saluted. A door on the right side of the stage opened, and a man who had caused Wade an *immense* amount of pain in the past came through it. He was dressed in a green, stiff jacket, with two sets of brass buttons running down its length. Braided gold cords decorated his shoulders, and a wide-brimmed hat sat perfectly atop his head. And of course, two large revolvers rested in holsters at his waist. A Master Gunner of his rank would *never* be caught in public without them.

As Master Ulysses walked to the podium, the spurs on

his boots clicked and echoed across the silent room, and Wade swore he could hear the heartbeat of the cadet next to him. Whether it was making Wade reload and empty his dual revolvers as fast as he could until his fingertips bled, or lashing him across the back every time he messed up his blindfold disassembling process, it was all the same bullshit—and Wade grew to hate him with a passion.

"At ease," he said at the podium, and all at once, the cadets took their seats. "It is my greatest pleasure to be here today—the day before your bestowment—to deliver one *final* test to be passed in order to graduate as Gunners. Let me be the first to say that this class of cadets has been one of the greatest the Order has ever seen. I would like to personally congratulate you all for fighting through the pain and making it this far in our examination and screening process. If you pass the final test, you will be ready for Bestowment tomorrow. This is Master Gunner Ulysses' final message."

He saluted, and the entire crowd cheered—everyone *except* Wade, who gritted his teeth with anger. He hated him—hated him more than he hated cleaning the shitters, and he was happy to finally be given the rank of Gunner so he could go fight for the Order in the Farlands and never have to see him again.

Another horn blew, and the cadets shot up and formed into a single file line in between the tables. Together, they marched toward an exit at the other end of the refectory. Standing in front of the exit was a tall, burly Master Gunner named Leroy. As each cadet approached, he directed them to their respective lawn.

"Colt, South Lawn, John, North Lawn, Westin, North Lawn, Elenor, South Lawn, Jess, South Lawn." The moment Wade approached, he stopped giving orders and held out an arm in front of Wade. *"Wade Russell."*

Wade froze. The other cadets behind him stared at him, noticing the difference in Master Gunner Leroy's tone.

"Yessir?"

The Master Gunner looked left and right before leaning forward until he was mere inches from Wade's ear. "I have special orders from Master Gunner Ulysses."

Shit.

"You are to report to the shooting range, *immediately.* Do not go to the North or South Lawns with the others."

"What? Why not!"

"That is an order, Cadet!" the Master Gunner yelled in his face, sending droplets of spit at him. The other cadets laughed.

Wade balled up his fist, but ultimately forced himself to relax.

"Yes sir…" Wade forced a salute and exited the cafeteria.

Trying not to draw attention to himself, Wade quickly made his way past the other cadets on the South Lawn. Just as he neared the end, they noticed him and flashed confused looks.

"Wade! The final test is this way!" Colt yelled from behind.

Wade turned and shrugged as if to say, *I don't know,* before continuing on to the shooting range where his final test awaited him.

• • •

The shooting range was located on the East Lawn, and Wade had to walk nearly the entire length of the property to get to it. Although he knew the other cadets had been sent to the North and South Lawns, a part of him still hoped others would be waiting for him when he arrived. But as he neared and saw the range empty, that hope was quickly replaced with an ever-growing fear.

The range itself was basic but vast, containing hundreds of targets for shooting practice. Bullet casings littered the ground beneath his feet, crunching and scattering in different directions as he dragged his heels. Rows of padded blankets for long-range rifling dotted the ground, and weapon racks filled with shotguns and revolvers surrounded him.

As Wade stood there, scanning the area for any potential threats, his nostrils filled with the stale scent of gunpowder and brass. All at once, long-forgotten memories rushed back to him, as if a dam had been broken within the walls of his mind. This was where he had spent thousands of hours of his life–blistering heat, rain, snow, or fog, it didn't matter, they still practiced, firing every weapon type and caliber of bullet from varying distances.

Although the practices were tough, Wade still had great times here–shooting with his friends until the early hours of the morning and losing a lot of his hearing in the process. This place seemed to be the only thing he ever really understood; in some ways, it was the only home he ever had.

But the grueling practices all led to a final shooting assessment: twelve perfect bullseyes in a row. Those who passed moved closer to Bestowment. Those who didn't were never seen at the castle again.

Wade wondered why he had been sent here and what would be required of him, and as he pondered these things, he noticed Master Gunner Ulysses standing twenty yards in front of him. His stomach dropped, and his heartbeat kicked up so fast, he thought it might explode. He gulped, trying to swallow the dry taste in his mouth, and walked toward him as best he could on unsteady, shaking legs.

"Cadet Wade!" Master Gunner Ulysses yelled, standing with his arms behind his back. "It's good to see you."

Wade was now face to face with his master. He tried his hardest to steady his legs with no luck.

"Good to see you too, Master Gunner Ulysses," Wade said with a quick salute.

Master Ulysses signaled for Wade to walk alongside him, and they started down the range.

"I know you're wondering why you're here—away from your peers, but I think this is fitting." The Master Gunner looked off toward the horizon, as if recalling a fond memory. "When I first found you, I couldn't believe my eyes. A small child covered in dirt and blood, standing before me, holding an empty revolver, with fallen foes around him—the light of Nor was shining down on you, boy, like a *monument*. Some even say you were born with a gun in your hand."

"I was just defending my village, sir—trying to protect those I loved."

"And did you?"

Pain crossed Wade's face. He wanted to respond, but nothing came out.

"Huh, after all these years, you still *only* focus on that failure and miss the true significance of that moment," Ulysses said with a sigh while shaking his head. "And maybe you always will."

"What was the significance, sir? Being brought here and

turned into a grunt to fight in the kingdom's wars?"

"That's not for me to answer, Wade, that's for you to learn on your own. But when you first arrived, I noticed you were faster, stronger, and better than the other cadets in every way. You've always been different, which is why you're with me and not among them right now. I know you don't believe it, but you're better than them, Wade, and legends do *not* surround themselves with average fools—"

"You're talking about my friends, sir."

Master Gunner Ulysses chuckled and said, "I do not believe in friends, Cadet."

Shocking, Wade thought to himself, but he knew better than to say it aloud. Over the years, Wade had learned that the mind was a sanctuary for unspoken words that would put you in the dirt.

Instead, he asked a safer question, "And why is that?"

"In war, you have soldiers and the dead. Nothing more. The definition of friendship is attachment, and friends are the first thing you lose in war. The burden of losing them can weigh heavily on a soldier, making them lose focus, making them distracted... making them a worse Gunner. You can be the best, Wade, perhaps even better than Shar himself, just as the Council of the Gun believes, but you will achieve *nothing* if you carry attachments with you onto the battlefield. My tip for you, Wade, is to not have friends. Do you understand me?"

Wade didn't respond, he only continued to stare at the oxidized casings embedded in the dirt.

"I thought so," Ulysses scoffed, "which is why I doubt your legendary status. I see the potential in you, just as everyone else does, but I also see your faults. The faults of a chosen one are never seen by their believers as they are blinded by a powerful thing called hope. They'd hold their breath until they died before ever admitting they chose the wrong person. But you see, Wade, I am no believer in you, and I will prove it to you by betting my freedom on it."

Faster than lightning, Master Ulysses drew his revolver and aimed it at the side of Wade's head. Wade's body tensed, and his hands shot to the grips of his own iron.

"*Don't.*"

"What the hell are you doing!" Wade shouted, anger boiling inside him.

"Don't move another inch, or I'll blow your damn head off."

"You're fucking insane!"

"No, Wade, I'm the *only* one who sees the truth! You want to reach Bestowment, but I will not allow you to inherit his guns unless you are worthy!" He pressed the barrel further into Wade's temple, digging the cold tip deeper into his skin. "Now, slowly draw your revolvers."

As Wade drew his iron, he thought about gunning down his master right then and there. He would have milliseconds to react and fire, but in that time, he would most likely be killed, as Ulysses was no slouch. He earned his rank within the Order for a reason.

So, Wade was paralyzed by fear and had to make a choice, but perhaps that was exactly what the deranged old man wanted—for Wade to try it, just so he could claim he killed a traitor. The risk was too great, and there was nothing he could do.

He was *powerless.*

"I can see it in your eyes, Wade, you want to kill me, and

to that I say, *fair enough*. I wasn't kind to you during your training with the Order, but you became the best, didn't you? I pushed you to your limits, farther than any other Master was willing to, and that is why you're receiving Rose & Thorn tomorrow, but before you do, I have one final test. If you fail, it will be the last test for *both* of us. Twelve shots, perfect bullseyes. If you miss one, you die."

What? That was it? That was the final test?

Wade fought back laughter. All of that buildup, all of that anticipation, and all of those theatrics with a gun pressed to his head led to *that*. Wade almost believed he could do it with his eyes closed, and, truthfully, the test felt like an insult.

"You can shoot me, Wade, I give you permission. I've had a long life, and I'd even be happy to go–maybe I'd finally get a good night's sleep, but we both know you want to prove to me why you deserve the iron waiting for you."

Wade hesitated, then gripped his revolvers and yanked them free of their holsters, but instead of gunning down his master, he aimed them at the target in the distance.

"That's what I thought," Ulysses said as a devious smile grew on his face.

Wade ignored him and readied himself for the test. A trickle of sweat slowly ran down his temple until his hand tensed, his finger contracted, and his revolver fired. A hole appeared in the target: a *perfect* bullseye.

Master Ulysses smiled even wider. "Eleven more."

Wade's hand tightened on the grip of the gun and he fired again. Another bullseye appeared. He did this four more times until his right revolver was empty. Then, Wade focused again, controlling his breath as he shot the first round from the revolver in his left hand. Another bullseye. His hand started to become sweaty, and he could feel the cold metal of Ulysses' gun pressing against his skull, waiting to be fired.

Another.

"You're almost there," Master Ulysses said. "Just 4 more."

More sweat accumulated in his grip. His hand had become unsteady, and he could feel his arm wanting to sway.

Another.

There were only three shots left–three shots left to get away from this madman and place forever.

Another. Come on, two more, Wade, he thought to himself, *just two more. Focus.*

Another bullseye appeared, and now there was only one round left in his revolver. This was it. It all came down to this final shot.

Wade focused once more, closing one eye and exhaling as his finger slowly pulled back on the trigger. The tension built up and beads of sweat dripped down his forehead and ran to the bridge of his nose. His hand shook violently now as he pulled further, and further, and…

BANG!

Wade stood with his revolvers outstretched before him, smoke pouring from the left barrel. A singular, perfect hole sat in the middle of the target–not one shot missed. The revolver that pressed against his head lowered, and Wade let out a massive sigh of relief.

His weapons started to lower and…

"HOLD!" his master yelled. "Did I order you to move?"

"No sir," Wade responded, quickly raising his revolvers again.

"And you *won't* until the next horn blows."

"When will that be, sir?"

"I guess you shall find out, won't you? *This* is your final test, Wade. Good luck."

Ulysses began to walk out of the shooting range, kicking bullet casings with his boots as he went.

"And Wade?" Wade turned his head slightly, not lowering his guns an inch. His master stood pointing into the distance. "Do you see that out there?"

Wade quickly scanned the horizon, and in a sniper's nest, he could see a faint shimmer of light.

"We both know what that means. I shall see you tomorrow at Bestowment, Cadet."

His master didn't come back, and Wade continued to stand with his weapons outstretched before him for *hours*. The sun beared down on him, burning his skin. He could feel blisters start to form on his face. Sweat poured down his forehead and ran over his eyes, tortuously stinging them. He tried his best to find relief by rubbing them with his shoulders while making sure not to drop his weapons.

I want to kill Ulysses, but who am I if I cannot complete this test? If Shar's guns are not mine, then what do I deserve besides death?

• • •

Hours had gone by now, and Wade's muscles felt as if they were on fire. The sun started to dip below the horizon, providing a moment of relief that was immediately replaced with more pain. The faint shimmer in the distance remained, and nausea and brutal aches consumed every ounce of his body. Wade began to hyperventilate, attempting to hold the weapons up high, but his muscles were shutting down. He couldn't do it, he *couldn't*. But what did he have to lose?

Rose & Thorn did not wait for him if he failed, no, only death, along with the smug smile that would eternally rest on his master's face as he rotted in a jail cell for killing a cadet in training, knowing that he proved the Council *wrong*.

Fuck him and fuck that.

Wade wouldn't allow Ulysses to win.

He focused on what he had learned during his time here, and remembered a state of being that a Gunner could enter in times of war to ease their mind. Wade was told to imagine a rabbit running across his field of view. After some time, the rabbit would leave his world and carry him away with it. Wade tried to picture this rabbit, and eventually, he saw it running in front of him. He chased the rabbit and entered a catatonic state, traveling deep into the far reaches of his own mind. He was delirious, exhausted, and dehydrated, but as he chased the rabbit, the seconds seemed to fly by and he lost all sense of time. He knew it was night by his shivering, and he knew it was morning when he felt the rising sun on his burned face again, but he continued to chase the rabbit.

In his mind, Wade could hear the horn going off and filling his ears with the beautiful sound of relief and salvation... but it *never* came.

Suddenly, the rabbit started running faster and faster. Wade couldn't keep up and watched as it ran over a hill and out of sight. Wade lost it and was sucked out of the confines of his mind, and all at once, pain surged over him like a great wave crashing onto a beach. His muscles began to cramp and fail, screaming for him to give up. His entire body shook violently, as if he were seizing and maybe he was. Then, the guns started to dip, and he could still see the shimmer in the distance, watching him, waiting to strike him down.

"NO!" Wade screamed. "No, you bastard! NO!"

But the guns dipped further and further. Wade fought with every ounce of might he had, screaming and hyperventilating, but they continued to plunge. Finally, they dropped below his waist, and a gunshot echoed across the land.

DG

CHAPTER SIX

THE TWO RULES OF WEAPONRY

Wade awoke with a jolt, shooting upright and breathing heavily. Beads of sweat ran down his forehead and onto his shirt. He immediately brought his hands to his biceps, expecting to be overcome with pain, but was relieved to feel none. The fog of the dream started to dissipate, and he remembered where he was: in a cave with the girl. He covered his face in embarrassment, before dragging his fingertips across his coarse skin and clearing away the sweat that pooled on it.

"I'm sorry about that," Wade said preemptively. "I just… had a bad dream."

He turned to his left, expecting to see Sarah, but she was *gone.*

His heart rate immediately picked up as he frantically scanned the cave, looking for her, but she was nowhere to be found. He shot off the ground, sending sand flying into the air before grabbing his guns and sprinting toward the mouth.

"Sarah!" he yelled, emerging into the bright sunlight that the cave had shielded them from.

Wade brought his hand above his eyes, giving them a

chance to adjust. As the brightness faded, he spotted the girl a few yards away, picking up dead poppy flowers from the dirt. A sigh of relief followed.

He watched her for a moment, gathering the flowers and attempting to turn them into some sort of crown, but the petals and stalks were too brittle, and they immediately broke away to dust within her palm.

"How long have you been out here?" Wade asked as he holstered his revolvers.

"I don't know, maybe an hour?" she responded. "I let you sleep, you looked like you needed it anyway."

I wish you had woken me up.

Wade fully exited the cave and looked across the hazy horizon. The sky was clear with not even a cloud in sight. Then, he bent down and picked up one of the dried out petals from the gray dirt.

Dead. Just like everything is or will be.

The petal fell from his fingertips and didn't waver an inch in any direction, dropping like a coin.

"Good day to shoot."

"What?" Sarah asked.

"No wind. It's a good day to teach you."

"Was that your idea from last night?"

The Demon Gunner nodded and said, "If we're going to do this, you're going to need to learn how to shoot."

"Can you teach me?"

A smile crossed Wade's face.

"Let's eat first."

• • •

After breakfast, Wade delicately stacked multiple rock

towers in the dirt for Sarah. Then he retrieved her father's repeater rifle and revolver from the saddlebag before returning to her, the iron held in his hands.

"These were your father's guns, Sarah. Have you ever shot them before?"

"No, never."

"Well today, that's gonna change." He spun the revolver on his index finger before presenting it flat on his palm to her with the barrel pointing away. "This is a single-action revolver, .45 caliber, with recoil that kicks up and to the right. It's an impressive tool, and your father had good taste in iron."

Wade took a step back, creating a decent gap between them.

"Two rules with weaponry. *One–*" He aimed the gun down at the ground, away from Sarah. "You never aim a gun at someone you don't intend to kill. Why? Because of rule number *two–*" With a flick of his wrist, he flipped open the cylinder revealing six bullets within it. "A gun is *always* loaded." He shook out the bullets into his palm and tossed them into his ammo pouch.

He then spun the gun around, keeping the barrel pointed at the dirt, and handed it to her.

"Now, go ahead and get a feel for it," he said with a nod.

Sarah flipped the gun back and forth while inspecting it.

"It's heavy," she said, which made Wade chuckle.

"They all are, but you'll get stronger. You'll *have* to."

Sarah looked up at Wade with wide eyes as he stepped forward and stood next to her.

"Now, go ahead and get a firm grip with your right hand and raise it up." Sarah did as instructed. "Good, now press your thumb into that recoil shield there. That's gonna help control the kick. Next, place your left index finger across the trigger guard."

"Like this?" she asked, her hand shaking with nerves.

"Just like that."

"Should I wrap it?"

"No," the Demon Gunner responded. "All that hand is doing is pulling the hammer back. Hold and *aim* with your right hand, pull with your left thumb. That left pointer finger is only resting on the guard. Now, stagger your stance, extend your arms, and lean into the shot."

Her legs staggered, her arms extended, and the shaking picked up.

"You're doing great, Sarah. Cock that hammer back." Her small thumb rose to the hammer and drew it back. "Close your left eye, look down the sight, take a deep breath, and exhale as you fire."

CLICK!

The hammer dropped.

"Just like that, now, do it *again*." She repeated the steps just like before. "There you go. You think you're ready for the real thing now?"

She nodded, excitement replacing nerves.

"Ho, now. First, repeat the two rules."

"Never aim a gun at someone you don't want to kill. And..." she thought for a moment, "guns are always loaded?"

The Demon Gunner nodded and smiled. He took the revolver from her and loaded a single bullet into the cylinder before handing it back.

"You got this."

"I'm nervous."

"Remember when you saved my skin? You've already

done this, but this time, the gun won't shoot out of your hands."

"Alright, I can do this. I can do this."

She prepared herself and raised the gun, aiming at the rock tower in the distance. Her skinny finger danced on the trigger.

BANG!

The gun fired, kicking up high in her hand. The bullet ripped past the target and buried itself in the dirt.

"I missed," she said in frustration, quickly wiping the few tears that ran down her face.

Wade could practically hear her heartbeat from where he was standing. Her hands and legs continued to shake.

"It's alright," Wade assured with a pat on the back. "You rushed it, that's all."

He took the gun and reloaded another bullet.

"Get it on up and try again."

"Okay..."

She repeated the steps, pulled the hammer back, and fired, but she missed *again*. Sarah stomped her foot and shook her head.

"I'm doing everything you said!"

"You're aiming with your eye, Sarah."

"Isn't that what I'm supposed to be doing?"

"If you're going to be a true Gunner, you need to aim with your *heart*."

"What does that even mean?" she asked.

Wade took the gun from her and began to reload it.

"This is a powerful tool, Sarah, one that can take a life or a *Demon* from this world forever. When you aim, you aim with your heart. You've got to *believe* in what you're about to do, because once you pull that trigger, there ain't no getting that bullet back." He handed the gun to her.

"*Again.*"

She raised the gun before her and focused, drawing the hammer back. She closed one eye, took a deep breath, and fired.

BANG!

A rock tower exploded, sending a cloud of dust into the air.

"There ya' go!" Wade said as she turned around with a big smile, accidentally aiming the gun directly at his chest. "Nor almighty!" He jumped to the side. "Rule number one!"

The firearm was snatched out of her hand with lightning fast speed.

"Sorry, I was just excited, I forgot."

Wade shook his head in disappointment, but he couldn't help it as a soft smile cracked through his stern expression.

"You did good, Sarah." He began to load the rest of the rounds into the cylinder. "Now, do that again. You've got 3 shots left. Make 'em count."

Sarah nodded as she once again took the gun into her hands, making sure to keep the barrel pointed *down* this time. She aimed, cocked the hammer back, and fired, striking another rock tower in the distance. She immediately fired again but missed.

"Focus," Wade said. "Slow it down."

She took a deep breath, fired again, and hit another tower.

"Well done," he said as he took the gun from her. "Now for the rifle."

"Are you sure? Last time–"

"Forget last time. Look how good you just did. You've got this, I promise. Same rules apply to all weapons, alright?" He held the rifle up in front of her. "This is a

Harvester repeater rifle, .22 caliber, lever action. It'll kick up and to the left, so you need to dig into 'er."

She nodded and took hold of the iron.

"Get that rifle sittin' firmly there," he said as he helped guide the weapon into position.

"Like this?" she asked, placing the stock into her bony shoulder.

"Yes ma'am, that's what you didn't do before, which is why the gun shot from your hands. Dig it in there, grip the forearm, place your cheek on the stock, stagger those feet, and push *into* the weapon. You gotta apply equal force in the opposite direction."

He took a moment to let her get comfortable.

"Focus and fire."

Click!

"Very good, I'll let you load it this time." Wade pulled a cartridge from his ammo pouch and handed it to her. "Slide this into that loading gate there. Yep, just like that. Now, put three fingers into the lever and push forward and pull back."

The loading mechanism slid the round into place.

"Very good." Wade carefully stepped back, giving her ample room. "Fire when you're ready."

She focused, took a deep breath, and blasted a rock tower in the distance. The kick pushed her back a bit, and Wade extended a hand to catch her.

"Ow," she said as she rubbed her shoulder. "That kicked like a bull!"

Wade patted her on the back once more and said, "You'll get stronger, I promise. Now *again*."

She loaded, aimed, and fired.

"Now load five more shots and shoot them in succession.

When you work the lever, take your index finger out and keep it alongside the trigger guard. Pull the trigger and crank, pull the trigger and crank, pull the trigger and crank. Do it with rhythm. Now prepare yourself, the bullets will keep coming."

Sarah cocked the gun and pulled the trigger.

BANG!

"AGAIN!" he yelled.

She cranked the lever and fired.

"AGAIN!"

She kept doing this over and over until there was nothing left to shoot. The gun clicked empty.

"I did it!" she cried out.

Wade wanted to hug the girl, but he held himself back, remembering the words of his old master and the world they still lived in.

"You're a natural, Sarah. You would've made for a fine Gunner for the Order."

"Really? You think so?"

Wade nodded.

"Now I reckon we've got enough sunlight for a hunt. You think you can get us dinner?"

"I can try."

"Good, then follow me."

• • •

Wade and Sarah lay flat against the hard-packed dirt, leaning over a rock. In the distance, a malnourished rabbit attempted to nibble on a dead plant.

"There," Wade said, pointing with two fingers. "You see it?"

Sarah leaned in closer, trying to get a better look. Her eyes focused on the animal.

"I see it."

"*Take it.*"

She gripped her repeater rifle tighter and said, "Are you sure?"

"Yes, remember what I told you."

"I aim with my *heart.*"

Wade nodded.

"Alright then, here goes nothing," Sarah said, bringing the rifle up and aiming it at the rabbit.

"Take your time and focus. Don't rush it, or you'll scare every rabbit away for miles."

Sarah closed one eye and aimed down the sight of the rifle, lining up the bead on the center of the animal.

"*I aim with my heart.*"

She took a deep breath and pulled the trigger. The sound of the shot echoed across the barren wasteland, and the rabbit bolted. A clear miss.

"Damn it!" she yelled, slamming her fist into the gray sand.

Wade smiled and brought out her father's revolver from his waist band.

"You rushed it."

"I didn't, I swear to ya'!"

Wade shook his head and took his sweet time loading a single shot into the revolver.

"You see, becoming a marksman takes time. It won't happen overnight, tomorrow, or in a week, but it'll come eventually if you stick with it." He cocked the hammer back. "But it'll *never* come… if you rush it."

Wade raised the gun before him and focused on the

running rabbit in the distance. He accounted for the drop in elevation from the hill they stood on, the soft breeze from the East that ruffled his clothes, and the speed of the animal running for its life. His arm was stiff straight, not swaying an inch. A quick breath and the pull of a trigger caused the headless rabbit to tumble across the dirt.

"I aim with my heart, and so will you."

• • •

A small flame extended from Wade's index finger, lighting the last candle in a row at the mouth of the cave.

That should do for tonight.

The sunlight outside was fading fast as the great ball of fire finally dipped below the horizon and disappeared from sight. The dull sound of metal clinking together from Wade's waist announced his arrival next to the girl. She sat cross legged in front of the fire, biting into the small rabbit's cooked leg. For a long time that night, they didn't speak. Wade instead fiddled with a piece of the rabbit's fur and a leather string.

The silence was finally broken with, "I'm sorry I missed the rabbit."

He didn't look up, passing the string through a hole in the skin he had punched out.

"You're eating it, right?"

Sarah smiled and said, "Yeah, I just... I feel like I disappointed–"

"What did I say?"

"Don't rush it."

"So *don't*. It'll come, I promise."

He continued to fiddle.

"Thank you, Wade, for today."

"You saved my life—"

"You saved it *first*."

Wade looked past the fire at Sarah and nodded. Then, a large yawn overtook her.

"I think I'm going to get some sleep now. That shooting tired me out."

"Sleep well."

"You should too."

"I'll try when I finish with this."

Sarah peered over the flames at the pouch-like item he had now created.

"What is it?"

"You'll see tomorrow."

"Alright." Sarah came around the fire and laid down across the sleeping pad next to Wade. She placed her earplugs in. "Goodnight, Wade."

"Goodnight, Sarah. See you in the morning."

As Sarah drifted to sleep, Wade continued working the rabbit skin into its desired shape. The crackling of the fire filled the otherwise silent cave, and he glanced to his right and stared at the frail girl. His fingers stopped moving; he looked back at his creation. In front of him, the flames danced, casting long shadows across his scarred face.

My tip for you, Wade, is to not have friends. Do you understand me?

Goosebumps raised on his arms as the Darkness began to grow outside the cave. He heard the familiar sounds of Bone Eaters screeching into the night, followed by the singing of the Demons.

Wade knew he was out of time.

He situated his earplugs in their rightful place and went

back to his work, but it did nothing to block out the words of long forgotten men that continued to echo in his mind.

Do you understand me?

DG

CHAPTER SEVEN

A GUNNER'S LAST STAND

Wade awoke in the early hours of the morning, finding himself leaning against the wall of the cave. He didn't remember when he had fallen asleep, but the rabbit skin still sitting in his hand indicated that it had been abrupt and in the middle of his work. His back and neck were cranked; only movement and smoke would help them now. To his right, Sarah lay peacefully on the feather and cotton sleeping pad. He would let her continue to rest.

The air outside the cave was cold and crisp–a sign that the Consumption had retreated only moments ago, and bones lay littered across the barren wasteland in front of him. With each step, the dirt and sand beneath his boots crunched, as if he were walking across snow. It made his teeth ache.

Quicksilver stood hitched on a dead tree a few feet away, unscathed and unbothered by whatever horrific events had transpired in the night. He dug into the horse's saddlebag, fumbling around for two very small, very specific items. Finally, he found them and pulled them out. Within his palm sat a short piece of paper and glass vial with a cork wedged in the top. He popped the cork and shook out a small amount of dry, thinly sliced brown leaves onto the paper–the morning remedy to *any* ill feeling. He rolled it up and placed the dart between his lips before leaning toward Quicksilver's muzzle and waiting for an exhale. Blue fire was expunged from her nostrils, lighting the tip of the cigarette and immediately sending its rejuvenating power into Wade's lungs. The Master's of the Order used to tell the cadets that they were no good, and if they were caught with one, they'd get flogged, but that didn't stop anyone. Besides, all of the Masters secretly smoked too.

How else were you supposed to get through training?

Nor knew he needed them now more than ever.

As he exhaled, the memories of sitting on the roof of the castle with his friends poured over him. Not a worry in the world, only the sunrise in front of him and good people beside him–people long since gone now. A sharp pain grew in Wade's chest, not from the smoke, but just a pain only nostalgia could bring.

The sound of crunching behind him brought Wade out of his thoughts. He didn't react or turn toward the girl, he just continued to smoke and lean against Quicksilver, admiring the beauty of the still morning.

"Do you ever worry about her?" Sarah asked.

"What is there to worry about?"

Sarah held her arms crossed over each other in an attempt to stay warm.

"She's always out here alone," she said, kicking a small pebble in front of her. "Aren't you afraid she's going to get eaten?"

"They don't bother her," Wade said with a long exhale of smoke. "At least I don't think so."

"Why not?"

Wade rapped his knuckles against her exposed ribs, "What's there to eat?"

Sarah came closer and ran her fingers across Quicksilver's body.

"Where did you find her again?" she asked.

Wade's mouth opened as if to respond, but he slowly closed it instead, as he realized he didn't have an immediate answer.

Finally, he uttered, "I've just... always had her."

Wade took one last drag of the now pathetic, burnt cigarette and tossed it into the dirt. He dug the heel of his boot into it–a habit that was no longer needed as there was nothing to accidentally set ablaze for *hundreds* of miles.

"So, what are we doing today?" she asked.

"Shooting."

• • •

Slowly but surely, the girl was improving. The more Wade observed her, the more he believed she would've made for a fine Gunner indeed. Sarah was a natural, and seemed to pick up on the small nuances of marksmanship all on her own. She would adjust her body positioning before a shot, becoming as still and relaxed as possible. Her breathing was consistent, and the sway of her gun decreased. They practiced shooting standing up, laying down, crouched, on her back–any position that she might find herself in while needing to make a life or death shot. Wade made sure to emphasize that *all* shots could be life or death out here.

Of course, her aim wasn't perfect. She would often

fumble with the lever on the repeater rifle, jamming it in the process and requiring the assistance of Wade to clear it and start again. But she had a steady hand and her aim was *mostly* true. To say the least, the Demon Gunner was proud.

"How have we not run out of bullets yet?" Sarah asked, laying on the ground and continuing to fire at the newly positioned rock target in the distance.

"Well your father kept a good amount in his carriage," Wade responded as he continued to pack candles into the saddlebag. "I collected it all when I found the guns."

But he didn't get a response.

He turned to the girl and saw her slowly lowering her gun while staring off into the distance, as if in a trance. The barrel of the gun made a *thud* when it finally hit the dirt. Wade turned back and latched the top of the saddle bag, but stopped.

Say something, damn it.

"Sarah, I'm sorry again for what happened to your parents," he finally muttered.

"It's alright," she said, but he could tell it wasn't.

"Come here, I want to show you something," he said, waving her over.

Sarah got up from the ground, wiping the tears from her face and the dirt from her dress.

"You see this ammo pouch I carry?" he asked.

"Yea?"

Wade wedged his finger into it and widened it by easing a leather string before Sarah leaned forward and inspected it.

"I can't hardly see the bottom?"

"Because it's enchanted with magic."

Sarah froze and looked up.

"*Magic?*" the girl asked. "Magic is real?"

"*Very,* which is also why we don't have to worry about running out of ammo. *Here.*" He grabbed her skinny wrist and directed her hand into it. "All you have to do is just think about what you need," her fingers rustled around in the pouch, "and it'll be in your hand when you pull it out."

She closed her eyes for a moment before pulling out her hand, revealing a handful of bullets for the repeater rifle.

"What! That's amazing! Where on Rhodahn did you get this?"

Wade tried to think, but he drew another blank. Quite frankly, he couldn't remember how he obtained it. He just knew he had it his whole life, like a preference for food or music.

"A gift from… the Order," he said, the only logical response he could come up with.

"Wow," Sarah responded. "So the Order knows magic too?"

"Indeed."

"Lucky you. We could've used some of it the night you found me."

"Sadly, I don't know any."

"Then what's that fire thing you do? Isn't that magic?"

"No, that's just a gift. Something I was born with. I don't know how to explain it either."

She flipped a bullet back and forth between her fingers, mulling over what was just said.

"Well you did the best you could."

There was a long silence.

"You know, they're not regular bullets either," Wade finally said.

"I thought something was up with them. They're much *heavier.*"

"Because they're Hellfire."

"Hellfire?"

"Special bullets designed for killing Demons. They're magical, just like the pouch. It would take many rounds of regular ammo to kill a Bone Eater, but with Hellfire, you can do it with just one shot if you place it right."

"How?"

"They explode and ignite the Demons insides, and let me tell ya', these bastards *hate* fire."

"Can I try and shoot one?"

"Go for it, but it kicks harder than the regular stuff. Just be prepared for it."

She quickly slid the bullet into her repeater rifle, aimed, and–

BANG!

A bright flash of fire followed the bullet out of the barrel. The round hit the rock in the distance and exploded it into a thousand pieces. Sarah jumped back in shock.

"That's Hellfire for ya'."

She smiled and turned to Wade. "I think I like it."

"Sarah, do you remember how I told you these were your father's guns?"

"Yes…" she meekly muttered, hanging her head. "I remember."

"Well, they're *yours* now."

Wade presented what he had been working on in the cave: a holster made of rabbit fur and skin. She took it into her hands and looked up at him with wide eyes.

"Really? You made this for me?"

"Yes, but you must now protect your iron with your life,

as it will always protect you," Wade said, climbing up onto Quicksilver. "I will teach you how to dismantle, clean, and rebuild your guns, just like a Gunner. They are a part of you now, and they will forever be a part of you until death. Do you understand that?"

"Yes, but when will I learn that? Right now?"

Wade looked up into the sky and saw that the sun was now overhead.

"No, not now. Perhaps at the next campfire, later tonight. We need to get moving before the sun sets again."

She didn't argue, and they both climbed onto Quicksilver and took off across the cold desert.

• • •

The pair rode for a hundred miles, making good time to beat the setting sun, but as Wade steered Quicksilver, worry began to set in. The desert they rode across was flat with little to no rock formations. If they had to sleep in a tent for the night, Wade didn't know if the candles would be enough to ward off the monsters who lurked in the Darkness. The combined scent of their flesh could possibly be too much to mask, and they would most certainly be hunted. Fear rose in his chest, smothering him. Wade never had these feelings before, but things were different now, and the girl who sat behind him proved that.

Then, in the far distance, he spotted something: dark storm clouds that were growing and quickly approaching. It was a desert storm—the *worst* of any kind he had seen before. Wade suspected that the Consumption was affecting the environment in more ways than one, and now he was certain of it.

Wade turned over his shoulder and yelled, "Hang on! We gotta outrun this storm!"

He felt Sarah's grip tighten around his waist as he whipped the reins twice and sent them on their way.

"Come on, Quicksilver, we need to move fast!"

Quicksilver rocketed across the land, hooves colliding with dirt and blue fire pouring from her nose. The wind picked up tremendously, whistling and howling around them. Light rain quickly turned into a torrential downpour, soaking them and causing Wade's vision to blur. He could barely tell East from West.

At the speed they were traveling, the droplets felt like sharp thorns, stabbing into their skin. Wade pulled up his kerchief and bent his head down, using the brim of his hat as a shield in an attempt to protect himself from the rain that was thrashing them. Luckily for Sarah, his body was taking the brunt of it.

BOOM!

Giant streaks of lightning crashed down, and as Wade looked around, he saw that the storm had fully engulfed them now. The wind violently beat against them, nearly pulling Wade off the back of Quicksilver. Their momentum had ceased, and the horse let out a painful neigh before kicking up and halting in place. The fog of rain and sand had grown so thick, Wade couldn't even see which direction they had been traveling in.

"HANG ON!" Wade yelled as another violent gust of wind ripped past them.

The sand had transformed into painful projectiles, bashing their faces and blinding them.

BOOM!

Another bolt struck down so close to them that it sent

a searing shock through their bodies. Behind him, he felt Sarah's grip tighten then slip from his waist. Her body went limp and the wind ripped her off the back of the horse and sent her flying into the storm.

"SARAH!" Wade yelled as another gust threatened to rip him off too.

He could feel his body lifting from the saddle and his grip on the reins failing him. Then, a *giant* gust of wind lifted Quicksilver off the ground and sent them flying into the air. They were thrashed around, spinning and flipping as if they were in a tornado. The only hand Wade kept on the reins was now white from gripping it so hard. He couldn't hang on any longer; this was it. His grip finally gave out, and he was sucked into the distance, tumbling over himself, blinded by sand.

• • •

When Wade finally awoke, he found himself half buried in a dune. His body ached, and his mouth was incredibly dry. He forced a harsh cough, purging the sand from his throat. His eyes finally blinked open and adjusted to the red moonlight that shined down upon the wasteland. An immediate chill ran across his skin.

The Consumption had begun.

He forced himself to sit up, breaking through the frozen sand that he was trapped under. He immediately scanned his surroundings; Sarah and Quicksilver were nowhere to be found.

"Sarah!" he yelled as he got to his feet. "Sarah, where are you!"

Nothing.

The Demon Gunner started up the dune, trudging through the sand while attempting to run. His body was weak and unsteady, and with every movement, audible cracks and pops emanated from his joints. He finally made it to the top of the dune and looked out across it. Nothing but sand, rocks, and a wall of Darkness.

His sand covered fingertips graced his dry lips, and with all the air in his lungs, he attempted to whistle, but nothing more than a pathetic squeak came out, as if trying to extinguish a candle.

"Fuck!" he yelled into the night. The horse... The girl... They were both gone. "FUCK!"

Then, his heartbeat skipped a beat.

My iron.

His hands shot down to his sides, and he immediately felt the cold metal of Rose and Thorn, allowing him to breathe again. They were still sitting on his waist, right where they belonged.

Thank Nor.

He had his guns, but other than that, he was lost and alone. The Blood Moon was rising fast, and the terrible cold he felt only grew stronger, causing goosebumps to rise on his arms. His candles were also gone, along with his rations and the Demon blood. There was no denying it now: he was fucked.

In a final act of desperation, Wade *ran.*

He didn't know where he was going, but he ran as fast as his legs would carry him. And as he ducked down into another dune and came out on the other side, he thought he could see a faint light in the distance. It was small–just a shimmer of one, but what could it be...

A screech echoed behind him, and in a split second,

Wade had unholstered his guns and fully spun around, pointing them into the Darkness, ready to shoot anything that dared attack him.

All at once, three Bone Eaters launched themselves over the dune in front of him and landed at his feet. Wade took aim and fired, striking each one between the eyes. Their heads exploded with fire, sending green blood spraying into the air.

Now Wade took off again, running toward the light. He was moving faster and faster, frantically climbing up and down dunes and picking himself up when he fell. The light in the distance grew brighter, and he could almost make out a large structure *within* it.

BANG!

A gunshot sounded off next to him, and Wade turned to the source of the noise.

Sarah.

He bounded up a dune and cleared the top, only to see Sarah at the bottom of another, desperately attempting to reload her repeater rifle as a Bone Eater drew closer. The bullets accidentally fell from her hand, spilling onto the sand. And just as she bent down to pick them up, the Bone Eater lunged at her. Wade tracked the monster through the air and delivered a shot, exploding its head before it reached her. Blood and guts sprayed onto her, causing her to scream. Wade stumbled down the dune and ran toward her.

"Sarah!" Wade yelled.

"Wade!"

"We need to move! Come on!"

Wade ran next to her and grabbed her hand, pulling her across the sand. They ran as fast as they could as more screeches echoed behind them. The source of the light was now much clearer, and Wade couldn't believe what he was seeing. Standing before them was a giant fort, with high stone walls and bright torches lighting the exterior. An impressive wooden gate sat in the middle of the fort, and like moths to a flame, it *called* to them.

"Keep running!" Wade yelled.

Behind them, a herd of Bone Eaters closed in. The fort was closer now–right in front of them. Without stopping, Wade turned back and began firing off shots, striking the Bone Eaters square in the face. As their corpses dropped into the sand, more launched out from behind them, stomping over the fallen.

"Go!" Wade yelled. "To the gate!"

Wade fired the rest of his bullets, mowing the Demons down one by one. He flipped open the cylinders and reloaded before shooting at them again. Sarah was now at the gate, banging on it, hoping someone was there to save them, but no one answered. Wade kept shooting, but no matter how many bullets he pumped into them, the pack wasn't thinning, and soon they would be overwhelmed.

It grew abundantly clear that this would be his last stand.

"Come on you filthy bastards! TAKE ME!" Wade unloaded his guns, exploding more Bone Eaters before him.

The Hellfire daisy chained to the other's, causing them to explode like dynamite. Giant plumes of fire and smoke erupted in front of him, and for a split second, he thought he was safe. Then, through the smoke, green eyes *appeared*. Their wretched bodies followed. Wade brought his guns up once more and gritted his teeth.

"COME ON!"

CLICK!

Rose and Thorn were empty, and he was shit out of luck. This was it—this was the end. No one was coming to save them. Wade looked down at the guns in his hands. He didn't know much, but he knew one thing: when the Consumption retreated and the Demon Gunner stood no more, they wouldn't find his cylinders empty.

Wade flipped them open and—

BANG!

A gunshot sounded out next to him.

BANG! BANG! BANG!

More and more, from all directions. Bullets whizzed past his head, and Bone Eaters were picked off left and right. Out of instinct, Wade dropped to the sand and looked up. On top of the walls stood men and women with repeater rifles, firing off into the herd of Bone Eaters.

"MOVE YOUR ASS!" one of them yelled to Wade.

He didn't hesitate, scrambling to his feet again and taking off toward the fort. More Bone Eaters emerged, clambering over the fallen as they chased after him. He could feel their warm breath and hear their teeth snapping together mere inches away from his boots.

Then, in front of him, a loud groan echoed across the desert. The wall split into two and slowly opened, followed by bullets that narrowly missed Wade.

"Come on!" a person yelled from within the fort.

Wade ran and jumped, diving through the opening.

DG

CHAPTER EIGHT

FORT CARN

W ade landed *hard* on the dirt, gasping for air, but he had no time to focus on the pain. He rolled over, groaning, as he attempted to reload his guns. Within his sights, he could see Bone Eaters charging forward. His fingers tensed on the triggers, but the heavy, wooden gate was already closing. Bullets continued to fly past until the gate had fully sealed again.

The Demon Gunner looked to his right and saw a man and woman releasing thick ropes attached to a pulley, causing a large plank of wood to fall across the door, securing it with a loud *thud.*

Others stood facing him with guns in their hands. They all wore blue jeans, button-downs, and wide-brimmed hats–similar to the one that currently sat atop his head.

Gunslingers.

Behind them, contained within the giant stone walls of the fort, was a small village. Wooden shacks with orange clay tile roofs had been constructed, and stairs and wooden walkways connected different levels that went up three stories high. Under the walkways, stacks and stacks of TNT were piled high. The fort was a thing of beauty and something that reminded him of his old world–something he had not seen since beginning his journey long ago.

But Wade couldn't admire it any longer, as more gunslingers poured down the steps and surrounded him, each with revolvers on their waists or repeater rifles in their hands. They stopped within a few feet of him and whispered amongst themselves, watching him intently.

Then, goosebumps ran down his arms.

Sarah.

His head whipped back and forth as he searched for her, but she was nowhere to be found. The gunslingers stepped closer, now *glaring* at him. Wade couldn't tell what their intentions were, and he wasn't going to wait to find out. He jumped to his feet, and in a fraction of a second, he had his guns aimed at the crowd.

"Where is the girl!" Wade shouted.

No one responded as they raised their own guns.

"Where the hell is she!" Sweat dripped down Wade's temple; his finger's danced on the triggers. "ANSWER ME!"

"Woah there partner!" a man yelled from the back of the crowd.

Wade aimed toward the sound of the voice, and he watched as the gunslingers started shuffling around, forming a part down the middle of the crowd. A *large* man with two gold revolvers on either side of his waist and criss-crossed belts of ammo across his chest, painfully limped toward him. His potbelly was pronounced, and it caused his shirt to bow at the buttons and flare outward as if it were about to burst through. He finally snorted loudly before spitting a giant wad of mucus into the dirt and rubbing it in with the heel of his boot, which his leg *barely* fit into. Atop his head sat a black hat with gold threading. He readjusted it before looking Wade dead in the eyes.

"Take it easy now, will ya'? There ain't no need for violence," he said, flashing what was left of his brown, rotted teeth. "Name's Butch–Butch Thompson."

He held out a hand to shake, but the Demon Gunner ignored it.

Butch frowned and placed his hands on his hips.

"Is it the girl?" he asked. Wade only responded with a nod. "Well, rest assured, she's well taken care of. We were just having her checked for bites."

"I want to see her."

"And you will, but we have to do the same for you first. Now just lower your guns…" Wade held them high. Butch shook his head and dropped his hand toward one of the gold revolvers at his waist. "I'm afraid I'm not asking."

Wade's hands started to shake, not wanting to drop the guns. He felt like the scared boy at the practice range again, but this wasn't Ulysses standing before him, this was someone who had just saved his life. Wade flipped looks between the crowd and Butch, and at the same time, both of his guns lowered.

Butch smiled and said, "Now you gotta hand yer' iron over."

He flapped his fingers, as if signaling for someone to come closer.

"*No*," Wade said sternly. "These weapons are a part of me. They stay in my hands and my hands only."

"Not in Fort Carn they aren't. You're a stranger to us, but we still saved your skin. Now, unless you want to be hog-tied and thrown back out there, then I suggest you cough 'em up. It's for our safety and yours."

Wade flashed looks between him and the crowd; they seemed to be closing in.

"How about the girl for the guns? Deal?" Butch asked.

Every instinct told Wade not to give up his iron, but he had no choice. The weapons wouldn't do him any good anyway, as he was greatly outnumbered. Besides, he still had the fire within him; he *always* had the fire.

Finally, Wade gave in and began the process of unhooking the magical chains that were bound to the grips of his guns. Once they were detached, he tossed the revolvers over to a gunslinger next to him, nearly impaling him with the knives that jutted off the ends of the barrels.

"I ain't never seen iron like this before, Butch," the gunslinger said while inspecting the raised gold engravings that ran across the guns like a web. "Where'd you get 'em?"

Wade stepped closer and clenched his fists.

"*The girl.*"

The gunslinger stepped back in fear as Butch placed a hand on his shoulder and said, "He knows better than to be talking." The gunslinger stepped back and carried the guns off to an unknown location. "A deal's a deal, my friend. Follow me this way!"

Wade walked behind Butch and passed through the crowd. The gunslingers continued to glare.

Weird fucks.

"Ignore 'em," Butch said, hiking up his blue jeans with his oversized belt. "Let me tell ya', we don't get a lot of newcomers around these parts. They're just surprised to see you, that's all. How about we start with your name?"

"*Wade.*"

"Well, Wade, welcome to our humble abode."

Wade looked around at the armed, patrolling gunslingers moving along the walkways that sat flush against the walls.

"What is this place?" he asked.

"This is Fort Carn! Established 1 AC," Butch said while raising his hands upward. "Our home, our commune, *our family*."

After Consumption… That's new.

"I didn't think anyone could survive out here this far into the Veil," Wade asked with genuine curiosity.

"Well, we make it work."

"How?"

"Torches, and *lots* of 'em. We dip them in kerosene and place them all around the perimeter of the fort before lighting them each and every night. It keeps them demonic bastards away. Hell, even them singing Demons don't come near this place, and if they do, we blow their damn heads off!" Butch yelled with a mighty laugh, slapping Wade hard on the back.

Wade stretched, attempting to recover from the surprisingly hard hit, and started to notice the impressive number of people that resided within the fort.

"*Food*, where do you get it?"

"First time in the Veil?"

"No."

"Well then you should know that the bastards out there don't go for animals, which leaves plenty for us! They want humans—real, delicious flesh…" Butch stared off into the distance. "*Souls*… It's like they can smell 'em." He continued walking. "We hunt and forage during the day and return here before the sun sets and Consumption begins."

Wade wondered how this could be true. Anyone he had met on his journey who had spent a decent amount of time in the Veil had been driven crazy by the Darkness, but these people seemed civilized. It couldn't be easy keeping a functioning village like this running, and truthfully, the Demon Gunner couldn't believe what he was seeing.

"We can even sleep without earplugs here. But you'll see for yourself tonight."

Wade nodded and continued to follow him into one of the shacks. Inside, small lamps and candles illuminated the space. A sign that said *infirmary* rested above a door.

"Right through there is where you'll find your cute little girl. Hopefully y'all ain't got no bites, or I'll have to dispose of you myself!" Butch said with another slap on the back and a big chuckle.

Wade ignored him and hurried toward the infirmary door. As he grabbed the handle, his heart rate picked up, hoping she'd be on the other side. He took a deep breath and pushed through, immediately finding Sarah sitting on a flat bench with her back turned toward him. The air his anxiety had held up finally released like a bellows.

She's safe, he thought to himself, relief washing over him.

A woman sat to her right, inspecting the girl's arms. Her dark brown hair was covered by a wide-brimmed hat, and she wore a button-down, just like the others, though she had left the top three undone. Her wrinkled face told a stressful story, but even with the toll the sun had taken on her skin, she was still *beautiful*, and Wade couldn't deny her resemblance to Jess. He tried not to stare, but he just couldn't help it. It had been a long time since he had seen anyone like her. After a while, the woman glanced up toward the Demon Gunner, and he quickly looked down at his dirty boots.

"Well, it looks like you're clean," the woman said as Sarah finally turned around and saw Wade standing in the doorway.

"Wade!" she yelled as she ran toward him, giving him a big hug. "I didn't know you made it!"

Wade could feel his shirt dampening at his chest. He wanted to hug her back, but *couldn't.*

"I'm here, and I'm glad you're alright," Wade whispered before she finally released him.

"As for you," the woman said. "I still need to check you over." She slapped the bench next to her. "Take a seat."

Wade looked down at Sarah, who gave him a reassuring nod, before shaking his head and following her orders.

"You can leave, sweetheart," the woman said. "It'll only take a minute."

"I'll see you outside," Sarah said, leaving Wade and the woman alone.

The mysterious woman stood in front of him, inspecting his body.

"I need you to take your shirt off first," she instructed.

The Demon Gunner didn't question it. He started by removing his thick leather jacket, and then one by one, he unbuttoned his tan shirt before fully taking it off. Scars littered his body, including a *large* one across his midsection.

"I bet you've got some stories to tell," the woman said as she brought her cold hands onto his body.

She began to run them over his shoulders and down his biceps, tracing his bulging veins to his forearms, then continuing to his calloused, weathered hands. She brought them back up to his chest, before she ran them across his abdomen and along the scar that rested there. She leaned forward and reached behind him as if bringing him in for a hug, then rubbed his back, checking for bites. For a moment, Wade wondered if this was even necessary, but he had a feeling that he didn't have much of a choice for what went on within these walls.

Don't make a fuss and just get this over with.

Finally, she stepped back and faced him.

"Your upper body is clean," she signaled to his faded blue jeans, "but I need to check down *there*." Wade flashed her a questioning look. "Trust me, I don't want to either, but the quicker we finish this and figure out if you're clean, the quicker I can start drinkin'."

"Can't argue with that," Wade said with a chuckle.

He undid the button on his pants, dropping them to his ankles. She got onto her knees and ran her hands along his thighs before moving to what lay between them. Wade couldn't see her face down there, but he could feel her cold hands on it, making him wince. He only continued to stare straight ahead at the wall, trying to make the time pass quicker. She finished by going down the back of his legs to his feet, before finally coming off of him.

"You're clean," she said as she helped pull his pants back up.

Wade started fastening his belt, "Usually I start with a name first."

"*Beth*, and yours?"

"*Wade.*"

"Well, welcome to Fort Carn, Wade. Hopefully I'll see you again," she said with a quick smile before leaving the room.

Wade froze for a moment and then shook his head, before buttoning his shirt and putting his jacket back on.

Outside the infirmary, he found Sarah sitting on a wooden crate talking to Butch.

"Ah! Thank Nor! You're both alright. Now we can feast

without worry!" Butch said while wiping a bead of sweat off his forehead with the back of his wrist. "Will you two be joining us in the mess hall?"

Wade glanced at Sarah and saw her heavy eyes fluttering.

"I think… we might have to pass tonight, Butch. We had a *long* day."

"Ah, no worries, friend! Let me tell you, I can only imagine the hell y'all went through to get here. There's a reason why we don't go outside these walls after dark! Now, we can get y'all into your room and talk again in the morning. How does that sound?"

"I'd appreciate that. Sarah?"

Sarah nodded, followed by a yawn.

"Right this way!"

• • •

For a fort in the middle of the desert—especially this deep into the Veil—Wade was incredibly surprised by their plush accommodations. A large animal skin rested in the center of the room, stretched across a wooden floor between two twin beds. Stationed between the beds was a small dresser with a lamp on it, and above the dresser was a holding rack for guns.

Butch had dropped off a hearty amount of food for them, which consisted of vegetables and buffalo meat, and of course, Wade and Sarah dug into it as soon as it arrived. By the time they finished it, they were both so full that they laid on their beds, exhausted and stuffed.

"What do you think of this place, Wade?" Sarah asked, staring up at the ceiling.

Wade looked around at the walls and thought about it

for a moment before saying, "I'm not sure. It just doesn't make sense, and I'm still trying to wrap my head around it."

"Have you ever seen anything like it?"

"*Never,*" Wade responded. "I would've thought that anyone who lives this deep into the Veil would've been driven mad, yet, they seem… normal?"

"*And* they saved us."

"They did indeed."

There was a long silence.

"I thought you were gone, Wade. I didn't know what to do."

"I almost was…"

Silence filled the room again, except for the occasional creak of the beds they lay upon.

"You should get some rest," Wade finally said. "We will need to get moving tomorrow morning. I don't want to stay here long."

"Why not?"

Wade stared at the ceiling and said, "Back at the Order, they used to tell us that it's common to see an oasis in the desert when you're thirsty. They're called mirages, because the closer you get, the more you realize it was never real."

"Why do you say that?"

"The Darkness can play tricks on the mind, Sarah, and I fear we may be in one now."

"But we're safe for the night, right? I mean, at least we're not camping in the desert?"

"You're right, at least we're not out there."

"At least we're not out there," she repeated. "Goodnight, Wade. I'll see you in the morning."

"Goodnight, Sarah."

But it didn't take long for Wade to realize that he wouldn't be able to fall asleep—not here, not *now*. Falling asleep would require a stiff drink, something heavy to ease his racing mind.

• • •

Soft music echoed across the fort as Wade *quietly* shut the door to their room, attempting not to wake Sarah. He followed the soothing sound of a banjo to a small shack in the corner of the fort where dozens of gunslingers stood talking and dancing. Inside the shack, drinks were being poured into tin cups. With his thumb and index finger, Wade tipped his hat down lower on his forehead and stepped inside. In front of him, a wall of various liquors sat on shelves. Wade caught himself from cheering with glee, not believing his eyes.

"What are you having?" a bartender asked as Wade approached.

"Whatever you'll give me."

The bartender smiled and waved a hand toward the bottles. "You can have anything you want, *sir*. It's on the house."

Wade's eyebrow raised with suspicion, but he wasn't going to argue with the man. He had been alive long enough to know that you *never* turn down a free drink, and Nor knew he needed it now more than ever.

Wade pointed toward a bottle of whiskey on the top shelf, but instead of getting him a glass, the bartender grabbed the entire bottle and placed it on the bar with a *thud*.

"All yours, newcomer," he said with a smile, sliding it

forward.

Wade inspected the bottle, popped the cork, and took a sip. The sharp liquor burned his throat, followed by a warm hug that enveloped him.

"*Ahhhh,*" Wade let out.

"Good stuff, huh?"

"*Good stuff.* Thankya," Wade said with a tip of his hat.

Wade took another long sip and looked around at the laughing and talking gunslingers, noticing the peace and tranquility of the scene. Fort Carn reminded him of his time at school with his friends… with Jess, and it nearly brought a tear to his eye.

Perhaps he had overreacted with Butch, or maybe it was his training that he just couldn't seem to shut off no matter how hard he tried. Here, with these people, there was nothing to worry about. But although it was nice, he still didn't want to leave Sarah alone in the room for long, so he took one last sip and began to push his way back through the crowd that had formed in the bar. Just as he stepped outside the shack, a soft hand grabbed his own and pulled him back inside.

"Howdy, Wade," Beth said with a big smile. "Glad you found your way to the ol' watering hole."

Wade ripped his hand out of her grip. "I was just leaving."

"Really? What's the rush? Not like you got anywhere to be right now."

"I…" Wade looked around at the dancing–the camaraderie of the gunslingers.

For the past few months, Wade had traveled alone across the desert, inhaling sand and fighting Demons. Staying a little longer wouldn't hurt, and besides, he didn't know when he would *ever* see a woman like this again.

"I guess I could stay for one song," Wade finally said, attempting to hide the smirk that was begging to crack through his stoic expression.

Beth quickly patted the stool next to her, which he pulled out and sat down on.

"So, where should we start first, Wade? I want to know why the hell you were out in the desert with a young girl, and how you got all those scars?"

"How about neither," Wade said, taking a long pull from the bottle.

"Oh no, you're not getting off that easy. We pay our dues around here with stories."

"Is that how it works?"

"Well that's *one* way," she said with a smile as she brushed against his leg with her hand.

Wade ignored this and took another sip. "I'm on a mission–a quest if you will."

"What kind? To get the most scars in the least amount of time?"

Wade gagged, causing some whiskey to spill on his chin. Beth extended her thumb and wiped it off before licking the residue from the tip of her finger.

"I guess you could say that's a part of it."

"Really?"

"Well I'm in search of answers, and those usually don't come easily."

"Aren't we all…" Beth said, taking a long sip from Wade's bottle without asking. "Tell me, what *kind* of answers?"

Wade thought for a moment, before finally responding with, "What happened to the world… Why the light went out… Who took it and how to get it back."

"Have you ever thought that this was a punishment?"

"For what?"

"*Sin.* You believe in Nor, don't ya'?"

Wade thought for a moment, then responded with, "He would never do that."

"How do *you* know? What if his creations got off the rails. Perhaps he wanted a fresh start. It's what I'd do, at least." She took another pull.

"Well good thing you're not Nor."

"Who says I'm not?"

Wade didn't respond.

"Or, how about this? What if this were Hell? I know I belong there," Beth said with a chuckle.

"The girl I'm with, *Sarah,* she doesn't. Maybe I do, but she doesn't."

"You say so much with absolute certainty. How do you know that to be true?"

Wade glared at her and then took his longest sip yet.

"*I know,*" he finally muttered.

"Well, if I were you, I'd stop looking for your answers. Instead, focus on what's right in front of you," she said as she began to run her hand up his inner thigh.

Wade's pants grew tighter.

What's a little more sin when you're already in Hell?

And before he knew it, they were bursting through the door to her room. Their lips were locked, tongues buried in each other's mouths as clothes were being ripped off and thrown onto the floor. She tackled him onto the bed and thrust his hands onto her plump breasts. As they kissed, he brought his hands down her sides and past her hips, feeling their width.

She quickly pressed her mouth to his neck and sucked *hard.* Wade's entire body pulsed, but the sucking became tighter and stronger. She pulled off with tremendous force, causing Wade to wince in pain.

Her hands then ran down to his jeans and slipped under the fabric, feeling the stiff shaft that rested there. She began kissing him on the lips again, but this time, she bit his lip forcefully. He groaned and recoiled back, checking to see if his lip was still there with his finger. A small drop of blood rested on the tip; she moaned and licked her lips.

"I'm sorry," she whimpered as she sped up what she was doing below his belt. "I just got excited." She licked down his neck and chest. "Don't worry, I'll make up for it."

His pants were ripped off and thrown away as she began toying with him in her mouth. Wade breathed heavily as she worked her way back up and climbed on top of him, sliding onto his shaft. A rush of warmth and pleasure poured over him, but he couldn't focus on it for long as she had started to ride him like a horse, smashing the headboard into the wall and yelling with pleasure.

Wade thought that she was going to wake up every gunslinger in the fort, including Butch, but then she brought her mouth down again and bit into his neck, *hard.* The pain was too much to bear and Wade pulled back, yelling out in pain.

"*Shhhhh,*" she said, licking down his neck. "We don't want to wake up the others. They would be jealous."

He wanted to protest, but an incredible feeling was building below his waist. Everything else left his mind, and only pleasure remained. She bit into his shoulder, but now the pain mixed with the pleasure, providing an intoxicating sensation. And then she saw his face, causing her to moan even louder. He knew he couldn't fight it any longer. His legs tensed, and he let go; the release was powerful and *binding*, causing them both to shake and moan. Beth finally collapsed forward and hugged him tight, twitching and shuddering as the pleasure slowly left their bodies.

"That... was *incredible*," she whispered in his ear, gently nibbling on it.

Wade's head spun as he breathed deeply, running his hands over her ass. They lay together, without exiting, until they both fell asleep and the Darkness had retreated.

DG

CHAPTER NINE

THE KING'S FEAST

The door to Sarah's room slowly creaked open. Wade peered in through the crack and saw the girl sleeping peacefully in her bed. Next to her, dust hung in the air, illuminated by the faint morning light shining in through a nearby window.

Wade tried entering as quietly as possible, but a loose floorboard under his boot quickly ruined that plan. Sarah stirred in her bed before rolling over and facing Wade, who had just taken off his hat and placed it beside him on the fur blanket that stretched across his bed.

"Where were you?" Wade didn't respond. "Wade?"

"I had a long night…" he finally muttered.

Sarah gave him a questioning look before sighing and pulling the blanket off of herself. She spun sideways so that her feet dangled off the edge of the bed and stretched her arms above her head with a big yawn.

"Well, if you don't want to talk about last night, how about we talk about today? What's the plan?" Sarah asked.

Wade scratched his head and thought about it for a moment. Truthfully, he didn't have a plan, not even a faint *idea* of one. Quicksilver was gone—lost in the storm, and she was their only means of travel across the wasteland. Perhaps Butch could provide a horse, but how could they feed it or quench its thirst? His sleeping pad, candles, and tent were also gone, which meant he had nothing left besides the clothes on his back and the revolvers that should've been sitting on his hips.

He imagined that the gunslingers would be more than happy to provide rations for their journey, but that would only fix *one* of their problems. And traveling at the regular speed of a horse would get Sarah and Wade killed if they didn't manage to make it to shelter in time. Besides, Wade had nothing to mask their scent. The Demons would surely sniff them out; they wouldn't even make it through the first night.

"So..." Sarah said, leaning forward inquisitively. "Do I need to ask—"

"I don't have one," Wade sheepishly admitted.

"You don't have a plan?"

"No."

"But you always have a plan?"

"Not this time."

• • •

The heatless sun hung high in the sky now, and Fort Carn was *alive*. Hunting parties had gone out in the morning and returned with rabbits, birds, and buffalo. Anyone who stayed behind either lounged around the fort, played cards, or practiced their aim, but as Wade and Sarah walked through the main courtyard, he couldn't seem to shake a strange feeling. No matter what the gunslingers were doing, their gazes still seemed to find them.

"Good morning, you two!" Butch said, hobbling over toward them. "Slept well, I hope?"

"I definitely did!" Sarah enthusiastically blurted out. "Nothing beats a proper bed after sleeping in a cave."

"Ain't that the truth," Butch chuckled. "What about you, Wade?"

"It was a good night."

"Love to hear it! Now, what are y'all wanting to get up to today?"

"That's something I actually wanted to discuss with you," Wade said.

"Lay it on me!"

"My steed got lost in the storm before we arrived. We don't have any means to carry on our journey."

"Well, I could give you a horse–perhaps two of 'em, but I can't promise you'd be able to get out of the Veil. Trust me, we've *tried*. No matter how far out you go, the Consumption still finds you. It seems to go on forever, with no end in sight."

"I'm afraid it does…" Wade said while pondering this.

He assumed that where he had started his journey had already been consumed. There was no turning back now; nothing could go fast enough to escape it, not even Quicksilver. The only option that remained was to go *further* into it.

"Wade, if you want to stay, all you need to do is ask," Butch said with a soft smile. "There ain't much of a world out there beyond these walls for the young one."

Wade glanced down at Sarah, who was admiring the gunslingers target practice.

"I'll need some time to think, but we greatly appreciate your hospitality."

Butch nodded and said, "Of course. In the meantime, make yourselves at home!"

Butch began to hobble away as the Demon Gunner called out, "Butch?" He turned around. "I meant to ask, I *need* my iron back."

"Consider it a loan," Butch said, flashing his rotted teeth. "Once you figure out if you're joining the brotherhood, I'll give 'em back to you. It's a safety thing, remember? What's ours is yours, and what's yours is mine! It's an old gunslinger sayin', I bet you've got a few of 'em yourself."

"Sure do..."

Wade stared at the obese man as he limped away, tipping his hat to passing gunslingers. Butch had been kind to them, but his friendliness still didn't stop Wade from loathing him. There was a time when Ulysses had been kind to him too. Regardless, he wanted his guns back, and he wanted them back *now*.

By the time Butch had hobbled out of earshot, Wade turned to Sarah and said, "How about you go and practice your shot. I bet they'd be willing to give you a rifle."

"Alright," Sarah responded. "And what are you going to do?"

He caught a flash of Beth tending to an injured gunslinger on one of the upper levels of the fort. She looked down at him and waved with a big smile.

"I need to talk to someone."

Sarah followed his eyeline.

"*Someone*, huh? You like her, don't ya'?"

Wade smiled and shook his head. "Get on outta here."

Sarah ran off, giggling the whole way. Wade then made his way up to Beth, just as the injured gunslinger got up off a crate and thanked her. After he left, Wade approached and tipped his hat before standing with his thumbs resting on his belt.

"Good morning," Wade said.

"Mornin'," Beth responded.

"Mind if we talk?"

Beth looked around in search of other injured gunslingers who might need her services, then finally said, "I think I can spare ya' a few minutes."

• • •

Wade and Beth carefully climbed a tall ladder to the top of a stone tower. It sat on one corner of the fort and offered an unobstructed vantage point overlooking the desolate valley. Tumbleweeds blew across the dry, desert landscape, and the cold sun hung in the sky above them.

Below them, Wade could see Sarah practicing her rifling. Another gunslinger–a teenager with shaggy brown hair and a friendly look on his face–was helping her aim. He stood behind her, holding her arms up as he guided the barrel of the rifle toward a target. What he was doing was incredibly dangerous and *not* the correct way to teach someone proper aim, but Wade knew that wasn't the goal. His suspicions were quickly confirmed, as each time she ran out of bullets, she would turn around with the gun pointed at the ground and talk with him. Wade couldn't hear what they were saying, but he didn't need to. He could see a twinkle in her eye and a bright smile on her face. It made him *happy*.

"I had a great night with you last night," Beth said, running her hand down his arm.

"So did I," Wade responded, pulling her in closer.

"Do you think you're going to stay?"

"I'm not sure yet. But it doesn't seem like I have much

of a choice."

A long silence followed as they watched Sarah laughing and talking with the young gunslinger.

"She seems happy here," Beth finally said. "Do you see it too?"

"I do, and I'm not sure if I want to be the one to take that away."

"Who says you have to?"

Wade shook his head and looked out toward the desert, the wind ruffling strands of brown hair that had escaped his hat.

"This was why I didn't want to bring her along. One way or another, I knew I'd have to choose between her and my quest."

"The quest? You're still thinking about that, huh?"

"I have to, what else is there to think about?"

Beth looked down at the roof they sat on, as if his words hurt her to hear—and maybe they did, but he didn't *care*. The fate of the world was still at stake, and it was up to him to figure out how to save it.

"The Darkness... The Demons... This isn't living, Beth. Can't you see? I thank you for welcoming us, but this fort isn't a home, it's a cage. Your entire world is confined to four walls and a bar. Don't you remember how it was before? The people, the animals, the *color?* We need to bring it back—we need to bring life back to Rhodahn!"

"Says who?" Beth responded defensively, raising her voice. "I feel more alive here than I ever did before the light went out. Just because *you* can't see that, doesn't mean it's not true!"

"Maybe so, but I know this isn't where I'm meant to be. I'm meant to be out there—on my quest," Wade's eyes slowly grew wider, "but maybe *she* isn't." He looked down at Sarah again. "Maybe this is as far as she goes; this is where her journey ends."

"Are you saying you'd leave her?"

Wade turned toward Beth and met her eyes. "Think about it. You could train her to become a gunslinger. She could join the brotherhood and live here, until I brought the light back!"

"But you still want to leave?"

"Beth, I have to. There's no other choice. You'll protect her, won't you?"

Beth shook her head and said, "Fine, I promise I will. And I won't stop you, but if this is the end of a short friendship..." And without another word, she grabbed Wade and kissed him.

Wade kissed her back, but it didn't take long for a sharp bite to come down on his bottom lip. He tried to pull away, but she rolled on top of him and pinned his arms back.

"If this is the last time I will see you," she said, reaching into his pants, "then I want to make it *count*."

• • •

Wade stood outside the door to Sarah's room. He could hear her rustling about inside, and he raised a balled fist to knock but stopped an inch from the wood. He had already rehearsed what he was going to say, but still, his conviction wavered. He didn't want to see her cry. Then, the door flung open, and Sarah stood before him.

"Wade?" She immediately noticed the solemn look on his face. "What are you doing out here?"

"Sarah," he sighed, "we need to talk."

"About what?"

"May I come in?"

"Of course, it's your room too."

A smile broke on his face as he entered.

"Is everything alright, Wade?"

Wade didn't respond. He just sat on the edge of his bed and removed his hat, revealing a head of sweaty, matted hair.

"You're in love, aren't ya'?" Sarah said with a giggle.

"I could say the same for you."

Sarah's face flushed. "It's just been a while since I've talked to a nice boy, that's all."

"Trust me, I understand." Wade looked down and scooped up his hat into his hands. "But that's not what I came here to talk about."

"What is it then?"

He took a deep breath and rubbed the brim of his hat with his index finger and thumb.

"Do you remember what I said about the mirage?" Wade asked.

"Yes, of course. Do you still think we're in one?"

Wade looked up at Sarah. "When we first got here, I thought this place was no good–a roadblock on our urgent quest. But the more I think about it, the more I realize we were *meant* to find this place."

"Wade–"

"When I saved your life, I made a promise to you. A promise that I would protect you to the best of my ability, but this journey–my quest–I'd be lying if I said it wouldn't get more dangerous. The more I toil with it, the more I realize it was never meant for *you*. It was something I decided to do on my own–to find answers, and perhaps to fix this fucked up world so that one day you can live in a better one."

"What are you saying?"

"What I'm saying is, Nor brought us together. Nor also brought us here... but I think this is where we part ways." Sarah froze; tears welled in her eyes. "Sarah, *I'm sorry,* but my quest was never meant for the both of us. You can stay here–learn their ways and live among them. We both know it's safer that way. I don't have Quicksilver any more, and I can't see what lies ahead in the Darkness. If you come, you could die."

"And so could you!"

"I know, but it's what I signed up for when I set out on this journey. But you, Sarah, you didn't, and you don't deserve to be dragged along by something that doesn't concern you."

"So you're just going to leave me here?"

Wade nodded, and Sarah hung her head.

"I *have* to, as I couldn't live with myself if something were to happen to you out there. You'll be safe here, and that is all that matters." Sarah sat in silence. "Sarah?"

She ran forward and hugged him.

"Thank you, Wade."

"For what?"

"For saving my life again."

Wade slowly wrapped his arms around the girl and hugged her back.

"I'll miss you," she said, not letting go.

"I'll miss–"

A knock came from the door, causing them to finally release. Wade put his hat back on and made his way to the door. He swung it open and saw Butch standing before him.

"Wade! It is good to see your fresh face. Would you and Sarah like to join us for dinner?" He looked between them and saw the girl's tears. "Oh… Is this a bad time?"

"No," Wade assured, wiping his own face. "We'd love to."

Butch nodded, "Alright, I'll see y'all down there then. No rush! I promise, the food will stay warm!"

Butch hobbled away, and Wade closed the door again.

"Well, we should probably–"

Sarah hugged him once more.

• • •

The mess hall contained a large wooden table that stretched the length of the room. A sizable revolver insignia, engraved into the wood, sat at its center. It reminded Wade of the Order's very own, and the barrel pointed directly toward his heart. Plates and chalices waiting to be filled rested on top of the table, and large platters of food, concealed by silver covers, lay on either side of the insignia.

All of the gunslingers in Fort Carn were in the room, and Wade could see that the Blood Moon was rising through one of the windows, casting its all-too-familiar red glow across the wasteland. Butch stood at the head of the table, while Wade faced him from the other end with Sarah and Beth beside him. One by one, they all took their seats.

"Before we begin our feast, I think Wade has an important announcement to make," Butch called out, causing Wade's eyebrow to raise in surprise. "Come on now, Wade, you *know*." Wade still sat in confusion, unsure of what he was referring to. "Don't keep us waiting. What have you decided to do? Are you stayin', or are you leavin'?"

All of the gunslingers stared at him in fascination.

"Oh... Well, I hoped to have a word with ya' privately, but I guess I can speak on it now." Wade released a small cough to clear his throat. "To start, I greatly appreciate your hospitality. Sleeping in caves and dealing with the Demons that lurk beyond these walls has not been easy, *especially* for poor Sarah here. So thank you for bringing us in, truly. But, before we arrived on your doorstep, I was on a quest for answers. Unfortunately... I am *still* on that quest, and I will be unable to stay here as I need to finish what I started. Tomorrow, I will set off into Darkness once more and carry on my journey."

Silence filled the room, and then, one by one, devilish smiles crossed the gunslinger's faces. Then, everyone sitting at the table erupted into laughter. Hands slammed down hard on the table, and feet danced madly on the floor, causing the entire room to shake. Butch was laughing so hard, he could barely breathe.

He finally slammed his fist down on the table and yelled, "Quiet, quiet, I don't think the man is even finished!" which caused the room to laugh *even* harder.

Wade and Sarah looked around with confusion. He glanced over to Beth who stared at him with wide-eyed fascination. She reached out a hand and took his, rubbing it with her thumb.

"Please, Wade, *continue,*" she whispered. "You're almost to the best part."

Wade's brow furrowed as he started again, "*But...* I believe it is in Sarah's best interest... to stay."

The crowd erupted into cheers and hollering. They

began bouncing in their seats, violently whipping their heads back and forth, mere inches from slamming their faces onto the table. Sarah looked to Wade again with great fear, but he didn't know what was going on or why they were acting so weird. Out of instinct, Wade stealthily brought his hands to his holsters, but they still sat empty on his legs.

Fuck.

Butch leaned forward and swooped up his chalice before raising it into the air.

"To the fresh blood of the brotherhood... Wade and Sarah!" Butch signaled for them to take up their chalices and raise them high.

"To the fresh blood!" the rest of the gunslingers said in unison, as they all took long sips from their chalices.

Wade glanced at Sarah, as if to say, *No.*

"Wade, *Sarah...* Go on now. Git you some of that sweet liquor," Butch said, but his smile had morphed into that of a hungry pig.

Still, the Gunner signaled, *No.*

"Hey, don't look at him, look at me." His voice was demanding, and he raised his gold revolver and placed it on the table with a loud *thud.* "I said drink, girl."

Wade felt heat growing within his balled fists, but the other gunslingers stood up, lowering their hands to their iron. Wade wouldn't be able to summon his fire without them noticing and striking him down. So, he looked at the girl and finally nodded, *Yes.*

All the gunslingers in the room watched as Sarah drank, uncanny smiles growing on their faces. When Sarah finished, she gagged and coughed before wiping the dark liquid off her chin with her dirty dress sleeve.

"Now you, *Gunner.* Drink up."

Wade didn't move.

"I SAID DRINK!" Butch slammed his chalice down onto the table, causing Sarah to jump in fright.

Wade swooped up his own chalice and drank it before tossing the empty cup aside. It bounced across the room and rattled to a halt on the floor.

"Very good," he said, licking his lips and flashing his rotted teeth. "I like you soldiers, so good at following orders. Now, what did you say again at the bar?" Butch took a long sip. "*Ahhhhh…*" he mocked, wiping the liquor from his mustache. The other gunslingers laughed. "Well, Wade, that speech you gave was beautiful, and I commend you. Wanting to save the world and all that stupid shit, ha, just like them heroes of those old tales we all read as wee, little children. But, let me spoil something for you, Gunner, this ain't no children's tale, and I've got a few words of my own for you."

Wade's heart was now beating out of his chest as he scanned around the room. In the time it took him to drink his chalice, it seemed as if the other gunslingers had pressed in *closer* to him.

"Let me be the first to say, we were *so* happy you showed up on our doorstep. We don't get many visitors around these parts, but when we do, we never waste the opportunity to take them in. And of course, they never say no! They all show up with the same scared and bewildered look, so happy to find *us,* as if they stumbled upon Nor's very own home in the sky! And we don't even know how we got so lucky! Whether it's the storm that circles this place, them nasty Demons, or the Darkness itself, it's almost like you poor suckers are guided here."

Butch stared up to the sky, as if looking at something or *someone*. The other gunslingers seemed eager to jump out of their seats. Their feet and hands tapped wildly, as their empty eyes pierced *deep* into Wade's soul.

"So let me just cut to the point. You're a gift, and we don't give up our gifts that easily."

Wade glanced at Beth, and the smile that had once sat on her face transformed into a devilishly twisted one. He barely recognized her now.

"Do you remember what you said, Wade–how this whole thing shouldn't exist? The Darkness corrupts, drives people crazy. You... You remember all that, don't ya'? Tell me you remember, Gunner?" The gunslingers looked between each other. Their smiles widened. "Well, guess what? You were right."

"Wa...Wade..." Wade flipped his gaze from Butch to the girl, just before her head dropped and slammed hard onto the table.

"Sarah!" Wade shouted.

Two men grabbed him from behind and forced him down into his chair again. He tried to fight from their grip, but he felt his strength waning. Next to him, Beth inched closer and continued to run her hands up and down his arms.

"Easy there, Wade. It's almost over, then we can feast," she whispered in his ear.

Butch stood up, facing Wade, and readjusted himself by pulling on the bowing belt that held up his oversized pants.

"The thing about the Darkness," Butch said, "is that it only drives you crazy if you fight it. If you succumb to it–let yourself be taken by its power, then it actually sets you free."

All at once, their eyes shifted to a glowing, green color.

"We see the truth now, Wade. I know you want to find your answers–something or someone to tell you how to 'save' this world, but who ever said it needs saving? Who says we need to go back to the way things were? When the Gunners ruled us? When them weird and self-righteous fuckers ran around with the glowing sticks? No. Oh no, no, no. We're the kings now, and we're *not* going back. I won't let you drag us back to the light, Wade. I like it, just how things are." Butch walked down the length of the table and approached Wade, mere inches from his face. His putrid breath made Wade gag. "Now listen to me, Wade, when you stare into the Darkness for long enough, you'll see someone staring back. When you stop and listen to him, he'll give you the answers you so desperately seek. But what you fail to realize is that we don't need the light to come back, and you must accept that fact and learn to live in the dark."

Next to Wade, Sarah continued to lay with her head forward, unmoving. Butch sauntered behind the girl and grabbed a bundle of her hair in a closed fist. He pulled her head back, so that she was looking toward the sky, and forced one of her eyes open before dropping her head back down onto the table with a *thud*.

"What the hell... did you do... to...her."

"Oh, just the same thing that's happening to you now, Wade. I'm honestly surprised it took this long. You're a fighter, aren't ya'. You know, way back when, I tried being a Gunner myself. Them arrogant fucks didn't let me in the Order, so, I created my own. The day I heard you killed each other was the best damn day of my life." Wade's eyes grew wide, but then their heaviness became apparent, and they slowly began to close. "The good news is, all of this will be over soon." Wade fought with all his might to stay awake. "Still awake, goodness me! Well then, I might as well keep talkin'! You wondered how we survived out here? Well, we adapted—evolved to the new world we found ourselves in."

Wade's vision started to blur, and his head grew heavier and heavier, as if someone were stacking weights upon it. He swayed back and forth, attempting to stay conscious.

"You see, Wade, it's only darkness if you're blinded by the light. You're smart, so I know you know it too. The world you remember is gone, and there's no bringing it back now. I'm sorry you couldn't see that before. I think you would've made a fine gunslinger of the brotherhood. All that training would've been useful for us, and it's a damn shame we're letting it go to waste, but you'll make a fine meal instead."

A silver platter was pushed before Wade. Butch grabbed the lid and pulled it off, revealing a man's severed head with his mouth hanging open as if perpetually screaming. Blood trickled out of his dug out eye sockets, and his tongue seemed to be missing. Next to Wade, he saw a female gunslinger chewing on it, as if it were a broken-off stalk of sugarcane.

"As for the girl, she's too pretty to be eaten like you," Butch said, tossing the lid to the side. The others in the room cackled at the sound of this. Butch ran his stubby fingers through her long blonde hair before reaching her face. He touched her lips, her cheeks, and neck as his lips trembled. "*Thank you* for delivering us such a beautiful girl, Wade. I just know she's going to be delicious."

Drool seeped from his mouth and dripped onto her arm, then Butch's hand reached down and gripped her neck. His breath shook, and his lip quivered even more. "So, so delicious."

"Get… off…of…" Wade's head fell forward again, but it was caught by sharp fingernails that dug into his forehead before it could fall.

"You're in my house now, Wade. You don't tell me what to do with my food!" Butch signaled to the men behind him, and they grabbed Wade and yanked him up. His legs felt weak and shaky, and he could barely stand on his own. "Take him to the hooks while we have some fun with the girl."

The other gunslingers cheered and hollered as Wade was dragged backward, out of the mess hall. As he was taken away, he watched them surround the girl. The door slowly shut, trapping her alone inside with the *monsters*.

CHAPTER TEN

LEAD & BLOOD

The tips of Wade's boots squeaked as he was dragged across the floor, suspended by his armpits. His vision faded in and out, and the long hallway he found himself in seemed to stretch and twist endlessly, disorienting him.

Finally, they reached a dark, descending flight of stairs that led to a cellar. Wade was thrown forward, flipping and crashing down the stairs before slamming hard against a solid iron door. Footsteps echoed behind him, until a gunslinger reached the door and unlocked it with a brass key. It groaned as it opened, and immediately, a horrible stench filled Wade's nostrils. He gagged before being pushed face first inside the room. He was too weak to catch himself, and he fell hard onto the floor. As he lay there, he heard mumbling behind him, but he couldn't understand it. It sounded as if they were speaking underwater. The world in front of him continued to spin, yet, all he could think about was *Sarah.*

His bruised face rose from the cold, stone floor, attempting to get his bearings. Then, he saw them: sharp iron hooks dangling from the ceiling by thick chains. Corpses hung from the hooks, suspended by the skin on their backs or pierced through their mouths. They had long since died, and trails of blood ran down their pallid skin from slits on their necks, pooling at their feet.

More mumbling came from the gunslingers behind him. Wade tried to focus on their voices, and slowly, they became clearer, like ear plugs being pulled out.

"Can you hear me, Wade?" He looked up to the source of the voice. "Good, because I wanted to tell you that I did enjoy making love with you. I will carry our baby with pride," Beth said as she rubbed her stomach. "He'll never know you, but I promise, he will make for a fine gunslinger one day, just like his daddy."

"Enough talking," the other gunslinger interrupted. "Let's get him hung up and cut open so I can have my turn with the girl."

Immense rage poured over Wade. He felt sensations growing in his limbs, as if he were regaining control over them. His blurred vision became clearer, the world stopped spinning, and heat grew in his body. He pictured Sarah in the room upstairs–what they were doing to her, the revolting smiles and mouths filled with rotten teeth, as they had their way with the one person he made a promise to protect.

Beth stepped forward and holstered her revolver before grabbing one of the hooks to keep it steady. The other two gunslingers fished their hands under Wade's armpits again and started to lift him off his feet. His fingers twitched; his muscles contracted.

Sarah.

Wade yelled out in rage. In one move, he pushed off the floor and grabbed the heads of the two men holding him before slamming them hard together.

CRACK!

Their bodies dropped, and blood seeped out of their

shattered skulls.

"NO!" Beth screamed, fumbling for her revolver, but Wade had already lunged at her.

He pried the hook from her grip and forced it through her opened, screaming mouth. The sharp point of the hook tore through the back of her skull, raising her hair and sending blood spraying across the room in a stream. Her eyelids twitched as her body went limp and fell forward, dangling lifeless, suspended by the hook. Blood steadily trickled out of her mouth and ran down her neck.

Breathing heavily, Wade stared at her corpse for a moment. Then, a rustling sound came from the two men at his feet. He turned to see them scrambling on the floor, disoriented, groaning, and clutching their cracked skulls in pain. Gritting his teeth, Wade lifted his leather boot over one of their heads and brought it down with such tremendous force that the gunslinger's skull exploded, painting Wade's other leg in blood and brain matter. The last living gunslinger—who had gotten a mouthful of it—looked up at Wade in horror.

"N… No..." the man muttered as he attempted to crawl away from the Demon Gunner, slipping and sliding in the pool of blood beneath him. "Please… don't hurt me."

Wade grabbed the man by the neck and lifted him off the floor.

"Would you have hurt her?" Wade asked.

The man's eyes went wide; Wade lowered his face toward a hook.

"HAVE MERCY!" the man yelled as the tip of the hook pierced his eyeball and passed straight through it.

He screamed and writhed within Wade's grip while the hook drove deeper into his brain. His arms and legs flailed, scraping against the ground, but Wade didn't stop. He pushed the hook in *farther* until he felt the tip reach the inside of his skull and drag along it. The gunslinger's body shuddered one final time before Wade dropped him fully onto the hook, leaving him dangling in the air by his eye socket. The metallic smell of blood had now overpowered the rot in the air, and Wade didn't want to stand in it any longer.

He grabbed two revolvers from the corpses and left their bodies in the darkness before stumbling up the stairs. He felt weak and dizzy again, suspecting the adrenaline from his rage was wearing off. But once he reached the top of the stairs, he saw the doorway to the mess hall in the distance, and his heart began to race. He fought to stay upright–the hallway stretching in and out–and every few feet, he caught himself on the walls to keep from tipping over. Yet with each step toward the door, more rage and *heat* surged inside him.

Then, he heard voices from within the room.

"I get to go first!" one yelled.

"No, she's mine!"

"Stand the fuck back!" A gunshot rang out. "If you think anyone is touching her but me, you're wrong," Butch yelled over the chaos. "The girl's *mine,* and let me tell you, I've never tasted a beauty like this before–"

Wade screamed as blue fire erupted from his eyes. He kicked the mess hall door open, exploding it into a thousand wooden splinters. Immediately, he saw dozens of naked gunslingers standing before him. Sarah lay on the table, still motionless, and Butch stood before her, naked, with his pants at his ankles and the hem of her dress bunched up in his hand.

BANG! BANG! BANG! BANG! BANG!

Shots rang out across the room. Heads exploded, spraying blood onto the walls. Their bodies dropped instantly as Wade stepped fully into the mess hall. The naked gunslingers dove for cover, scrambling for their weapons, but Wade was too quick for them. He slid forward and pressed the barrel of his right revolver into the side of a gunslinger's head. He pulled the trigger, blowing a hole clean through it. His other revolver tracked around the room, shooting and picking off any stragglers that attempted to hide.

Click! Click!

His guns were empty; he tossed them aside. In front of him, a gunslinger attempted to grab a gun from her holster. Wade leapt forward, sliding across the embossed table and snatching up a piece of cutlery as he went. While falling off the other end, he jammed the knife into the wood, inches away from the insignia. The frantic gunslinger raised her shaking gun at Wade, but it was too late. He grabbed her wrist and disarmed her before slamming her face onto the table and driving the knife through her skull.

Just as Wade turned to face Butch, a bowie knife came down on top of him. Wade managed to catch his attacker by the wrist with one hand, holding him off as he thrust the barrel of his revolver upward into his attacker's chin. The gunslinger screamed; terror filled his eyes.

BANG!

His head exploded, painting the ceiling with blood and brain matter that dripped down in giant globs. Wade breathed heavily, the revolver clutched in his bloody hand.

"Now, Wade... just listen to me," Butch pleaded behind him.

Wade heard boots frantically squeaking across the blood covered floor. He turned to the source of it and saw Butch desperately attempting to pull up his pants. Wade walked toward the pathetic man, wiping blood from his face with the sleeve of his jacket.

"I didn't do nothin' yet," Butch said as he backpedaled, holding his pants up by the belt.

"*Yet?*" Wade said, holstering his revolver as he stared Butch dead in the eyes.

The blue fire that emanated from his own illuminated the terrified man's face, and Wade slowly began to wrap the chains that dangled from his forearms over his knuckles.

"What the hell are you?" Butch uttered, his lip quivering.

The Demon Gunner lunged at Butch, tackling him onto the ground. Punches flew back and forth across the fat man's face, and with each hit, blood and teeth sprayed across the room. Wade continued, not letting up as Butch coughed and choked on his own blood, which rapidly filled his mouth.

"If I hadn't survived," Wade said, laying another hard punch across his face, "what would you have done to her?"

"P…P…Please…" Butch pleaded, blood pouring from his torn apart mouth.

Wade scooped up the man's head into his hands and began to push inward, *hard*. He could feel his skull start to flex within his grip.

"This is the world you wanted to live in, right, Butch? Okay, then let me show you what I like to do to the Demons hiding in the Darkness."

Wade thrust his thumbs into the man's bulging, horrified eyes. He screamed and writhed in pain, as Wade gritted his teeth and dug in *even* deeper. Wade could feel Butch's legs relentlessly kicking underneath him, sliding across the bloody floor. Finally, he pulled Butch's head back and slammed it forward, over and over and *over* again. And with each hit, more pieces of his skull broke off into the pool of blood that had formed underneath them. But he didn't stop, he just kept slamming his head into the floor until there was barely anything left to hold onto. With all of his strength, he pulled it apart and tore Butch's head clean in half, decapitating him in the process. His neck expelled blood like a geyser.

Then, there was *silence,* broken only by the occasional drip of blood from a corpse somewhere in the room. Wade breathed heavily as naked bodies all around him slid down the walls and dropped onto the floor with a *thud.* Their bullet wounds leaked, combining with the others until the entire room was painted red, with hints of dark green blood mixed in.

Wade still rested on his knees. His hands trembled; blood ran down his forearms and off his fingertips.

They're dead... They're all dead.

Finally, he painfully got to his feet. The effects of the poison he consumed earlier were starting to wear off and leave his system, marked by the clarity of his vision.

"Sarah..." Wade mumbled, stumbling toward her unconscious body.

He pushed a finger into her neck, feeling for a pulse.

Beat... Beat... Beat.

It was faint, but it was there.

"Thank Nor," he whispered between breaths.

He wrapped his arms under her but hesitated before lifting her off the table.

Do you understand me? Ulysses asked in his mind.

"I do…" Wade responded out loud. "And I don't give a fuck."

Wade lifted her up and hoisted her onto his shoulder.

Click!

Behind him, a woman stood pointing Rose and Thorn at his back. Wade turned around and faced her.

"Don't you move another fucking inch!" she yelled. "I'll blow you away and take the girl!" Her hands shook violently. "I'm hungry! I'll do it, I promise I will!"

Wade stepped forward.

"I'M WARNING YOU, NOW! DON'T MOVE ANY CLOSER!"

Wade raised his foot to do just that, and the woman pulled the trigger… except, the trigger *wouldn't* pull. She strained incredibly hard, attempting to fire the weapon, but the trigger still wouldn't budge–not even an inch.

Wade lunged forward and swiped Thorn from her hand. Her eyes grew wide just before he thrust the silver blade through her face, skewering her into the wall. Then, he pulled the heavy trigger and blew her head clean off. Her decapitated body dropped and slid down the wall, leaving a trail of blood on it. Rose still rested in her hand, and he reached down and pried it from her stiff fingers before continuing on down the hall.

Once Wade was outside and back in the main courtyard, he honed in on the massive containers of dynamite hidden under the walkways. He raised Thorn to shoot them, but a loud bell rang in the distance, breaking his concentration. The gunslingers on guard ran along the wooden walkways, attempting to locate the threat, but Wade wouldn't give them the chance. He aimed again, and this time, nothing prevented him from pulling the trigger.

BOOOOOOOOOMMM!!!!!!!

The barrels *exploded,* sending a giant wave of fire and debris into the air. The gunslingers screamed and cried out as they were engulfed in flames. They fell from the walkways and splattered on the dirt in front of him, burning to a crisp.

Wade bolted for the gate, picking off any stragglers that had managed to escape the explosion. Their heads were blown off, and their bodies dropped to the ground. Bullets began to whizz past him, tossing up clouds of dirt at his feet. One nearly grazed his leg.

Then, a series of explosions erupted behind him as more containers detonated. Wade shot the rope that held the counter weight of the gate, causing it to unravel and open the large wooden doors. Once they split apart, he dove out of the fort, just as the entire structure combusted and went up in flames.

Wade collapsed onto the sand and laid Sarah down next to him as more and more explosions erupted within the walls of the now burning fort. Screams and cries of agony, that no one but Wade would ever hear, echoed across the endless desert. He hung his head back in the sand and attempted to breathe, feeling the intense cramp that had now formed in his midsection. His eyes started to close…

"You're a killer, Wade," Jess said from behind him.

Wade shot up and spun around. A wall of Darkness was rapidly closing in on him, and within it, green eyes began to appear. Wade unholstered his guns again and aimed them at the approaching Demons. There were *hundreds* of them, and Wade knew he couldn't take them all. They had survived the cannibals, only to walk right back into death's open arms.

"It was a valiant effort, Wade, but even the best Gunner the Order has ever seen can't fight his way out of this one," Ulysses said in his ear. "You're in deep shit, boy."

Wade looked around and saw a Soul Stealer floating in front of him. It resembled a woman, draped in a tattered and torn dress, but he wasn't convinced. Its skinny arms waved him over, as if it were drawing him in for a warm embrace. He aimed and fired, exploding it into ash. Bone Eaters appeared and inched forward, creeping out of the Darkness but stopping just before the light of the fire. Their mangled and jagged teeth snapped at him; black goo dripped from their mouths.

But, although it wasn't real, his master was right, Wade *couldn't* fight his way out of this. There were too many of them, and even with his infinite ammo, he couldn't take them all. The fire would eventually burn out, and they would charge him. He looked down at Sarah laying in the sand–her white dress soaked in blood. Then, he did the only thing he could. He brought his fingers to his lips and whistled, over and over again. The Demons inched closer, the fire behind him diminishing with each passing second.

Again and again, he whistled over the snapping of their razor-sharp teeth that begged to tear him apart. The monsters were inches from his feet now, gaining more and more confidence to approach the fire.

But in the distance, Wade spotted something. Small at first, but growing in size and intensity. Another set of eyes appeared in the Darkness, but they weren't green, they were blue. Wade recognized them *instantly.*

Quicksilver burst through the Darkness and leapt over the Demons, landing in front of Wade and squashing the head of a Bone Eater in the process. The Demon Gunner quickly lifted Sarah from the sand and hoisted both of them up onto the saddle. Holding Sarah with one arm and Thorn in the other, he fired at the Demons, dropping them and clearing a path for Quicksilver to run through before whipping the reins twice. The fiery horse neighed and took off, blowing past the Demons and crushing more beneath her hooves. Quicksilver began to pick up speed, faster and faster, ripping through the Darkness of the night.

Ulysses called out behind them, "RUN, WADE! RUN LIKE THE COWARD YOU ARE! YOU ARE ONLY DELAYING THE INEVITABLE! WE KNOW IT'S COMING! WE BOTH KNOW WHAT YOU CANNOT RUN FROM FOREVER!"

Wade, Sarah, and Quicksilver disappeared into the night, as the fire at Fort Carn slowly burned out, and the Demons began to feast on what remained of the monsters within the walls of death.

PART TWO
THE
FOREST

CHAPTER ELEVEN

SNOW FALLS, THE VEIL DARKENS

Snow fell upon a canopy of dying trees as a harsh, cold wind blew through the forest, rustling the whithered leaves scattered across the ground. Sarah was disoriented and dizzy, fighting to stay awake while laying flat on her back in the dirt. It was soft and damp, and all she could do was dig her tingling fingernails into it. The sensation made her shiver.

Where am I? she thought to herself.

This was not the last place Sarah had been, but then again, where *had* she been? She remembered that she was running–being chased by Demons through their town. All around her, friends, family… They were torn to shreds and devoured.

Next thing she knew, she was being thrown into the back of her family's covered wagon. The man who hoisted her in–her uncle, Lee–had been killed seconds after by a Bone Eater. Her father didn't hesitate. He whipped the reins twice on the horses' backs and took off. Her mother told her to close her eyes, but Sarah didn't listen. As they sped away into the desert, Sarah heard screams and cries for help echoing from the now-burning town.

But that *wasn't* the last thing she remembered. No... She remembered her parents ultimately meeting the same fate as her town, despite their desperate escape. She could still hear her mother crying for help, calling out endlessly within the confines of her mind. Then she remembered being saved by a man–a strange and kind man, but strange all the same. And, he was a Gunner of the Order. She had heard stories of Gunners before, but she thought they were all gone–dead, after the fall of Gadriel. She agreed to join him on his quest, and they had been traveling together across the desert, fighting Demons, carrying out his mission, and running from the Darkness. Until they found...

Fort Carn.

Memories started to flow back into her mind like a dam opening into a dry riverbed. She saw people sitting around a dinner table... Butch... Beth. That was the last place she had been, yes, but now? Now she found herself laying on her back in a dark forest.

It was freezing, and her breath was visible with each exhale. Her arms and legs were littered with bruises, and every ounce of her body ached. But as she looked around the forest, a terrible realization grew: she was *alone.*

"W..." she mumbled, feeling slowly returning to her limbs, allowing her to raise her head. "Wa..."

A hand thrust in front of her mouth, silencing her. She followed the arm upward with her eyes until they met Wade's–his gaze filled with fear. He raised a finger to his lips as if to say *shhhh.* Then, he pointed in the distance. Sarah sat up slightly, following the direction of his finger. Looking over a fallen tree, she could barely make out a large, tenebrous figure sauntering through the forest. She couldn't focus on it for long–it kept vanishing behind the thick foliage. But from the few glimpses she caught, the monster appeared to have long, spindly legs like those of a spider. Towering trees toppled effortlessly as it moved *through* them.

Sarah's heart rate quickened. She watched the monster pass by another tree and disappear from sight. Wade looked down at her, and she wondered if he wanted them to move positions. She tried sitting up further, but Wade thrust her back down into the dirt. He then shook his head, *No.*

Wade looked back into the distance, and Sarah moved ever so slightly to catch a glimpse of it again, but when she found it, she saw that the monster had stopped. It just stood there, sniffing in the air. Then, it *turned.*

Wade grabbed Sarah with force and dragged her behind another tree–just as the monster swung its head to their previous position. The way he had pulled her made her wonder if she weighed anything at all.

But now he was unfastening something–a rusted flask, its dented tin stamped with the shape of a revolver. He poured out its contents into the palm of his bare hand and began to smear the cold liquid over her arms and face. She knew the vomitous smell instantly: *Demon blood.* Sarah wanted to scream, but she held it in. Wade then caked the blood on himself before pressing his back hard against the rough bark of the tree.

Behind them, they heard scuttling, then silence. The monster sniffed again.

Boom.
Boom.
Boom.

Trees came crashing down, nearly crushing them as the monster drew closer. Sarah couldn't hold it in this time and screamed, but Wade's scarred fingers muffled her cries. Tears ran down his hand as she squeezed her eyes shut and clung tightly onto his arm. The monster was now only a few feet from them, and Sarah heard the familiar dull sound of Thorn being drawn from Wade's side. The monster sniffed again and exhaled; a cloud of warm breath floated past them. Then, the tree they hid behind started to bend forward with a loud groan. Sarah felt its enormous weight pressing down on her and wondered when it would snap and crush them like ants. Fear caused her to shake uncontrollably; Wade held her mouth *even* tighter. More and more the tree bowed, bending them fully over. The pain was indescribable, and Sarah nearly passed out again–but a loud screech came from the monster, and the weight of the tree immediately lifted off their backs. They heard the scuttling once more, and when they finally looked, the monster was gone.

Simultaneously, Wade and Sarah exhaled a sigh of relief, sending out a cloud of condensation in front of them.

"Wade…" Sarah whispered as she gripped him once more. "Am I dead?"

"No, you're not dead," Wade responded while scanning the surrounding area. "But unless you want to be, we need to keep moving."

"Where are we then? What happened to Fort Carn?"

He didn't respond, and she could see that something was wrong–*very* wrong.

"We need to find shelter. Let's move."

Wade grabbed Sarah's hand and pulled her up from the dirt. She looked around for their trusty steed, and luckily found her hidden behind a tree only a few feet from them. They mounted the undead horse and took off through the forest.

• • •

As they rode, Sarah's mind raced, wondering how they could've ended up here. Her body was badly bruised–especially near her rib cage, as if a rope had been tied around it, and Wade looked more worried and scared than he had *ever* before. The desert landscape that she had known all her life was now gone, replaced with snow and trees taller than she had ever seen before. And it was even colder here than in the desert; it felt as if they had traveled to a new world.

Were they even still on Rhodahn?

She didn't know, and she was too afraid to ask. Besides, Wade would probably give her answers in due time. Sarah also didn't know where they were going, but Quicksilver seemed to be following a slushy, mud covered trail that twisted and turned through the forest. Her hooves collided with the dirt and crashed through streams before picking up the single-track again and racing further down it with tremendous speed and nimbleness.

Sarah began to wonder if even Wade *himself* knew where they were going, or perhaps he was just following the only thing he could, hoping it would lead them to some form of shelter. The trail had to lead to something after all. Whichever it was, she knew she would not be able to ride in these conditions much longer–although she didn't think she had much of a choice. Her fingers were now turning blue from frostbite, and her dress was tattered and torn, providing little protection from the cold that grew stronger as they traveled deeper into the forest.

"Up ahead!" Wade said over his shoulder while pointing into the distance with his free hand that wasn't gripping the reins.

Sarah leaned past him and saw a dilapidated log cabin standing alone in a clearing. Wade steered Quicksilver toward it. Once they were a few feet from it, he brought the horse to a grinding halt before they quickly dismounted and moved to its rear. Wade flung open the saddlebags, revealing her repeater rifle and revolver.

"*Here*," he said, tossing her the repeater rifle, which she caught with both hands.

After she slung it across her back, she reached into the saddlebag and pulled out her revolver. She flipped open the cylinder–six bullets. With the flick of her wrist, she snapped it shut and turned to Wade.

He raised two fingers to his eyes, then to the house, and said, "With me," before drawing Rose and Thorn from their holsters.

They crept toward it, carefully watching their steps to avoid any unnecessary noise. It was a basic, two-story cabin; its rough-hewn log walls were beaten down by countless winters, marked by the crumbling chinking. The roof sagged slightly under the weight of snow and fallen pine needles that had gathered there over time, left uncleared. Three wooden steps led up to a covered porch, each one creaking beneath their feet as they climbed.

Wade once again pressed a finger to his lips, urging Sarah to be silent while she watched Rose slide gently back into its holster. He laid his now-free hand on the weathered wooden door and held it there for a moment.

Then, he looked back at Sarah for reassurance, and she nodded to press on.

Crrreeeaaakkk…

The door swung open, and Wade quickly aimed Thorn into the dark room. Sarah crouched down beside him, doing the same with her revolver, scanning for any sign of movement. To the right stood a stone fireplace, and next to it, a small table cluttered with dozens of empty glass bottles. Overturned, broken chairs and dirty rags lay scattered across the floor; it looked like it had been abandoned for *years*.

As they stepped further into the cabin, glass crunched loudly beneath their feet. Wade immediately stopped, waiting for something to jump out and attack–but nothing did. They continued on.

Next to them was a set of stairs leading to the second floor, and Wade signaled to Sarah not to follow as he climbed them and disappeared. She heard multiple doors creak open and the familiar, heavy sound of Rose and Thorn being raised and lowered as he cleared each room. Finally, Wade came back down.

"*Clear,*" he said with a nod, then pointed to the only door on the main floor. "That's the last one that needs to be checked."

Wade approached and gripped the brass knob; Sarah quickly readied her revolver, aiming it at the slowly opening door. The revolver shook in her hand, and she tried to steady it by holding her breath as the door creaked further open. Wade looked back at her with a worried expression, but she couldn't see what lay within as the doorway was cast in darkness.

"Stay here."

"Let me come—"

"*Stay.*"

Wade then descended a flight of stairs and disappeared. Sarah waited, silence filling the room. She could hear her heart…

BANG!

A single shot sounded off.

"Wade?" Sarah yelled, but he didn't respond. She ran to the doorway and saw an ominous staircase leading to a basement with no sign of him. "WADE!"

Silence.

She readjusted her grip on the revolver, gulped, and began to walk down the steps. One by one, they creaked and groaned beneath her feet. On the last step, she raised her iron and turned—Wade stood in the basement, barely illuminated by the light spilling in from a small window just above ground level. At his feet lay a young girl's corpse. Green blood drained from a bullet hole in her head, pooling on the floor. Behind them, a decomposed family sat in a circle of wooden chairs. Sarah's stomach turned; puke filled her mouth and hit the floor.

"Are you alright?" Sarah asked while wiping her face with her sleeve.

"Yes," Wade responded sullenly. "She caught me by surprise."

"Was she…"

"A Nightwalker. Not sure when she turned."

"What about the rest?"

Wade sighed, "You should see for yourself."

As Sarah stepped closer, crossing through the light, she saw a shotgun resting between the legs of an older man. A gaping hole marred the back of his head, and the wall behind him was stained a darker shade than the rest of the room. There were two others—a woman and a young boy, both with the same wounds. Their mouths hung unnaturally wide, and their eye sockets were empty.

Dear Nor...

"What happened to them, Wade?" Sarah asked as she covered her mouth, attempting not to puke again.

Wade brought the tip of Thorn's blade onto the father's collar and pushed the fabric *down*, revealing a large bite mark.

"They were bit—infected by the Darkness," Wade said as he shook his head. "I had hoped that we saw the last of the Nightwalkers in the desert, but I'm afraid I was wrong." Wade inspected them further. "They were a family, and it looks like they went out on their own terms before the infection fully took over."

Sarah stared at the corpses in disbelief.

"You're saying they killed themselves?"

"Yes, and it looks like the father was the last to go."

"How do you know?"

"Because he's the one still holding the gun. They went in a circle, taking the shotgun from each other's hands after the deed was done. The little one *here*," Wade said, pointing at the young girl who had just been killed. "She must've turned too soon."

"Or maybe she couldn't do it?" Sarah added.

"Perhaps so..."

They stood in silence, staring at the corpses. Sarah wondered what she would do in the same situation. Would she have been able to pull the trigger like the others, or would she have let herself turn like the girl?

"It looks like they've been preserved by the cold—or the

Veil, maybe *both*," Wade said as he broke off the father's dried out finger. "Death seems to linger in the Darkness like a shadow—as if it thrives off of it." He tossed the finger aside and saw that there was a bulkhead next to him with two wooden doors leading outside. "I'll go ahead and clear out these bodies and meet you upstairs when I'm done."

Sarah nodded and began to walk back up the creaky basement stairs. There was a single thought that echoed within the walls of her mind.

Would I pull the trigger?

• • •

Later that night, just before the Consumption began, Wade and Sarah sat together in front of the fireplace, staring at the frozen ash that rested within it. Beside them sat a pile of firewood that Wade had found outside, next to the bulkhead. He tossed a few pieces into the firebox, then rested his hand on top of the logs. Drawing in a deep breath, Wade summoned a small blue flame from his palm, its glow illuminating their faces as it continued to grow.

"So you've always just been able to do that, huh?"

"Yes ma'am, *always*," he said as he got up, watching the blue flames start to overtake the logs.

She didn't press further, which relieved Wade as he didn't have any other explanation.

The fire had helped ease her constant shivering, but he could tell that she was still very cold. He unfurled a blanket from one of the saddlebags and laid it gently across her shoulders.

"This should help."

"Thank you," she said between chattering teeth. "Are…

you not… cold?"

"My jacket is well insulated."

"Lucky you."

Wade chuckled and said, "I'll go look upstairs and see if I can find anything to help keep you warm. If not, I'll hunt for something tomorrow."

"I would appreciate that," she said, still staring at the flames, their shadows dancing upon her pale face.

Wade got up off the floor and turned toward the steps, but he stopped and watched the girl for a moment. It was a peaceful scene, and he wanted to cherish it just a little longer. Then, he started up the stairs.

"Wait." He stopped once more. "Before you do that, can you just tell me what is going on—how we got here?"

No, he thought to himself. *How could I?*

"Wade? Please talk to me. Why are we here? What happened at the fort?"

"*Nothing,*" he finally said. "We needed to leave—to continue the quest."

"That's not true, Wade. That's not the last conversation we had."

"It is."

"Then where'd I get these bruises?"

"I had to tie you to me, so you wouldn't fall off."

"Just tell me the truth!" she yelled.

Wade ran back down the stairs and peered through the windows, expecting to see the monster that they had just evaded. But he saw *nothing* creeping in the Darkness and sighed out of relief.

"Please, for the love of Nor, keep your voice down."

"I'm sorry, I didn't mean to yell, it's just… Please don't lie to me, Wade. You're the only person I feel like I can trust in this world." Wade's heart dropped, and he hung his head. "Please just tell me the *truth*."

Tears welled in his eyes, but they didn't fall. He fought them back, not letting them break from his eyelids.

"What was the last thing you remembered?" he asked.

"We… We sat down to eat. We were having dinner?"

Wade shook his head and said, "Fort Carn wasn't what we thought it was, Sarah. There was something in the chalices. I never saw them slip anything, so they must've done it before we sat down."

"They poisoned me? Is that why I can't remember anything?"

"They poisoned *both* of us." Wade took a deep breath. "You drank it first, and I watched your head fall to the table. Butch then forced me to finish mine, and I immediately felt dizzy—disoriented. Within seconds, my arms and legs barely worked. The room was spinning, and I… I couldn't move."

"Why would they do that?"

Wade hung his head once more and said, "I don't know."

"Yes, you do!" Sarah cried out. "Tell me what happened, please!"

"Sarah… it's behind us now. We need to move on. Focus on the mission."

"I can't move on unless I know!"

"Why not?"

"Because *you* know the truth, and you don't deserve to carry that burden alone."

There was a long silence that followed her words, and a single tear ran down Wade's face.

"They showed me the last visitor who showed up on the fort's doorstep. His head was on a platter, and I watched as they chewed on his tongue." Sarah covered her mouth in disgust. "Then, I was being dragged down a long hallway. The world was stretching in and out, and I couldn't fight back. They took me into a cold cellar with the other visitors, strung up on hooks."

"Where was I?" Sarah said through tears.

Wade gritted his teeth, fighting with all of his strength not to break down in front of the girl.

"They had you upstairs, Sarah. "

"*No…*"

"Just before they hung me up, I felt rage—something I haven't felt in a long, *long* time. I killed them, Sarah. I saw them around you, and I killed them all."

Sarah cried into her hands.

"What did they do to me?"

"I don't know, Sarah. I got to you as soon as I could. *I'm sorry.*"

He remembered the faces of those he killed. He saw them licking their lips, the devilish smile on Butch's face as he stood naked over her, and the eagerness of the boy from the range to have his turn with her. Rage grew within him once again. He needed to release it.

"I'll see if I can find some more wood outside," he quickly said while turning to the door.

Sarah reached out and grabbed Wade's jacket sleeve.

"Wait…" She quickly got up off the floor and hugged him, wrapping her arms around him as tightly as she could.

Wade hugged her back, and he felt the rage inside dissipating.

• • •

They continued to sit together on the floor of the cabin. Wade gave her his jacket, because she didn't want him to leave her alone to go look for clothes. He used the fire within himself to keep warm, while occasionally raising his hands in front of the logs that burned brightly. For a long time, neither one of them said a word.

"What is this place?" Sarah finally asked.

"I'm not sure. I'm just as confused as you are."

"Well can you start from the beginning? How did we even get here from the desert?"

Wade racked his brain and tried to remember the details of the journey.

"After I killed Butch and the others, I burned the fort down to the ground. Quicksilver came back for us, but you still weren't awake. I loaded us onto her back, and we took off–riding all night. Surprisingly, the Demons didn't bother us. They instead seemed to be drawn to the fort, as if the death that lingered there called out to them like a beacon. I just wanted to get as far away from that place as possible, so we didn't stop–not once. I steered Quicksilver until I fell asleep, yet, she didn't stop either. It was almost as if she knew we were running from something." Wade paused and stared at the flames. "When I awoke, we were no longer in the desert. We were now in a dark forest covered in snow, but we were moving much slower than before–following a trail cut through the trees. That was when I saw *it*."

"That monster from before?"

Wade nodded and continued, "It was moving through the woods, but then it stopped dead in its tracks. I didn't want us to be seen, and Quicksilver's trot was too loud, so I pulled you off her back and hid behind a fallen tree. That was when you woke up."

"What the hell was that thing? Did you recognize it?"

"No, I've never seen anything like it in my life–not even in the desert."

There was a long pause before Sarah asked, "If you *had* to guess, where do you think we are?"

"Somewhere in the Forest of Delfar. It feels colder, which means we're heading West," Wade said, glancing through the window into the encroaching Darkness. "We're getting closer to the source of the Consumption, I can *feel* it. I think we may have some answers soon."

"I hope so," Sarah responded. "Do you think that monster will find us here?"

"I don't know, but I'll set up some torches around the house before we turn in for the night. We will also need to keep our voices down as I believe it is drawn to sound. That's the best we can do."

"That's a good idea."

Wade got up from the floor, but Sarah continued to stare at the slowly dying flames.

"Wade?"

"Yes?"

"Can you make the world go back to the way it was before the light went out?"

"I'll try, Sarah, I'll try my best."

Wade turned to the door.

"Do you think Nor is punishing us?" she asked. "Did we do something wrong, Wade?"

"He wouldn't do that."

Sarah brought her knees closer to her chest and said, "When I woke up and asked you if I were dead, you said *no*. But how do you know we aren't?"

The shadows of the flames whipped back and forth across Wade's half-lit face; he didn't have an answer for her. She looked at the Demon Gunner with tears in her eyes.

"It feels like I am."

CHAPTER TWELVE

THE BESTOWMENT OF THE IRON

Wade's muscles tensed in fright. He knew he wouldn't have any time to react to the bullet, and soon he would be *dead*–laying flat on his back with blood slowly trickling out of his skull. Another cadet would eventually find his body, but he wondered if it could even be proven that Ulysses was responsible for his murder. Knowing the Master Gunner and how he operates, Wade believed he would never have killed him *himself.* Ulysses always had plausible deniability for his abuse of the cadets, dating all the way back to Wade's arrival at the School. Their training had been nothing more than a facade for his sick games and sadistic pleasure–and it worked beautifully. No one suspected a thing, and of course, no one ever spoke up against it either.

So, Wade surmised that Ulysses had recruited a strung-out drug addict, high off the devil's root, to shoot him and run off into the woods before anyone even knew he was dead. But while Wade was lost in thought, he realized *nothing* had happened to him. He wasn't shot or injured, and he even wondered if a bullet had been fired at all. For all he knew, he might have just hallucinated the sound.

Thank Nor.

Wade chuckled and then collapsed forward, slamming hard onto the dirt. His entire body felt numb, and every limb ached and burned intensely. He couldn't move, even if he wanted to, as his body wouldn't listen to his commands. It felt as if his soul was disconnected, and he was floating in a void within the confines of his flesh. Then, his vision began to fade.

"Wade!" someone yelled in the far distance.

He couldn't make out who had called his name–the constant ringing in his ears muffled everything–but he felt vibrations in the ground growing more and more intense, as if someone was running toward him.

He has come to finish the job.

Strong hands wrapped around his shoulders and flipped him over.

"Are you alright?" Jess asked while checking over his body for bullet holes. "What the hell happened to you! Wade? Can you hear me?"

"U... U..." He attempted to speak, but nothing more than pathetic whimpers came out. His lips and throat were as dry as the dirt he lay upon. His world spun, and he fought hard to stay awake. If he lost the battle of consciousness, he might never wake again. So, he focused as hard as he could and uttered a single word, *"Water."*

Jess quickly unhooked the water sack that hung off her belt and unscrewed the cap. She poured the cool liquid into his mouth, and immediately, euphoria washed over him. He began to guzzle it as fast as he could. When the water sack was finally empty, he laid his head back onto the dirt and let the liquid run down the sides of his face.

"Wade, can you talk to me?"

Wade stared blankly at the rising sun before finally saying, "I'm... I'm alright."

"Thank Nor," Jess said, hugging him and pressing her head into his chest. "We've been looking for you all morning!"

Wade began to sit up, holding his head in pain.

"You're so sunburned! Please, Wade, tell me what happened. Why weren't you at the final test?"

"This *was* my final test," Wade said as the flicker of light in the sniper's nest caught his attention once again. "Master Ulysses personally administered it."

"Master Ulysses did this?" Jess stared at him in confusion and finally said, "That doesn't make any... Nevermind, you can explain the rest inside. We need to get you out of the sun, right now."

Wade didn't fight that order in the slightest. Jess extended a hand and helped him to his feet, and for a split second, his body felt fine—weightless even.

"Can you walk?" she asked.

Wade nodded and took one step forward. His knees immediately buckled, and he collapsed face first back onto the dirt.

• • •

When Wade finally awoke, he found himself laying in bed with a damp cloth on his forehead. He sat up slightly, and an oppressive soreness immediately fell upon him. It seemed he could now move–*barely*–and when he looked around, he saw his clothes strewn across the floor of his room. His basic cadet revolvers sat in their holsters next to his bed, and his wide-brimmed hat rested on the post of his headboard. *Someone* had undressed him and put him here.

His arms felt incredibly stiff and tight, and he could barely raise them to pull the bed sheet off. That small act alone nearly made him pass out again. Just as he started to swing his legs off the bed, the door to his room creaked open and Jess walked in with a cup of soup.

"You're awake!" she said before rushing over to him. She placed the bowl on the nightstand and pulled the covers back over Wade's body. "*Rest.* There's no rush to get up, you're not missing anything. Everyone is just relaxing."

"What day is it?" Wade asked, holding his throbbing head.

"*Bestowment Day.*"

"I slept an entire day?"

"*And* night," she added. "I'm just glad you're awake. Before you tell me what happened, you need to eat."

She scooped up some of the foggy broth and brought it to Wade's mouth. Just like the water, the soup tasted heavenly. She brought another salty spoonful to his lips, and he slurped it up before grabbing the bowl from her hands and downing it like a starving child.

"I'm sorry," Wade said before wiping his lips with his forearm. "I was so hungry."

"I know, it's ok," she said while gently rubbing his stubble. "Do you think you can tell me what happened now?"

Wade took a deep breath; the memories washing back over him like a wave of pain.

"It's ok if you can't. I can give you more–"

"When we were split up by lawns," Wade finally said, "Master Grant told me to meet Ulysses at the gun range.

I was confused, as everyone else was on the North and South Lawns. When I finally got there, it was just Master Ulysses standing there–no one else. He placed a gun to my head…"

Jess gasped and said, "What?"

"He told me to fire twelve shots–all bullseyes. If I even missed one, he would kill me and spend the rest of his life in jail. But if I succeeded, he would allow for Rose & Thorn to be bestowed upon me."

"Rose & Thorn? Those are–"

"*Shar's* guns, I know. Trust me, none of this makes sense."

"You didn't know you were in line for them before?"

"No," Wade said as he shook his head. "I had no idea, but with the way he was talking, it seemed like the Council had already made up their minds. It was only Ulysses who hadn't."

"So it was his test? The Council had nothing to do with it?"

"Yes."

"And did you pass?"

"I'm still here, aren't I?" Wade said, causing Jess to flash a soft smile. "But that was only part of it."

"What?"

"The bullseye shit was just a warmup. He knew I wouldn't miss and that wasn't what he was testing me on. The second I finished shooting, the *real* test came. As the smoke was still leaving my barrels, he told me that if I dropped my guns even an inch, a sniper would blow my head off."

"Why would he do this? What does that prove?"

"Jess, I don't know."

"But there *has* to be a reason for putting you through

that?"

Wade stared at a painting on the far wall. It depicted Master Gunners on horseback, led by Shar Vahn, scouting the beautiful, rolling green hills of Gadriel–the place where they would one day build their kingdom. It was his favorite painting in the castle, and perhaps the only reason Wade stuck with the grueling training of the Order. It was his dream to be like those first Master Gunners, riding across their future kingdom, protecting the innocent people who lived within it.

"Wade?"

Wade was brought back to the conversation. He closed his eyes and said, "Master Ulysses said something… It was just bullshit though."

"Wade," Jess took his hand into her own. "What did he tell you?"

The words hung in his throat like a lump of coal. He didn't want to say it, because it was bullshit. All of this was *bullshit*.

"The Council believes that I'm the Shar'La." Jess froze, paralyzed by these words. Her hand went limp within his grip. "But *he* didn't, and the test would ultimately prove that he was right. I had to hold my guns up until the next horn blew, but… I don't even think there was a horn."

"Dear Nor," Jess muttered, squeezing his hand once more. "Did you–"

"All day, and all night… until the sun came up again. Until my arms failed me."

"But you didn't get tagged?"

"No," Wade said, shifting his gaze from the painting to meet her's. "I must've passed the test."

Wade could almost see the thoughts racing behind her

pale green eyes.

Finally, she said, "He who receives Shar's guns... is the greatest Gunner of them all. That means you're the chosen–"

"*Don't.* Don't even say it. It's not me, Jess. I don't know what the hell Ulysses was talking about, and if anything, he was just saying that to mess with me. The test he administered was just his last attempt to break me before I left this place for good. I'm not the Shar'La, and I don't want to be."

"But what if you get his guns tonight?" Jess asked. "There will be no denying it then."

"Then I'll dismantle and melt them down. They can be my new boot spurs–the nicest in all of Gadriel."

"Wade..."

"What? They'll be worth more to me in pure gold and silver anyways."

"How could you say that!"

"Because I don't want the throne, Jess! Hell, I don't even know if I want to be a Gunner anymore. All I want right now is a bath."

Jess pulled up the sheet higher on his chest and said, "You need to keep resting, but if you don't think you're the Shar'La, then don't take his iron. But if you do, then you damn well better use them."

• • •

The bath house at the School had always been a great place for contemplation ever since Wade first arrived. It wasn't anything fancy–just a wooden shack built atop a natural hot spring, with several tin tubs that overflowed endlessly with warm water. There was one room for the men, and one for the women, but no one else besides Wade was in it now, leaving him alone with his thoughts.

Over the years, Wade used to sit in these tubs and incessantly mull over the stressors in his life. He often wondered whether he was saying the right things to court Jess, if he was keeping pace with the other cadets at school, and–most of all–why he was even a Gunner in the first place. He never believed in himself, and Ulysses' treatment of him didn't help anything either.

And now, a decade after the first time he sat and thought here, he was once again thinking about that evil man. Master Ulysses had always been a massive piece of shit–every cadet knew that–but one thing he was never known for was being a *liar*, and that terrified Wade.

If Rose & Thorn were to be handed to him this evening, then he would be forced to make a choice, and he didn't know which one was correct. Rejecting them could fracture the Order and send it into a civil war, as the Council would turn on each other for falsely picking Wade as the Shar'La–even if it were true. But if he took the iron, then by virtue, he would be accepting the throne of the Kingdom of Gadriel–a responsibility he *didn't* want to bear.

Truthfully, there was no right answer, and Wade knew that, he just hated that he was even in this position to begin with. All of this came from bullshit prophecies and made up stories, passed down over generations of Gunners and Master Gunners. Wade could still recite the words that had been etched into Shar's Rock hundreds of years ago:

When he is ready, a Gunner shall rise.
His aim steady, his soul wise.
Rose & Thorn seek their Master.
Foes shall mourn, he shoots them faster.
As the sun fades, fire he shall harness.
Bring him the guns, deliver us from darkness.

As he repeated it over and over again in his mind, he wondered what the hell that prophecy even meant. Shar was full of shit, but no one dared say so, lest they be labeled a heretic. For a split second, it had seemed that even Master Ulysses knew it too. Maybe he *should've* failed the test, then he wouldn't have to worry about leading an army or sitting on a throne that didn't belong to him.

Wade had never asked for any of this—he never even wanted it. He was now just the latest sucker to be caught up in this bullshit, and as he plunged his sore arms into the warm water, he pondered the same question he had for so many years...

Why am I even here?

• • •

Wade wore the finest clothes he had: a simple button down, blue jeans, a wide-brimmed hat, and of course, polished leather boots. For the first time since he arrived, his holsters sat empty—a tradition for Bestowment—as new guns would soon call them home.

Wade took one last look at himself in the mirror. His face was riddled with blisters, and his skin was peeling from the sunburn—but that wasn't what he was staring at. No, he was staring at something else—something that stared back. He didn't want to look any longer, for he hated seeing a *fraud*.

• • •

Later that night, Wade, Jess, John, Westin, Elenor, and Colt walked together toward the Great House with the rest of the elated cadets. This was a walk they had all done many times, but tonight was *different,* as this would be their last.

"Wade, we heard about what happened with Master Ulysses," John said with a soft pat on the back. "I'm sorry, man." He looked over his shoulder, checking to see if he was in earshot of them. "That guy always sucked."

"Appreciate it," Wade said under his breath, trying not to make this moment about himself.

"So, this is really it?" Colt asked. "We're finally at Bestowment. The end of the road…"

"You're making that sound bittersweet as if you didn't count down the days to Bestowment since we got here," Elenor responded.

"Hey, sometimes moments like these sneak up on you. All that time I spent wishing life would move faster could've been spent taking it all in instead."

"Come on, man, don't make this all sappy," Westin said, nudging Colt with his shoulder. "Let's just try and enjoy it, alright?"

"You're right, I'm sorry, I'm not trying to bum anyone out. I guess what I'm trying to say is, we don't know what the future holds. I just know that I'm going to miss these days with you guys. That's all."

"Me too," Jess said, squeezing Wade's hand.

They all packed into the Great House–a massive, domed room with hundreds of seats formed in a semi-circle facing the main, center stage. Each row of seats was progressively elevated higher and higher so that no view was obstructed. Hanging on the walls were large green banners with the Order of the Gun's insignia on it: an upward facing revolver. The Great House was exclusively used for Induction and Bestowment Day, and Wade was just as amazed now as he had been the first time he came here, many, *many* years ago.

One by one, all the cadets took their seats. They mingled and laughed amongst themselves without a worry in the world. Some tried to guess which set of iron they might receive, while others wondered where they would be sent to fight after graduation. But for now, all the pain and stress from training was behind them, and tonight was a night for celebration–despite what their unknown futures held.

Wade leaned over to Jess and whispered, "I didn't ask you, what was your final test?"

"Oh, you don't want to know. It was much harder than yours."

"Seriously?"

"Oh yea, we had to recite the Alma Mater," Jess said with a smirk.

Wade shook his head and chuckled, "Wouldn't that have been nice."

All of the chatter came to an *immediate* end when Master Ulysses took the stage. The cadets shot up at the sight of him and saluted.

"At ease, cadets." Master Ulysses cleared his throat. "That was the last time I will ever address you as such. You are all gathered here today for a very special tradition…

Bestowment!" The crowd erupted into cheers. "You have painstakingly fought and trained for this very moment, and from here on out, you will take what you have learned within these walls to the battlefield, protecting Gadriel's people and its way of life with your own.

"300 years ago, Shar founded the Order of the Gun with these principles: character, grit, resilience, and strength. I want you to know that each and every one of you sitting before me exemplifies those principles. I know that you are excited for the next chapter of your life–life *after* school–but I would be lying if I said it was going to be easy. Take a moment to look to your left and right. The brothers and sisters you sit with now may not be here one day. While they're here, love them, cherish them, and do not take them for granted. What comes next may be hard, but you are stronger than *any* adversity that you may face out there, for you are now… GUNNERS!"

The crowd erupted into cheers.

"And from this day forward, you are born anew. Use your training to protect yourself and those you love. You shall now forever live and die by the gun, for after tonight, it is a part of you until death. When you receive your weapons, raise them above you with pride, for you have earned your iron."

Everyone stood up at once, cheering madly, but Wade remained seated, attempting to nullify the anxious feeling growing in his stomach.

"When I say your name, rise and join me here. John Hancock," Master Ulysses said as the newly appointed Gunner rose from the crowd and made his way to the stage. "Passed down from Master Gunner Urie and bestowed upon you, Fire & Ice!"

His red and blue revolvers sat within a block of marble, shaped perfectly to the weapons. John grabbed and raised them above his head while the crowd cheered him on.

"Hell yeah!" he yelled, which sent the crowd into a frenzy.

One by one, more cadets were called up onto the stage. "Westin Faulkner, Smoke & Ash!"

Westin raised them into the air in triumph.

"Elenor Vance, Sun & Moon!"

"Colt Ward, Dust & Dreams!"

"Jess Westman, Fang & Talon!"

Wade clapped madly until his hands were bright red, before standing up and giving his girlfriend a big hug.

"Congratulations, Jess," Wade said with a smile, staring into her eyes. "I love you."

"I love you too." She gave him a kiss before running up onto the stage and claiming her new iron.

As the night continued, more and more Gunners were called up to the stage. Wade, of course, was *not* one of them. It was finally down to two cadets, and Wade hoped his name would not be called last. He didn't want Ulysses to turn this into a spectacle; he didn't even want to go up there at all.

"There are only two more sets of iron to be bestowed tonight," Master Ulysses said as he looked across the crowd. "Next... Ben Carpenter, Shadow & Bone!"

The crowd cheered as Ben ran up on stage and claimed his white and black weapons. Wade's stomach dropped, and his ears began to ring.

No... Please, no.

"That leaves one last cadet..." The crowd looked around, wondering who hadn't been called up yet. Wade sank lower into his seat, attempting to hide. "Wade Russell!" Ulysses finally shouted.

The crowd cheered, and Wade was pulled up from his seat against his will by his friends. Jess gave him a quick kiss on his cheek before he slipped through the crowd and made his way to the stage. He stood facing Master Ulysses, trying his best not to shake. It was the first time they had seen each other since the final test.

"Wade, you are our last cadet for Bestowment tonight. I would like to make it known to all in this room how special of a moment this is." The crowd was now silent, as everyone watched two Master Gunners carry in a gold and silver chest. Gasps echoed across the room. "This set was passed down from the very first Master Gunner... the founder of the Order... the original defender of Gadriel... *Shar Vahn.*"

The crowd stared in disbelief; Wade's stomach dropped.

"Bestowed upon you, Wade Russell, *Rose & Thorn.*"

Not a single person cheered; not a single person clapped. Wade wondered if they could hear his heart beating through his chest. A key was placed into the center of the box and turned to the right. With a click, it unlocked and opened, revealing two silver revolvers–noticeably bigger than any of the weapons that had been bestowed before. Gold engravings ran across their flanks, spiraling and interlacing in a beautiful, artistic pattern, as if the iron had been hand crafted by Nor himself. The engravings formed a raised T on the right one and an R on the left one. The guns glistened and sparkled in the light–the most beautiful iron Wade had ever seen in his life, but the admiration quickly faded as the weapons didn't belong to him. He felt sick to his stomach just looking at them.

A bead of sweat ran down the side of his temple as he felt every eye in the auditorium fixed on him. He told himself that it was a dream; it wasn't real. He was still at the gun range, he just hadn't woken up yet. These weapons weren't being bestowed upon him as he didn't deserve them. Out of everyone in that room, Wade Russell was, quite literally, the *least* deserving. He tried to wake himself up, but it wasn't working. This was real. There was no escaping the nightmare now. He slowly raised his hand toward them.

Come to us, Wade… the weapons whispered. *Bring us into the light.*

Wade knew what taking them into his hands would bring: the throne. He would officially become the Shar'La and king of Gadriel–at only eighteen years old. Rose & Thorn had never before been presented to any other cadet in the hundreds of years since Shar's death, and Wade wondered if the guns had even been seen since they were sealed in his casket and buried. If Wade refused them, they would be returned to Shar, never to be unearthed again. Staring at them now, in all their glory, Wade realized that would be a crime.

He reached into the chest and laid his palms on the engraved grips. They were cold as ice, and he felt an almost magnetic sensation growing in his fingers, forcing them to wrap around the iron. Wade didn't fight it, and before he knew it, he was holding the weapons within his hands.

"Pull the triggers, and they're yours," Master Ulysses whispered.

Wade aimed them at the floor and brought his fingers to the triggers. He hesitated for a moment before looking at the crowd. They continued to stare at him, dead silent.

Wade looked back at the guns, exhaled, and *pulled* the triggers.

Click.

The hammers snapped, and the cylinders spun.

"*As he intended,*" Master Ulysses muttered. Then, Wade raised the iron into the air. "The Shar'La!"

"THE SHAR'LA!" the crowd repeated, erupting into cheers.

Wade held the weapons proudly above his head, pumping them in triumph, and while he stood there, only one thought occupied his mind: Rose & Thorn were an honor as well as a curse, as the last man who held them in his hands died a tragic death, *lost and alone.*

• • •

That night after the ceremony was the first night the newly initiated and bestowed Gunners were allowed to drink, and they took *full* advantage of it. They danced and partied in the refectory, cheering and celebrating their accomplishments by passing around their newly bestowed iron–*always* keeping the barrels pointed at the ground–and inspected and compared their differences. Each weapon had a unique color scheme and design–all special in their own right. Of course, most of the Gunners spent the night hounding Wade, as everyone wanted to get a closer look at Rose & Thorn.

"I graduated with the Shar'La!" a Gunner yelled while standing on top of a table and raising his beer into the air. "Fuck yea!"

He downed the entire mug, swayed slightly, and finally collapsed face first onto the table with a hard *thud.* Later that night, Wade saw other Gunners carrying him out of the refectory by his arms and legs.

But as the hours ticked by, Wade was growing sick of the attention and looked for a way out. John raised his beer into the air and signaled for the rest to join him.

"To the Order, to Bestowment, to the Kingdom of Gadriel, and to a life of shooting guns and getting fucked up!" John started to chug his beer, and the rest of the Gunners followed.

Wade used the distraction as a means to escape to get a breath of fresh air. He stumbled outside the refectory and stood staring up at the stars. They were *beautiful,* and in his drunkenness, he wondered if he could just stand there and stare at them forever. But approaching footsteps behind him brought him out of his trance and made him groan.

"Rose & Thorn have grown shy. No more visitors tonight. Try again… tomorrow," Wade said with a burp.

"Really? You can't make an exception for *me?*"

Wade turned to see Jess, arms crossed and leaning against the doorway leading back into the refectory.

"I saw you sneak out," she said. "Running away already? The night just started."

"I wasn't running away, I just… needed a second to breathe."

"I figured." The smashing of mugs echoed outside, followed by more cheering and hollering. "How are you feeling?"

"Fine, I guess. Nothing's really changed, has it?"

"No, I guess not, besides you being the Shar La and all."

"The others are more obsessed with these stupid guns than I am."

"Can you blame them? It's been hundreds of years since anyone has seen them. They're relics, Wade, and now they're *yours*."

"Lucky me," Wade said, rolling his eyes.

Jess wrapped her arms around Wade from behind and laid her head down on his back.

"I know you're scared of what it means–being the Shar'La–but would you have had it any other way?"

"It's not about what I wanted. What if the Council got it wrong?"

"They didn't."

Wade stared back up at the stars; Jess hugged him tighter.

"I'm going to head up to the Shar'La's room, and when he is ready…" she whispered in his ear, "he can come find me laying naked on his bed."

She kissed his cheek and pulled away from him, disappearing back into the refectory and leaving him alone with his mouth hanging open in disbelief. But before he could join her, he had a loose end to tie up first.

• • •

Wade trekked across the range, crushing empty shells into the dirt with each step. He walked with purpose, as he only had one thing on his mind: the sniper's nest. He climbed up the ladder of the nest and laughed at what he saw sitting before him. Propped up against a small rock was a broken piece of a mirror.

Should've known…

Wade climbed back down the ladder, only to see Master Ulysses leaning against the nest with his hands buried in his pockets.

"You really didn't know, did you?" Master Ulysses said with a chuckle.

"I didn't think you'd be that predictable... or sane."

"Well, it looks like I was wrong about you after all, *Shar'La.*"

"But what if you weren't, even if your fucked up method for figuring that out failed."

"Huh, you think so?" He kicked a shell in front of him and it skidded across the dirt. "Holding that fancy iron doesn't make you feel like a hero all of a sudden?"

"No."

"Go figure."

"I'm not the Shar'La, Master Ulysses, no matter how hard you people try to force it on me."

"Your lack of belief in yourself has always been your greatest weakness, Wade."

"But I know I'm not! I can feel it!"

"So, you're saying the Rock, the Council, and the magic that is binded to those triggers is *wrong?*"

"Yes. I'm a nobody–nothing, always have been."

"I don't believe that, but I do believe I found you for a reason."

"So you believe *I'm* the one who is supposed to lead our armies? Everyone else back there would kill to have these guns, and I want to leave them right here in the dirt and never see them again!"

"Yes, I do, because you're the only one here who *doesn't* want them."

"What?"

"And maybe that's the point. Maybe that's why you're the only one in the history of the Order who could pull those triggers. You don't seek power like the rest of us."

Wade shook his head and said, "I don't want to die the same way he did, Ulysses."

"Do any of us? The man who fears death and the man who fears nothing both die all the same." Master Ulysses looked deeper into his eyes. "You know, I see a lot of myself in you, Wade. You want to control everything–always on your terms, but life isn't about control, it's about letting go. When you realize that, you'll finally be free." He began to walk off. "Enjoy this time while you have it, Wade."

"Why?"

"Because those who inherit great power also inherit great responsibility. Do you understand me?" Wade nodded. "Good."

"Wait, Master Ulysses, during my final test, you said I shouldn't have friends. Do you really believe that?"

"I do." He stepped into the darkness of the night. "I'll see you on the throne, kid."

CHAPTER THIRTEEN

THE BEAR

Wade's eyes fluttered open, and he stared at the bowing ceiling above him, riddled with cracks and splinters. He had just been *home*–now where was he? He shifted slightly, and the makeshift bed beneath him–which was nothing more than a wooden frame nailed together, stuffed with hay, and covered with a patched blanket– creaked loudly. He was back in the cabin with Sarah. A return to the nightmare. But he had to admit, it was the first decent sleep he'd had in days since escaping the fort, and Nor knew he needed it.

The Demon Gunner immediately wanted to retreat back into the depths of his mind and escape this place once more, but he knew it would only be temporary. There was no warm bed with Jess in it waiting for him, no friends ready to travel to the Farlands of Gadriel to begin their new lives as Gunners, no–there was only this reality now, and with it, only suffering.

As he sat up and drew in a long breath, he noticed the air in the room had a stale taste to it–turpid and unpleasant. His nose was stuffed from the dust drifting down from the bowing ceiling, floating in the air like a heavy fog. The silence in the room was broken only by the soft rumblings of the girl to his right.

Sarah lay asleep in her small bed at the far end of the

room. Her body jolted a few times, then settled again. Her breathing was slow and steady, and Wade was careful not to wake her. He'd let her sleep all day if she needed to. There was nothing outside these walls for her anyway.

He flipped the dusty blanket off of himself and quietly slid out of bed. The door to the upstairs bedroom creaked as it closed, and he made his way down the rickety wooden steps to the living room. Wade was thankful for the cabin they now found refuge in. It was a momentary safe haven from the Darkness, and he wondered if candles outside a tent would even deter Demons this deep into the Veil. Without the cabin, they would've surely been dead. Nor had guided them here, he could *feel* it.

Outside, Wade stepped onto the porch, quietly attempted to blow his nose, and immediately drew his shirt collar up. It was still cold–considerably colder than the desert, and Wade didn't exactly know why. He could only speculate that they were now closer to the source of the Darkness than ever before. The drop in temperature could also mean that the Demons in these woods were stronger–*bigger*, more dangerous than the previous ones. The spider-like monster they first encountered seemed to prove that theory.

But if Wade had any hope of venturing further into the Veil, he needed to get Sarah into warmer clothes. He searched through the house and managed to find a thick pair of blue jeans, a thin leather overcoat, and–to his surprise–a wide-brimmed hat much like the one he was wearing. Though they'd help momentarily, the new clothes alone would not be enough for the journey ahead. He needed fur.

• • •

Wade stalked through the forest, following animal tracks that twisted and wound between the trees. Some prints he recognized–deer, maybe bear–but others he couldn't place. They left behind strange, multi-point impressions in the snow, nothing like the anatomy of any animal he knew. There were even long, smooth trails carved through the snow, as if something had slithered through the underbrush. Just looking at them unsettled him, and he found himself glancing over his shoulder every few seconds, half-expecting to see something watching him from the shadows.

He carried a bow he'd found in the basement of the cabin and had used it to kill a few rabbits and foxes. It was clunky and not particularly sturdy, but it was effective and quiet enough not to attract the monster from before–and that was all that mattered.

During his time at the School, Wade had been trained in a wide array of weapons–throwing knives, axes, blow-darts, bows–anything that could be thrown or fired with enough force to kill. Cadets were required to achieve one hundred percent accuracy with each weapon by the time Bestowment rolled around; otherwise, they would forfeit their iron and face immediate expulsion. Though they had years to train, many cadets still failed–and Wade never saw them again. But above all else, Wade preferred to shoot guns. He used to wonder why they even bothered with such archaic weapons when they had powerful iron on their hips. Yet in moments like this, he found himself grateful for his time with Master Ulysses–even if he couldn't see it before.

Wade then focused back on the scene before him. A small rabbit stood in a clearing, foraging for the last scraps of nutrients buried beneath the forest floor. He crouched behind a bank, zeroed in, held his breath, and let an arrow fly. It struck true, piercing the rabbit's heart and dropping it into the snow where it convulsed. Wade crept forward and slid down beside it. He secured its head, then pressed the arrow in deeper, ensuring the kill. This would be his final catch of the hunt.

After he finished, he brought the carcasses back to the house and spent the morning skinning and processing them for meat and fur. The game in these woods was scarce, so he didn't get much–but it would be enough to create an insulated fur lining for Sarah's jacket.

Wade made sure to relight the makeshift torches he'd set up the night before, which were nothing more than sticks wrapped in fabric and dipped in Demon's blood, before heading inside. The gunslingers at Fort Carn might've been fucked in the head, but they had a solid system for warding off Demons–and even with being this deep into the Veil, it seemed to work flawlessly.

Next, he cooked the meat over the living room fire and spent the rest of the afternoon sewing fur into Sarah's new jacket with a needle and thread he had found in the basement. This was the scene the girl had walked into when she finally made her way downstairs. She yawned and stretched her arms over her head before taking a seat next to Wade on the floor.

"Who's that for?" she asked.

"The monster out there," Wade responded sarcastically, prompting Sarah to nudge him with her elbow and chuckle.

"No, it's for *you.*"

"Me? Really?"

Wade nodded and held it up in front of her. "Try it on and see if it fits."

She fed her arms through the sleeves and shimmied it into place. It was a *perfect* fit, and her smile proved that.

"And I've got something else for you," Wade said, dusting off a wide-brimmed hat and a small pocket knife in a leather sheath before presenting them to her.

Her eyes went wide as she said, "Where'd you find all this?"

"Downstairs. Now go ahead and put it on."

Sarah stared at the items for a moment before taking them into her hands and placing the hat atop her head. Immediately, she stood up and ran to a cracked mirror leaning against the wall, admiring it in the shattered reflection.

"I look like you!" Sarah shouted with excitement while turning from side to side. "Am I a Gunner now?"

"You'd need to pledge your life to the Order and the gun first."

"*Oh.*"

"*But...* you sure look like one," Wade said, cracking a smile. "Maybe one day, after we figure out where the light went, I'll show you where I was trained. They might even accept you into the Order."

Sarah chuckled while admiring her reflection and muttered, "I wish."

"Well, we should get moving soon. I don't want to stay here any longer than we have to."

"Are we traveling further into the Veil?"

"*Yes.*"

A worried look grew on Sarah's face. "I was afraid you were going to say that."

"We've got no other choice, but I'm planning on scouting out the trail on foot first—see if we can learn more about the path that lay ahead. Would you like to join?"

She thought for a moment and then said, "I could... *or* I could just sit inside this dusty ass cabin with the smell of death lingering in the air?" Wade smiled. "No thanks, I think I'll join you instead."

• • •

The pair moved through the forest, crouch-walking side by side in the snow. Wade guided them by feeling for changes in the air—warmer meant they were heading away from the Veil, colder meant... Well, that was the direction they *should've* been running from. But of course, they didn't. Instead, they pressed deeper into the woods.

The soft snow beneath their feet turned to ice, each step followed by a sharp crunch that echoed through the forest. Wade signaled to slow down by lowering a flat hand toward the ground. In this moment, noise was just as much the enemy as the cold.

After they crested a small hill, Wade scanned the foliage for the monster, but saw nothing. Relief washed over him, and he wondered if it had left these woods completely. But Nor knew he was never *that* lucky.

They continued on, slipping past towering pine trees, ducking under thickets, and crossing semi-frozen streams. With each tree that they passed, the Demon Gunner carved a notch into the bark with Rose, marking a trail they could follow later on Quicksilver. The ground began to rise, growing steeper with each step, until even lifting their feet became a struggle.

"Do you think… it's time… to turn back?" Sarah said between labored breaths.

"Almost," Wade said, noticing her struggling. "We can once we reach the top of this hill."

And when they finally did, they saw a frozen lake stretching far into the distance. Beyond it lay a cold, icy tundra, and behind that, towering mountains that seemed to stab into the heavens themselves. Wade narrowed his eyes and thought he saw a glimmer of light flickering in and out on top of one of the peaks.

"Is the Consumption doing this?" Sarah asked, breaking his concentration. "Making everything frozen?"

"Yes."

"Why?"

"I'm not sure. Perhaps it is what the *Demons* prefer." A strong wind picked up, causing Wade's leather jacket to flap against his sides. "Be prepared, Sarah, I suspect that the journey will only get harder from here."

A twig snapped behind them. Wade glanced over his shoulder and spotted a small deer at the base of the hill. He brought two fingers to his eyes, then pointed toward the animal, signaling Sarah. She turned, rose onto her tiptoes, and caught sight of it before nodding in agreement.

"Would you like to shoot it?" Wade whispered, drawing the bow from his back. "It would provide us with enough food for the journey ahead."

"But I don't know–"

"Yes you do," Wade insisted. "You're a Gunner now– anything you can aim with, you can shoot. *Trust yourself.*"

He handed her the bow, then an arrow, doubting she

could *actually* make the shot—but that didn't matter. He just wanted to see her try, remembering Master Ulysses' words…

One must never fear the act of trying, for true knowledge is only gained through experience, and once it is gained, it can never be called a failure.

However, he had to admit it was a tough shot—about twenty yards downhill, with a steady wind coming from the north. She would need to account for the—

SINK!

The arrow struck the side of the deer, piercing its heart. It kicked frantically before collapsing to the ground, convulsing until it died.

"Where the hell did that come from?" Wade whispered.

"I believed in myself and aimed with my heart—just as you said."

Wade brought his hand up and fist bumped her.

"Well done. Now, let's go get our kill."

They bounded down the hill and entered the clearing where the deer carcass lay. Its tongue lolled from its mouth, and its eyes stared blankly at the sky. Wade slid down beside it, grasped the shaft, and twisted it before pulling it from the midsection.

"How are we going to—" Sarah began, but before she could finish, Wade had already hoisted the full-grown deer onto his shoulder. She didn't ask any further questions, she just stared in amazement at this feat of strength. With his free hand, he wiped the mud and snow from his pants and signaled two fingers forward. "Let's move."

Suddenly, a dark shape moved between the trees. Sarah and Wade froze, expecting the spider-like monster to emerge—but instead, a decomposing black bear sauntered toward them, black drool dripping from its growling mouth.

"Sarah..." Wade said as he slowly stepped backward. "*Run*."

Sarah took off, and the bear charged forward, roaring as its claws tore into the snow-covered ground. Wade tossed the deer aside and, in one swift move, unholstered Rose and Thorn. He took aim, but just as he pulled the trigger, the sound of crashing trees erupted beside him. Wade dove backward, hitting the ground hard and narrowly avoiding the spider-like monster as it burst through the trees and slammed into the bear.

"WADE!" Sarah cried out as he attempted to crawl away from the chaos.

Behind him, the Demon had already overpowered the bear, pinning it to the ground with its long, spindly legs. One leg rose, tipped with a sharp point, then shot down in a lightning-fast strike, piercing the bear's chest. The bear let out a final roar of pain–then went still, its head slumping to the side.

Wade finally got a full look at the creature. It stood nearly ten feet tall, supported by at least eight spider-like, pointed legs. Its lower half was unmistakably arachnid, but its upper body was disturbingly human–gray skinned, with two elongated arms and a bald head. He couldn't see its face. The leg buried deep in the bear's chest slowly withdrew, a decomposing heart skewered on its tip. The creature brought it to its face, sniffed it, then flicked it aside in disappointment.

Wade used the distraction to bolt, sprinting after Sarah. Another small hill rose ahead, and he scrambled up it as fast as he could. Just as he reached the top, he glanced back–

only to see the monster *staring* at him with piercing green eyes. It had tusk-like mandibles that opened sideways, and it let out a screech so loud it rattled the trees.

"Keep going!" Wade yelled as he caught up to the girl. He grabbed the back of her jacket and helped pull her through the snow.

BOOM!

Branches and bark exploded behind them. Wade looked over his shoulder and saw the fast approaching monster. He swung one arm behind him and began shooting wildly, striking the monster multiple times in the chest. It screeched *even* louder and continued to charge forward.

Up ahead, the forest seemed to vanish–but it wasn't an end, just an incredibly steep drop off. Before Wade could react, his foot caught on a root, and he tumbled forward, dragging Sarah down with him. They flipped over and over until Wade managed to dig the blade of Thorn into the slope, slowing their descent.

When they finally stopped, he scrambled to his feet, reloaded his guns, and realized they were standing on the edge of a cliff. Then, the Demon appeared once more, staring down at them. Wade fired and hit it square in the face–but it didn't explode. The act only seemed to piss it off.

"Wade, we have to jump!"

He looked over his shoulder and saw a waterfall cascading into a pool veiled by mist. He had no idea how deep it was, but the girl was right–they didn't have a choice.

Without hesitation, Wade holstered his guns and tackled Sarah off the cliff just as one of the monster's legs swiped past behind them. They plunged into the mist, flipping over each other before crashing into the freezing water below. Wade took the brunt of the impact—it felt like slamming into a wall of stone. Pain immediately radiated from his broken ribs. He sank deeper into the dark water, unmoving.

Sarah.

His body jolted, and his senses snapped back. The cold water was striking, but it numbed the pain—if only for a moment. Adrenaline surged through him as he fought to reach the surface, desperate for air. But he wasn't rising. A strong current yanked him sideways, slamming him back and forth against the rocks along the riverbed. His brain screamed for air, his chest tightening with each passing second. Then—finally—he burst through the surface and gasped. The world was bright—disorienting, and he couldn't tell where the river was taking him.

"Sarah!" he yelled, trying to stay afloat. "SARAH!" He couldn't find her, he couldn't—

WHOOSH!

Sarah broke through the surface in front of him, coughing and gasping for air as they were taken further down the river. Wade swam toward her and grabbed onto her arm.

"I've got you," he assured.

With all of his strength, Wade paddled toward the riverbank and grabbed a tree root hanging over the water. He pulled himself up and swung Sarah forward, escaping the current's wrath. She managed to reach the shore and climb up the bank before collapsing onto the snow. Wade followed after, scrambling up the bank, and finally freeing himself from the ice-cold water.

"Wade..." Sarah murmured before passing out, shivering and convulsing from hyperthermia.

He slid down next to her and scooped her into his arms, channeling heat from within to warm her—but it wouldn't be enough. He needed a *real* fire. Nearby lay a gathering of sticks from a previous flood. Wade held out both hands, felt the fire within him, and unleashed it toward the bundle. Blue flames erupted, sending a giant cloud of smoke into the air. He pulled the girl closer, desperate to warm her.

"Sarah, please, *please* wake up," he said as he shook her, but she didn't wake.

He continued to hold her in his arms—praying to Nor to save her—as the sun dipped below the trees, and the Darkness grew around them.

CHAPTER FOURTEEN
ONE SHOT, ONE KILL

Wade sat there–holding her–and listened to the sound of the river running past.

"Come on," he said, drawing in deep breaths. "Please, Sarah, you gotta wake up."

The flame within him grew stronger, and steam began to rise from their damp clothes. Wade scooted them closer to the fire–as close as he could get without burning her–and held her there with outstretched arms. After what felt like an eternity, the girl's eyes *finally* fluttered open.

"W... Wade?" she asked, teeth chattering.

"I'm right here. I've got you."

Her body temperature started to rise, and color returned to her lips.

Thank Nor.

They remained by the raging fire for hours, until at last, Sarah was warm enough to be released from his arms. Slowly, she rose and made her way to the riverbank, where she sat down and buried her face in her hands. Wade stayed behind and rested on a log facing the woods, giving her a moment alone. He scanned the dense foliage, watching for any sign of movement. Now and then, a sharp crack of a twig snapping would break the silence, but nothing ever attacked.

"I don't want to stay here any longer," Sarah finally muttered from behind.

"Me neither," Wade responded. "We need to get moving."

"No, I mean I don't want to stay *here*–in these woods. I can't sleep another night in that cabin."

"Sarah, we've got nowhere else to–"

"We do," she interrupted. "We can continue on–to the source of the Darkness."

"And what about the monster?"

"Isn't it obvious? We're Gunners. We kill the damn thing."

• • •

When Sarah finally felt strong enough to make the trek back to the cabin, they rose from the fire and began walking along the river. After traveling a good distance down it, Wade spotted a thick overhang of tree limbs stretching above the water.

"*There,*" Wade said, pointing to the branches.

"What about them?"

"We're going to use them to swing across."

"How?"

"Like this."

Wade brought Thorn from its holster and tethered its grip to the chain that wrapped around his right forearm. He let out some slack, then swung the gun in a circle beside him, building momentum until he released it with an underhand toss, sending it flying toward a branch. The gun and the chain looped around the limb, and Wade gave a sharp tug, securing it in place with the blade pinned against another branch. He then hung on it, testing the limb's strength before turning toward the girl.

"You ready?" Wade asked.

"Let's do it," Sarah responded confidently.

Wade swept her up in his arms again, drew the chain back, and ran forward. At the river's edge, he lifted his legs and swung over the water. When they landed on the opposite bank, Wade gave the chain a forceful tug, snapping the branch in half and freeing his gun. As it fell, he yanked the chain backward and caught the weapon in his hand. Then, he began the arduous process of wrapping the chain back around his forearm after holstering Thorn.

"That worked surprisingly well," Sarah said with admiration.

"I'm glad, because we didn't have any other option. It would be nightfall by the time we reached the river's end—*if* we reached it at all. Now come on, we need to keep moving."

The cliff they had originally jumped from rose to their right, but it gradually gave way to a more mellow hill. Even so, it was still steep, slick, and all around a massive pain in the ass to climb. The rapidly setting sun didn't help anything either, as the air around them grew colder by the second, reminding them of the ever-ticking clock they were racing against. And as they walked, Wade could hear the girl shivering behind him. Whenever he felt like she began to slow and fall behind, he'd stop, inhale deeply, and raise fire in his palms, giving her a chance to warm up again.

The incline finally began to level out, and Wade spotted a notch he had carved in a tree—a sign they were close to the cabin. They moved as silently as possible, crouch-walking in case the monster was nearby. If it attacked again out here, they wouldn't have a river to jump into.

As they trekked through the snow, Wade wrestled

with a plan of how to kill the monster. The task would *not* be easy—it was faster, stronger, and more resistant to Hellfire than anything else they'd faced so far. Back in the desert, the Demons that lurked in the Darkness had been drawn to flesh—or as Butch put it, *souls*—and could smell them from a mile away. But this monster seemed to have a heightened sense for sound, which made an escape attempt on Quicksilver futile. Her hooves were far too loud, even in the snow. But regardless, the girl was right: they *needed* to kill it.

But how? Wade thought to himself. *What would Ulysses do?*

The forest around him faded away, and Wade saw his master standing before him, arms crossed with the same smug look on his face that was always there. Gunshots echoed across the practice range, and bullet casings bounced off the dirt, ejected from the rifles of dozens of training cadets. Wade was home once again.

"Now what could you possibly want?" Ulysses asked.

"*Help.*"

"Help? What did I train you for? The Shar'La is coming back for—"

"Please, Master Ulysses, we can't outrun it."

"I'm afraid you can't."

"We can't face it head on either. Hellfire has no effect on it."

"No it does not."

"I'm worried about the girl, Master. It has us trapped."

"It has *you* trapped?" Ulysses asked with a chuckle. "Did I hear that right? Tell me, Wade, when a rat chews through our rations, are we beholden to that rat?"

"Yes," Wade said sheepishly, but the way Ulysses smirked

at him told him everything he needed to know.

And just like that, Wade was back in the forest—his home gone once again, but his face now filled with hope, for he knew what his master was implying.

You are beholden to the rat only until you trap it.

Wade smiled, and sitting before them was their refuge. They ran the rest of the way toward it and shut the door quietly behind them. Wade wasted no time, throwing logs onto the fireplace and lighting them. The blue flames slowly grew in front of their faces.

"Here," Wade said, tossing her a blanket from one of the saddlebags.

She caught it and said, "Thank you," before tightly wrapping herself up in it. "Oh yeah, that's better. A few more minutes out there, and I think my teeth might've rattled straight outta my mouth."

Wade chuckled, and then they sat in silence, staring at the fire.

"I've got a plan, Sarah," Wade finally said. "That monster... it's attracted to sound—that much we know. The second the bear roared, it was on us. Which means we've got no chance of getting out of here on Quicksilver. We can't seem to kill it with the weapons we have either, so all we can do now is set a trap—" Wade held up a single round of Hellfire, *"with these."*

"But what are we going to do with them?" she asked. "I thought you said it's immune to Hellfire?"

"Not exactly."

Wade unholstered Thorn and fished the tip of its blade into the base of the bullet. With a faint *click*, the primer popped out and landed on the floor. He titled the bullet over and dumped out its contents into his cupped palm.

"This is a *highly* explosive, magical form of gunpowder," Wade said. "Enough of it concentrated in a single area would create…"

"*A bomb.*"

"Exactly."

"So we're going to blow it up?"

"We're going to *try* to, but unless you've got a better idea, that's our only option for now."

"No, I like that plan. I think it's just crazy enough to work."

"Good, then let's get to it."

• • •

All through the night, Wade and Sarah sat side by side, busting open rounds of Hellfire and dumping the gunpowder into mason jars Wade had found in the basement. Slowly but surely, dozens of loaded jars filled the room. Wade then broke down the beds, peeled up the floorboards, and nailed the wood together, creating multiple small boxes. One by one, they carefully placed each jar into the boxes and stacked them on top of each other, and by the time the sun rose again, four fully loaded boxes sat next to Wade and a now sleeping Sarah. He let her rest while he healed his broken ribs, knowing that it would soon be time to set the trap and face the monster once and for all.

• • •

The sun was now directly overhead in the snowy forest as Wade carried the boxes into the middle of a clearing and arranged them in a square. Behind him, Sarah double-checked Quicksilver's saddlebags, ensuring they were properly strapped down for the journey ahead. When she finished, she pulled Quicksilver by the reins into dense thickets that concealed her. She then hitched the undead horse to a tree and lay on the ground beside her, aiming at the boxes through the foliage with her repeater rifle outstretched before her.

Sarah gave a thumbs up that she was ready, and Wade hoisted himself on top of the boxes. He stood tall, staring off into the dark forest that lay in front of him. This was it, if he fucked this up, he was dead. He needed to be quick, he needed to be precise, and above all else, he needed to be brave.

Wade cupped his hands on either side of his mouth, took a deep breath, and yelled as *loud* as he could. "AHHHHHHHHHHHHH!!!!"

Black birds resting in the thick canopy above took off into the sky, but other than that, *nothing* happened.

He looked over toward Sarah, who shrugged.

"AHHHHHHHHH!!" he yelled again.

A few seconds passed, then, the echoes of trees cracking and breaking apart grew in the distance, growing closer with each passing second.

"AHHHHHHHHHH!!!"

Wade could see it now—the spider-like monster was approaching fast, and there was no mistaking that it was locked onto Wade. Trees crashed in front of him like great towers falling, exploding across the snow covered ground. Wade's hands lowered toward his revolvers. He fished into the holsters and gripped the cold steel of the magical iron.

One shot. One Kill.

CHAPTER FIFTEEN
THE RIFT

Wade unholstered Rose and Thorn as the monster drew closer, screeching and blasting trees out of its path. He raised the iron before him–his grip shaking violently–and it was now in his sights.

"Get ready!" he yelled to Sarah.

The Demon smashed through a set of trees fifty yards away, sending a wave of splinters and bark flying in every direction. Then, it stopped in its tracks and stood before him.

"I'm right here!" Wade shouted. "Come on, you ugly bastard!"

Its jaw opened sideways, flashing razor sharp teeth–almost as if it were smiling. Then it jolted forward and charged head on at Wade.

Come on, just a little closer.

It was only a few feet away now, and time seemed to slow. Wade waited–four heartbeats passed, and on the fifth, he crouched low and launched himself backward off the boxes. As he fell toward the ground, he leveled his iron sights, and just as the monster climbed on top of the boxes, he pulled the triggers. Two rounds of Hellfire launched from Rose and Thorn and flew toward their target, piercing straight through the wood.

BOOOOOOOOOMMMMM!!!!!!

A massive wall of fire erupted in front of Wade, and the explosion was so powerful, that it sent him flying. He crashed hard into the snow, flipping and tumbling before slamming into a tree and coming to a stop. Gritting his teeth, Wade shook his head and tried to ignore the excruciating pain pulsing through his body. He then looked up at the towering cloud of smoke and fire where the monster had once stood. Smoldering embers and ash rained down from the blown open canopy above, landing on his jacket and sprinkling it with soot.

"Are you OK?" Sarah yelled from her safe refuge a good distance away.

"I'm alright," Wade muttered, holding a hand over his freshly healed ribs that were most certainly broken again. He painfully rolled over and got up from the snow. "I... I think we killed it."

But then, the wind shifted; the smoke began to clear, and Wade saw the outline of a figure standing within it, still alive.

"Motherfucker," Wade said to himself before aiming his revolvers once more.

The monster lumbered out of the smoke, revealing its burned and crippled form. One side of its face and body was charred black, and its right arm had now been reduced to a stump, oozing green blood. But it didn't seem fazed, it just started toward him again, limping and stumbling, while dragging its mangled legs and leaving a trail of blood in its wake.

"Sarah," Wade shouted, gripping his revolvers tighter. "Time to rain Hellfire."

All at once, dozens of shots rang out.

BANG! BANG! BANG! BANG! BANG! BANG!

Spent casings flew from their weapons and scattered in the snow as bullets tore through the Demon's body, spraying bursts of green blood out from its back. Still, it marched on, refusing to fall, but Wade could see its strength waning–each step weaker than the last.

As Wade reloaded, Sarah kept firing her repeater rifle, racking the lever as fast as she could. Casings flew past her face like sparks, until the rifle finally clicked empty–but she didn't stop. In one motion, she tossed it aside, unholstered her pistol, spun it once on her finger, and fan fired it at the Demon. Its body was now so riddled with bullet holes that blood gushed from it like punctures in a water sack. It took one final step before its legs gave out, collapsing forward onto its knees, as if waiting to be judged by Nor himself.

Wade walked toward it, his spurs clinking softly against the leather of his boots. He stopped directly in front of the monster. Its jaw opened again, black drool dripping from jagged teeth–salivating, as if Wade was the most delicious thing it had ever seen. He stared into its defeated eyes, searching for some hint of life or thought within them, but found only hunger–an insatiable, *burning* hunger hidden within the green glow. Then in one swift move, Wade stabbed the blade of Thorn through the monster's face. It screeched and twitched before he pulled the trigger and blew its head off. Its limbs immediately went limp, and it collapsed backward into the snow.

Sarah stepped up beside him, rifle in hand. She leaned forward and prodded the monster's body with the barrel, giving it a few cautious jabs.

"Is it dead?" she asked.

"I believe so," Wade responded. "But you can never be

too careful." Wade emptied Rose and Thorn into its chest. "*There.* Always make sure to finish them off."

A threat isn't neutralized until you're back sleeping in your own bed. And even then, keep one eye open! Master Ulysses' words echoed in his head as he reloaded his weapons.

"Are you alright?" he finally asked. "Did you get tagged from the explosion?"

"No, I'm fine. How are you holding up? That landing looked rough."

Wade lowered his shoulder toward his hip and felt his stiff back pop and crack in multiple places. His ribs ached immensely.

"I'll heal..." he said with a groan, *"with time."*

Sarah giggled and said, "Good, because I can't go on without you."

A smile cracked through Wade's pained expression.

"I would've missed that shot too," Sarah said, brushing the snow off her jeans and adjusting the wide-brimmed hat on her head. "So, is it time we continue the quest?" She looked down at the bloated, leaking monster. "Find out where that ugly bastard came from?"

Wade watched its green blood run out of its body like a river, quickly soaking into the snow. "Yes, it's time."

"Quicksilver is tied up over there. She didn't move an inch during the explosion. Such a damn good–"

Suddenly, the ground beneath their feet began to rumble, then it erupted into a violent, earthquake-like shaking.

"What the hell is that?" Sarah asked.

Wade readied his weapons and scanned the forest. In the far distance, he spotted movement.

"Get Quicksilver, now!" Wade yelled.

Sarah sprinted toward the horse and unhitched her

from the tree. Wade squinted, focusing on the growing movement across the forest floor. At first, it looked like a flood rushing toward them, but he quickly realized it wasn't a flood at all. It was *thousands* of small, spider-like creatures swarming their way closer. Wade holstered Rose and Thorn and ran toward the now unhitched horse. He mounted her and scooted back in the saddle before extending a hand to Sarah and hoisting her up in front of him.

"You steer, I shoot. Got it?"

"Got it!"

Sarah whipped the reins twice, and they took off, weaving through the trees at breakneck speed. The spider-like creatures chased after them, gnashing and snapping their teeth. They looked just like the Demon they had slain—only smaller, not fully grown. Wade unholstered Thorn, twisted around in the saddle, and fired over his shoulder, blowing their heads off with dead-on accuracy. When his gun finally clicked empty, he fumbled to reload the cylinder as the bouncing of Quicksilver beneath him made it incredibly difficult, causing him to drop bullets into the snow.

The creatures continued to swarm after them, and even as Wade fired into the horde, he barely made a dent. For every six that fell, more charged in, trampling the fallen without hesitation. A shot cracked beside Wade's head, and he looked to his right to see Sarah holding a smoking revolver with one hand while gripping the reins with the other.

"Keep following the notches!" Wade yelled over the thundering of the hooves and the endless screeching of the horde behind them. "We should be at the lake soon!"

He twisted back around and continued firing Thorn.

More of them exploded, and as he went to reload once more, a single creature launched from the horde and flew toward his face. He jutted Thorn's blade into the creature's stomach and it passed through like a skewered piece of meat. Wade pulled the trigger, blowing the creature backward off the gun.

As the horde grew closer, more creatures started to leap forward into the air. They were quickly shot, exploding in bright flashes of green blood and fire, but one managed to latch onto Wade's leg. Its jaw opened wide, and just before it bit down into his soft flesh, Wade blew its head off. Its body fell into the snow and tumbled away.

Behind him, Sarah whipped the reins harder, causing Quicksilver to run faster up a steep hill. Wade looked past her and saw they were nearing the frozen lake.

We're almost there.

But even with the increase in speed, Quicksilver wasn't going fast enough. The creatures were closing in, and Thorn couldn't keep up with their onslaught. Wade had to do something and *fast*.

He holstered Thorn and began unraveling the chain on his left arm. Like a belt, he wrapped it around himself and then around Sarah before snapping the two ends together as if it were magnetic. Then, he drew in a deep breath, feeling the fire growing within him. He focused on it, outstretched his arms behind him, and blasted a wave of fire across the creatures and trees. The monsters screeched in pain as the forest exploded in bright blue flames.

Immediately, Wade felt dizzy and his grip on consciousness starting to slip. A heavy feeling washed over him, and before he knew it, he collapsed forward and passed out.

• • •

Wade awoke to the sound of Quicksilver's heavy footsteps thundering across the frozen lake. He could feel the air getting *even* colder, and heavy snow fall had started to come down upon them. Thankfully, the chain that wrapped around his midsection did its job to keep him from falling off the horse after he had passed out.

Wade glanced over his shoulder, half-expecting to see a wave of Demons charging them, but there was nothing. He sighed in relief, and Sarah noticed his movement.

"Wade, are you awake back there?" she asked. "You *need* to see this."

Wade lifted his heavy head from her back and glanced forward. At first, he didn't know how to describe what he saw. While he was asleep, they had nearly crossed the entirety of the frozen lake and were now facing an expansive mountain range. And above the towering mountains was the flickering speck of Darkness that Wade had seen before, but now that they were closer to it, it was no longer a speck, and its true form was horrifying. It looked as if a giant had punched a hole through the heavens, leaving nothing but a gaping black void in its place. The gray sky that sat above them was torn in *half,* and with each passing second, more Demons poured out of it like a waterfall of smoke.

"What the hell happened here, Wade?" Sarah asked horrified, covering her mouth.

Wade was speechless; the scene in front of him was worse than he could've *ever* imagined. He reached forward and pulled back on the reins, bringing Quicksilver to an immediate halt on the frozen lake. Wade unhooked the chain from his midsection and slid off the back of the horse, staring in silence at the tear in the sky.

When he had first begun this journey, he didn't know what he would find at the source of the Consumption, but now, standing here, seeing the Rift endlessly dump Demons into his world–into Rhodahn–caused an overwhelming feeling of guilt and hopelessness to flood his mind.

He glanced at Sarah, whose neck was craned up, looking at the Rift with a mixture of awe and horror, trying to comprehend what she was seeing, but she would never be able to, as no one could–not even Wade.

What have I done…

Wade knew he shouldn't have brought her on this quest. He was stupid–naive, and he had made a grave mistake, and Nor would surely punish him for it. He couldn't imagine the horrors that lay ahead, but now there was no way for her to go back–nowhere to return to; nowhere to escape to.

He should've left her in the town he found her in.

"I'm sorry," he finally said as he hung his head.

"Wade–"

"I shouldn't have brought you–"

"Just…" she interrupted, *"don't.* Look around, this is my life now–this has *been* my life since we left that town. There was no other option, and there's no going back now, and even if I could, I wouldn't leave you. I lost everything already, Wade. This journey–helping you in your quest–it's all I've got. If there's any chance we can fix what happened to this world and bring the light back, then I'll take it. And the only way we're going to do that is by continuing on and finding a way to close whatever the hell *that* is. I'd rather be here than dead in the dirt with my parents." She looked deep into Wade's eyes. "I'm a Gunner now, Wade, remember? This is what we do."

"Yes, yes you are," he finally responded. Then, he saw something: a faint, flickering glimmer of light that caught Wade's attention, drawing his gaze to the tallest mountain peak, which just so happened to be sitting directly under the Rift. "I don't know what lies on the path ahead, but *that–,*" he pointed toward the glimmer of light, "that is where we need to go, and I need you by my side to get there."

"Then there's no more time to waste. Let's finish this quest, Wade."

Sarah scooted back in the saddle, and Wade mounted Quicksilver and sat in front of her once again. They rode on toward the glimmer of light in the distance, calling out to them like a beacon of *hope.*

• • •

After finally getting off the frozen lake without incident, they started on a winding trail that took them between the mountains. The beautiful, vibrant, and alive world that he had once known was now devoid of life and gray. The bark on the dead trees had peeled away and fallen to the ground in piles. Decomposed, frozen human bodies and skeletons gripping revolvers flanked the trail, and not a *single* ounce of wildlife was seen the entire time they rode. No birds sang their tune, no wolves cried out, and no rodents scurried in front of their path. Life was gone here, and death had taken its place.

Wade also noticed that it was quiet–eerily quiet–and that

the death around them wasn't just visible, it was *palpable*, lingering in the air like a thick fog, sitting heavy on their shoulders, as if telling them that they were next. And as they traveled further down the trail, Wade's mind began wandering to its most depraved pits, as if the Darkness was growing within himself, urging him to betray Sarah. His hand itched to unholster Thorn and aim it at the small girl's spine. He would pull the trigger, and then once she was dead, he'd place the cold steel on his own temple and...

"Do you see that?" Sarah asked, pointing in the distance.

Wade shook himself out of his dark thoughts and looked forward. A small, decrepit shack sat next to the trail, half-buried in snow and fallen trees.

"If it's safe, we shall stay there for the night. I *need* to rest my mind," Wade sheepishly admitted.

As they approached the shack, he slowed Quicksilver to a halt.

"Be prepared for anything."

Wade signaled for Sarah to grab the reins, and she scooped them up. He pulled out Rose and Thorn and crept toward the weathered shack before kicking the door open and peaking inside. The floor was dirt, and the shack held nothing–no Demons, no rations, no beds. He just looked into an empty room with rusted sheets of tin for walls.

"It's clear," he said as he exited the shack and hitched Quicksilver to a dead tree outside.

Sarah slid off the horse and watched as Wade unhooked the saddlebags and handed her one. She hurried into the shack with it, and Wade began to lay out the candles and Demon blood around the perimeter of their refuge, but truthfully, he didn't know if these precautions would even protect them. They seemed to be on their own this deep into the Veil.

And by the time Wade finally entered the shack, Sarah had already unfurled the sleeping pads and laid them out across the dirt floor. He went to shut the door, but as it closed, he caught a glimpse of a dark figure in a black, hooded robe, standing on the edge of a cliff in front of the quickly setting sun, *watching* them. He swung the door open wider to get a better look, but the figure was gone. He scanned the horizon once more but saw nothing.

The Darkness is playing tricks on ya', kid. Just go to bed, Ulysses urged in his mind.

Wade slammed the door shut and retreated deeper into the shack.

"You sleep," he said with a nod. "I don't know what's lurking out there, so it would be best for us to take turns keeping watch for the night. I've got the first shift."

Sarah didn't argue; the day had been tiring enough, and he could see the dark, heavy bags that had appeared under her eyes. She gently laid down next to him on her sleeping pad, placed in her earplugs, and within two seconds, she immediately fell asleep.

For the rest of the night, Wade sat upright with Rose and Thorn across his lap, facing the thin tin door. He heard the flapping of winged Demons overhead and their screeches that echoed across the mountain range. Luckily, nothing seemed to notice that they were hiding beneath them.

As he stared at the rusted door, his mind began to wander again, mulling over the journey so far. He originally started this quest in search of answers, but everything they had found so far only led to more questions. Wade didn't want to admit it, and of course he would *never* tell Sarah this, but, truthfully, he was terrified of what lay ahead. The way that girl looked at him—as if he always had the answers and knew what to do—made him feel like a fraud. When Wade stood under that rift, as frozen as the lake they walked on, watching the Demons enter their world through a gaping hole in the sky, he felt something—something *terrifying*.

For the first time since Rose and Thorn had been bestowed upon him, Wade felt powerless.

PART THREE
THE
MOUNTAINS

DG

CHAPTER SIXTEEN

THE ORDER OF SHAR

Jutting out from the stone wall of a resplendent castle sat a grand balcony that hung over a sheer drop. Thick vines of ivy wrapped around the iron railings and snaked their way up the weathered ashlar. The balcony provided an incredible vantage point where Wade could gaze upon his kingdom and ponder.

The bright, beautiful sun sat high in the sky and graced his skin with its warmth, and Wade watched as an eagle took off from its nest and dove in front of him. The view from above Arcenia was spectacular, and down below, villagers bustled along cobblestone streets, slipping in and out of stone buildings with steep, pointed roofs built to shed snow in the cold winter months.

On the outskirts of the small city lay an imposing wall, and beyond it stretched rolling hills, emerald lakes, and green pastures where grazing cattle roamed. Ranchers on horseback wrangled them with long lassos, while Gunners honed their aim at shooting ranges nearby.

In the Innerlands, life at Fort Dennon and Arcenia was peaceful—how Wade wished it could *always* be. Just as the gun on his hip protected his beautiful kingdom of Gadriel, it also seemed to insinuate the same violence he tried so hard to avoid. Luckily, the fighting, the bloodshed, and the death was localized on the borders of the kingdom, painting only the Farlands in blood. But many of Arcenia's inhabitants did not know this–the true cost of the peace that they experienced, allowing them to live in blissful ignorance.

Behind Wade, the door to the balcony creaked open, pulling him from his thoughts.

"They're ready for you, King Master Wade," an older Gunner said before removing his wide-brimmed hat and saluting.

"I'll be right in," Wade responded, hoping to stay out there for just a little while longer.

Fifteen years had passed since Bestowment Day–the day he had been given the keys to this kingdom, and the day his life changed forever. And all of a sudden, things started to move very quickly. Unlike the others he had graduated with, Wade was not just a Gunner–no, now he was king. And as the leader of the Order and Gadriel, he was immediately granted a host of privileges: he slept in Shar's former quarters at the top of the castle–a lavish space with a large, plush bed draped in silk sheets; he bathed in a private bath house where he and Jess spent a *healthy* amount of time in; he had access to the finest food and mead he could ever desire; he commanded the Army of the Gunners; and, of course, he wielded all the power that came with the throne. If he woke up one morning and decided to orchestrate a full blown attack on the Kutarian Knights, he *could*, and virtually no one could stop him.

But the worst part was, they gave all of this power to an eighteen year old boy for being able to pull magical triggers. Wade always thought it was as nonsensical as it sounded, which is why he never did such things with his power. And for those fifteen years, he attempted to stay out of wars and instead focused on the people of Gadriel. But of course, there were always those who could not accept peace, and for fifteen years, Wade dealt with the pointless politics that power always seemed to attract.

Wade hated the long and drawn out ass-kissing conversations with the heads of the Order, begging him to bring Gadriel into another senseless war. He would travel across the kingdom to appease warmongers in the Far and Midlands, taking valuable time away from the needs of the farmers, the ranchers, the workers, and the youth of Arcenia who required his attention the most. But, above all else, he loathed the weight of responsibility that he now carried upon his shoulders each and every day.

Even though he had grown accustomed to his new life as king—at least the best he could—Wade still wished he could be that young, naive kid again, training and getting drunk with his friends at school without all this bullshit to worry about. Deep down, Nor knew he still felt like that same kid in his heart, even *if* everything else had changed since then—even if that life he had once known was gone and was never coming back.

• • •

Wade entered the Hall of the Gun—a large room with a vaulted ceiling, rows of mahogany pews, and a gold and silver mosaic of Rose and Thorn embedded in the floor. He walked past dozens of Master Gunners and Gunners, many of whom stared at him with disgust while whispering amongst themselves. Wade ignored them, as he always did, and continued to make his way toward the front of the room.

His throne, made of many rifles and revolvers pieced together and shaped into a chair, sat on an elevated platform at the front of the Hall facing the pews. Two sets of iron stairs flanked it on either side. Wade climbed the steps and took his seat on the throne, noticing for the first time how many people had now gathered in the Hall in front of him.

Lucky me.

"The Order of the Gun recognizes the official commencement of this emergency meeting. Master Gunner Kaldran shall be the first to speak," a Gunner, standing next to a scribe, called out loudly, his voice echoing across the Hall.

All of the Gunners in attendance placed their right hand over their heart, pulled an imaginary trigger in unison, and raised finger guns into the air.

Master Gunner Kaldran, an older man with a scarred face and a long gray beard, stood up from the crowd and bowed to Wade, before he cleared his throat and said, "King Master Wade, I humbly come to you for your approval on expanding our kingdom by moving our Gunners further south into Kutarian territory. The Knights have grown incredibly hostile in recent months, and we suspect they are gearing up for an invasion. We currently outnumber their soldiers three to one. If we do not strike now, they may make the first move on Gadriel once their ranks are rebuilt."

"Tell me, have they *made* any advancements on our land yet?" Wade asked.

"Well... *no*, but our scouts indicate that—"

"Then you know what my answer is."

"But sir–"

"I do not accept the move of aggression, Master Kaldran. Tell your men to stay put and hold our lines for the time bein'."

"But sir, we have suspicions that they are raising dragons!"

"That is a *final* order, Master Kaldran."

"Yes sir," he muttered, before he gritted his teeth and stormed down the center of the pews, exiting the Hall.

"Next, the Order recognizes Master Gunner Thomas to speak," the Gunner next to the scribe said.

A well built man with stubble stepped forward. His eyes were dark, and he stared at Wade with a look that could pierce through a soul.

"King Master Wade, our Gunners are growin' restless. It's been almost a year since they have seen combat. They are beginning to wonder what their purpose is–what they were trained for!"

"Aren't we all…" Wade said under his breath. "Maybe it's time for our Gunners to take up other disciplines, such as ones that don't revolve around killing their fellow Rhodahnian men? Have you tried to introduce the arts to 'em–music, writing, or even pottery?"

"*Pottery?*" Master Gunner Thomas scoffed, causing many of the Gunners in the Hall to chuckle. "With all due respect, sir, these are soldiers, *not* artists making bowls and cups."

"And? What's the difference?"

"They would never want to–"

"Let me ask you something, Master Thomas, have these men ever been taught anything besides the way of the gun? Have they ever been asked to create anything? To dream or stretch their imaginations? Or, have they been conditioned since they were children to give all of that up so that they can march headfirst into war and die a needless death!"

The Gunners in the Hall gasped.

"That's… That's blasphemous." Whispering in the Hall began to pick up. "This Order has stood by its founding principles for three hundred years! The way of the gun is what we know—what we built and protected the kingdom of Gadriel upon!"

"Well, maybe our kingdom was built on *false* principles."

The Hall broke out into complete and utter chaos. Gunners stood up from the pews, shouting and yelling, and in that moment, Wade expected a bullet to fly straight through his skull. Perhaps, he even wanted one to.

"FALSE KING!" a Gunner shouted.

"BANISH HIM TO THE DESERT!"

"Order! Order!" The Gunner next to the king yelled.

Wade stood up from his throne and said, "Has anyone come here with something *not* about war?"

The Gunners looked at each other, and no one said a word.

"We have villagers starvin' in the Innerlands—sleeping on our streets and numbing themselves with the devil's grass just to survive! Until you come to me with solutions to help our own people first, I won't approve of *any* of your requests to go kill others!" The Gunners stared at Wade with wide eyes and mouths hung open. "This meeting is adjourned!"

Wade stood up from his throne and made his way back through the crowd as the men and women on either side of him yelled and screamed at him.

"He is not the Shar'La! There has been a mistake!"
"The guns lied!"
"Shar failed us!"
"He should be shot!"
And with that, Wade left the Hall.

• • •

Later that afternoon, Wade lay outstretched in a bed of yellow sunflowers, staring up at the beautiful, blue sky above him. He brought his hands over the soft petals and felt their smooth texture as they blew in the wind and tickled his fingertips. Then, he heard a crunching sound approaching behind him.

"If you're here to kill me, all I ask is that you do not shoot me while I lay here. Let me die somewhere less peaceful than this. I would rather not taint these innocent flowers with my tarnished blood," Wade said.

"If I was here to kill you, you wouldn't have heard me."

Wade chuckled and shook his head as a warm body lay down beside him and wrapped around him.

"I heard about what happened in the Hall today," Jess said, settling her head on his chest before he planted a kiss on her forehead.

"Who hasn't," Wade said, his fingers tracing gently across her skin. "They made a mistake, and you know it. I'm no king. Hell, I ain't even a leader."

"Shar knew something we didn't. There was no mistake, Wade, we just can't see his reasoning for choosing you yet."

"But I don't believe in anything that he stood for. These guns that I carry, they've never gotten lighter since the day they were given to me. I thought I would get stronger–I thought this would get easier, but the burden still remains. I should just dismantle 'em and toss the pieces in the lake."

"And what would that accomplish? Someone else would just rebuild them and take the throne."

"Now wouldn't that be wonderful."

"And would they change the Order for the better?"

"Who's to say my ways are better? To them, I'm the Devil."

"Just because someone grows in a different direction than we hoped, doesn't mean they're not growing at all. You're being the king you need to be, Wade, and change is always hard. Don't let their hate and anger distract you."

"I just… I wish things could go back to the way they were. I was just another cog in the wheel–a mindless grunt standing side by side with my friends. We were so happy then."

"Were you really happy? And is that what you want? You took the guns, remember? Because you truly believed you could change things for the better, otherwise you would've left them in Shar's chest. Where has *that* man gone?"

Wade plucked a petal and tossed it in the air, letting the wind carry it away.

"He died a long time ago. I guess reality has a funny way of making us accept the facts we try our hardest to ignore."

"And what are you ignoring?"

"Look around, the Order is crumbling, aggression is rising in the south with the Kutarians, and my *own* Gunners wish to see me off the throne and executed by firing squad. For fifteen years I have tried to make a difference for Gadriel, only to fail. So tell me, what's the point of any of this?"

"Not all of the Gunners wish that for you, Wade. Perhaps they can't openly speak their truth, but they still believe in you. They haven't lost hope, even if *you* have. Things are changing, slowly but surely, and it'll continue to take time. Our kingdom and our way of life will one day thrive. Your work has the Innerland children of Gadriel aspiring to become more than soldiers—more than the Order thinks they're capable of. Perhaps our Gadriel is in a better place after all."

Wade looked down; their eyes locked, and they began to passionately kiss. As they made love in the bed of flowers, the sun fell and set on their peaceful kingdom—a kingdom without war.

• • •

That night, Wade tossed and turned in bed, haunted by the events that had transpired in the Hall. He saw the angry faces; he heard their yells—remembering every word they said.

He pictured himself being dragged from the castle, stripped of his garments, and taken to Arcenia where they would hang him in front of the people of Gadriel. Jess would scream and cry, begging for them to stop, only to watch the lever be pulled and the rope grow tight. Their leader, their king—their Shar'La, used as an example for what happens to Gadrielians who aspire to be more than killers.

His final resting place would be in Arcenia's city square, dangling and swaying in the wind, waiting to be plucked at and eaten by crows.

The horrific thoughts all became too much for him, and he quickly shot up from bed and put his face in his hands.

What the hell am I doing?

Jess stirred next to him but thankfully didn't wake. He gently lifted his side of the covers up and slipped out of bed before stepping out onto his private balcony.

The white drapes that covered the open doors flapped in the wind behind him, and he stood with his hands on the cold, worn iron railing, trying to get control of his emotions once again. There was a gentle and warm breeze on his skin, and he tried to focus solely on it, attempting to center his mind and his soul.

Then, the door to the king's chamber creaked open behind him. Wade rolled to the side and hid behind the stone wall, barely looking past it to see the intruders who had entered his room. Four men wearing bandanas and thick leather jackets–all armed with unidentifiable revolvers–approached the bed with their weapons raised. They hadn't noticed yet that Wade wasn't in bed, but he couldn't get the jump on them as his iron sat a few feet away, resting on his nightstand.

But a truly defenseless Gunner is not a Gunner at all. Isn't that right, Wade?

Wade reached down to his calf and slipped a small knife from the leather sheath strapped there.

"Where is he!" one of them shouted, jolting Jess awake, but she didn't scream. She just stayed focused on the approaching intruders.

Then, she glanced to the side and caught a brief glimpse of Wade on the balcony but made sure not to alert them of his location by quickly looking away.

"He's not here tonight," she finally said. "A meeting in

the Farlands. He left after dinner–"

He struck her hard across the face.

"You're lying, you whore! You two, check the balcony," the intruder said, signaling to his goons.

As they approached, Wade quietly slid up the side of the wall with his back pressed against, holding his knife to his chest. Just as the intruders walked out onto the balcony, Wade lurched forward and sliced across both of their necks in one swift move. They dropped their guns and clutched their wounds to stop the bleeding, but it continued to spill through their fingers until they collapsed forward onto the stone. Wade quickly swept up their iron and hid behind the wall once more.

BANG! BANG!

Wade's heart dropped, and he leaned out from the wall and took aim, expecting to see a horrifying sight, but the two other intruders were already laying dead on the floor. He looked to his right and saw Jess, still under the covers, holding her smoking revolver.

Wade ran to her and said, "Are you alright?"

"Yes, I'm alright," she said, holding her bruised face where the would-be assassin had struck her. "They can't say the same though."

Wade slid down next to the bodies and ripped off the bandanas, revealing Master Gunners Thomas and Kaldran.

• • •

"You can do this," Jess said, holding Wade's face while looking deep into his eyes. "Speaking to them now is a sign of strength. Show them that you're not afraid and why they should respect you."

A week had passed since the assassination attempt, and Wade and Jess were now sitting in a waiting room to the right of the Hall. Wade's leg shook uncontrollably, but he knew he had to do this. This would be the first time he had spoken to the Order since the attempt on his life, and there was now no other choice.

Double doors separated them from the rest of the Gunners, with his armed Royal Guard posted outside to ensure no one could enter. But in just a few moments, Wade would have to face those traitors again.

Any other king would probably advise Wade *against* putting himself in front of the same dignitaries who had attempted to assassinate him, but Wade knew he had to face this head on. There was nowhere to hide. If they wanted him dead, they would surely find a way to kill him, and Wade was not going to spend the rest of his life running or hiding. It's not what Shar would've done, and it certainly wasn't what the Shar'La would do either.

"I'm ready," Wade finally said with a nod to Jess.

She squeezed his hand, and they both stood up at once. The double doors swung open, revealing a packed hall filled with Master Gunners and Gunners from across Gadriel who had traveled to Fort Dennon after hearing the news of the assasination attempt. Within the crowd were *many* unfamiliar faces, but sitting in the front row was his old master Ulysses, along with his friends, Colt, John, Westin, and Elenor. After seeing them, a surge of confidence rushed through him.

Wade climbed the steps to the throne and stood before it. He glanced one last time at Jess who smiled and mouthed, *You can do this,* then, he took a deep breath and began his speech.

"Last week, while my wife and I slept in our chamber, an attempt on my life was made. I now stand here before you all, knowing that any one of you could strike me down and take the throne, but I'm not afraid. If that's how you wish to save yourselves, then I will not try to stop you. I gathered you all here to tell you that I am *not* the Shar'La, nor am I a king. I stand before you just as a Gunner–the same as my fellow man.

"We were taught from an early age that the way of the gun was the *only* way to live–strength through power, strength through iron, but I'm here to say that we *can* be better. These weapons, they are tools and nothing more." Wade raised Thorn into the air. "They protect us, our kingdom, and our families, but they do not define us. We are more than the iron we carry on our waists. The Gunners of the Order can be more than our name suggests.

"After the attempt on my life, I went back and studied our history, and I believe Shar would be disappointed to see what this bloodthirsty Order has become. That is why, from this day forward, the School and the Order of the Gun shall be officially disbanded." Gasps rose from the crowd. "We will build anew, in the original image that Shar had for the kingdom of Gadriel. And if our enemies ever threaten that which we have built, then I shall be there, side by side with you all, fighting for what is ours. From this day forward, we will now be known as the Order of Shar!" Wade yelled, thrusting a fist into the air.

The crowd looked at each other before Westin stood up and yelled, "For the Order of Shar!"

The rest of the Gunners erupted in cheers, and Wade looked at Jess who flashed a smile. He was finally freed from the iron that weighed him down everyday since it was first bestowed upon him, and while he stood there, he vowed to himself that he would only kill to protect the ones and the kingdom he loved. But, as what happens with all pure things, his dream for a better life for Gadrielians would one day be corrupted–taken from him, and the man who stood in front of that throne was painfully unaware of the war that was brewing in Rhodahn.

CHAPTER SEVENTEEN

THE FLIGHT OF THE DEMONS

The memories faded, and Wade found himself staring at the tin door of the shack once again. He unholstered Thorn and admired the beautiful iron. If only he knew then what he knew now, he would've never stood there and given that idiotic, self-righteous speech. Perhaps he would've even let his assassins kill him.

One life for many.

Sarah rustled next to Wade, but she didn't wake from her slumber. A peaceful look always rested upon her face, as if her dreams provided a lone sanctuary from this Norforsaken world.

Before she fell asleep, they had agreed that Wade would take the first watch but there would be no second. He doubted he'd be able to find sleep anyway. Thinking back to his days at Fort Dennon and the decision he made there kept him restless. It had been a long time since that place, those people–the land he admired while standing on that balcony–occupied his mind.

All of it was gone with the light–relics of a time before the Darkness took over their world.

Then, Wade noticed that faint sunlight had begun to seep through the gaps in the tin sheets that formed the walls of their refuge. Luckily, nothing had bothered them in the night, but he had heard countless footsteps passing by outside their shack.

Next to him, the girl began to wake.

"Is it morning already?" Sarah asked while stretching her arms over her head with a yawn.

Wade leaned forward and cracked the door slightly, noticing the faint silhouette of the sun beginning to rise through the Veil.

"Yes."

"Why didn't you wake me in the night? I was supposed to take the second watch?"

"No need, I'd rather you be sharp for the journey that lies ahead."

Wade opened the door fully now, glanced both ways, and saw no sign of Demons. He stepped outside, the bundled sleeping pads tucked under his arms, and began the onerous task of packing the candles into Quicksilver's saddlebags. Behind him, Sarah finally came out of the shack with a piece of jerky hanging from her mouth.

"Want some?" she asked through a mouthful, fumbling in her pocket before holding out a piece to Wade.

"I'm fine."

"You didn't sleep, you should at least eat."

Wade hesitated, unwilling to take any of her rations in case something were to happen to him, but he didn't think Sarah would take no for an answer. He swept it up and tossed the salty nugget into his mouth.

"Thank you."

"Don't mention it."

Sarah then threw her fur jacket on, settled her hat atop her head, and checked the cylinder of her revolver before snapping it back with a flick of her wrist like a true Gunner.

"Good to go," she finally said.

The singletrack trail they'd been following wound past the shack, twisting through the narrow slot between the mountains. Towering walls of rock rose on either side, making the Demon Gunner feel vulnerable and claustrophobic, like an animal walking into its own trap.

Wade did one last quick scan of their surroundings before saying, "Let's move."

Mounted on Quicksilver, they began down the winding trail. Wade couldn't decide whether to ride fast or slow, as he didn't know if there were more Demons drawn to noise lurking in the rock crevices that surrounded them, so, he kept the horse at a steady trot.

His heart raced, and the leather reins within his hands became damp with sweat. He felt as if they were sitting ducks, waiting to be torn apart, and he *hated* it. There were too many vantage points around them, and virtually no escape if they needed to make a quick getaway. If they were flanked from the front and rear, they were done for. No amount of shooting would free them if a horde of Demons descended upon them.

He also couldn't help but feel as if they were being *watched*. Every time he looked up at the steep cliffs towering above, he thought he caught a glimpse of green eyes peering over the precipices, only to vanish behind the rock.

"Wade?" Sarah asked quietly from behind him.

"Yes?"

"Can you tell me a story?"

A story? he thought to himself.

He couldn't remember the last time someone had asked him such a question. Wade wanted to remain silent, but he knew they'd be dead already if more Demons, like the one in the forest, lurked within this canyon; Quicksilver's hooves were too loud to conceal. So, he thought he owed it to the girl to tell her one.

"I will need to keep my voice down, but what kind of story are ya' looking for?" he finally responded.

"Well," Sarah said, thinking about it for a moment, "anything, really. Just to help pass the time while we ride, kinda like a distraction."

"A distraction…"

He racked his brain and found he had many stories to tell, but most were not suitable to share with her.

"I want to know more about Rose & Thorn," she added.

"My iron?"

"Yes, could you tell me about them? Perhaps where they came from?"

The birth of Rose & Thorn *was* a good story, he had to admit.

Why not?

"Rose & Thorn are special," Wade finally whispered. "In fact, they didn't even come from this planet."

"Really?"

"Indeed. They were born from the stars. It's said that the original wielder, Shar Vahn–the founder of the Order and the kingdom of Gadriel–saw a comet racing across the night sky from the balcony of his castle at Fort Dennon. It crash landed in a field a few miles away, and he immediately gathered his fellow Gunners and rode off to track it down. When they finally arrived at the impact crater, they found a glowing, silver rock embedded in the dirt. It hummed as if it were *singing* to them, and they listened to its tune for hours. The sun had begun to rise by the time they realized they were in a trance, enamored by the artifact's beauty. When they finally got their wits about 'em, they loaded the object into an open carriage and brought it back to the castle. Shar called upon the greatest gunsmith in Gadriel—an old man named Artorius—to melt the object down and reform it into a weapon of his choosin'.

"For weeks, Artorius fully committed himself to the endeavor, spending all day and night meticulously crafting and engraving the guns with pure gold. The process was so strenuous, that when Artorius finally finished it and caught his first glimpse of the iron, his heart failed. His apprentice told Shar that his dying words were, *'As I stare upon my creation, I see now that the beauty of the rose can be as sharp as the thorn.'* Shar then named the guns Rose & Thorn in his honor."

"That's an incredible story," Sarah said, enthralled. "Do you think I could shoot 'em one day?"

Wade chuckled and said, "You wouldn't be able to pull the triggers."

"Why not?"

"Have you ever heard of the story of Excalibur?"

"Maybe, but I can't remember it now. The name does sound familiar though."

"Well, the Kutarian Knights once said that there was a sword named Excalibur that could only be pulled from the rock it sat in by the *chosen one.*"

"But what does that have to do with your guns?"

"Well, Rose & Thorn function much like that legendary blade. The triggers can only be pulled by the Shar'La–which means 'the spirit of Shar'."

"How is that possible?"

"Just like my ammo pouch, the iron is imbued with magic."

"Who imbued it?"

"A wizard–one that no Gunner within the Order ever knew."

"A wizard? What's that?"

"Someone who wields Conviction."

"And that wizard made it so only *you* would be able to pull the triggers?"

"They made it so only the *Shar'La* could."

"Which is what you are, right? So that wizard technically made it for you."

Wade smiled, staring forward at the trail.

"Rose & Thorn are nearly indestructible and are said to be capable of killing gods. Each year, every cadet at the School was instructed to pull the triggers and attempt to fire the weapons. One by one, they all failed, and, eventually, they gave up and buried the guns with Shar again."

"Until you came along."

"*Until I came along.* Unknown to me, the Council of Masters had been watching my every move–studying me. Together, they came to the conclusion that I was the Shar'La and would be capable of pulling the triggers, but they never told me. There were even *some* Masters who disputed their claims." A shudder overtook Wade's body, thinking back to his final test. "But on Bestowment Day, I was presented with Rose & Thorn in front of all the other cadets. They instructed me to pull the triggers, and when I did, the cylinder spun. My school went into a frenzy, saying that I was the Shar'La and the prophecy would be fulfilled, except, I didn't *feel* any different. Things moved so quickly after that day, and all the things they tried forcing on me were wrong. I was the leader of an engine of war, but that was the last thing I wanted. All I could think about was that they made a mistake. I knew in my heart that I *wasn't* the Shar'La."

"Well, why not?"

"Because… Because I wasn't who they needed. I was a fuck-up–a troublemaker, and I hated the School and everything the Order stood for. I never even wanted to use Rose & Thorn to kill anyone unless I had to. I wasn't a king… I was barely even a Gunner."

"Then why do you still carry the weapons?"

"I don't know, *hope* maybe?"

"Hope for what?"

"That the Rock wasn't wrong."

"The Rock?"

"Yes, the Rock. It stood outside the entrance of the School in the Midlands. We walked past it everyday, and it held the prophecy of the wizard who imbued the guns."

"And what did it say?"

"*When he is ready, a Gunner shall rise.*
His aim steady, his soul wise.
Rose & Thorn seek their master.
Foes shall mourn, he shoots them faster.
As the sun fades, fire he shall harness.
Bring him the guns, deliver us from darkness."

Wade stared down the trail, reciting the words over and over again in his mind. "But it doesn't matter, it's all bullshit anyway."

"How could it be bullshit!" Sarah said loudly.

Wade shot her a frightened look over his shoulder and said, "Keep your voice down!"

"Sorry…" she responded meekly. "But–the prophecy–it's literally about *you*. Everything it talked about, it's happening right now, isn't it? It even mentions the Dark–"

"I've done nothing to stop it, Sarah."

"Well you saved me, and who's to say you won't save the world too?"

"Look around you, there's no bringing the light back."

"Then why are you still going? Why are we even on this journey if you really believe that?"

Wade gripped the reins tighter and sternly said, "You asked for a story, and that's it. These are questions I've been trying to answer since I set off on this quest. I don't think we're going to figure them out now."

"But–"

WHOOSH!

Wade's head snapped up at the sound, he couldn't see anything through the fog that surrounded them.

WHOOSH!

Again, the sound came from above; Wade drew Thorn from its holster.

WHOOSH! WHOOSH! WHOOSH!

The sound of powerful, flapping wings began to grow. Then, through the fog, Wade spotted the source of the noise. A pack of flying Demons descended toward them. They had twisted grins on their faces, glowing green eyes, red skin, and long, thin legs with razor sharp claws at the end of them. They flew straight down toward Wade and Sarah, claws outstretched as if ready to scoop up their prey.

"GET DOWN!" Wade yelled.

Sarah slid off the side of Quicksilver and ducked below the horse's torso. Shots exploded from Thorn, lighting them up with Hellfire, and the Demons at the front of the pack dropped like flies, splattering hard onto the trail and exploding like geysers of green blood from the ground. But more came down upon them, and one managed to knock Wade from the horse's back. He fell hard into the snow and stared up at the fog above them, attempting to catch his breath. Then, Sarah screamed next to him, and he quickly sat up to see a Demon clawing at the girl. She attempted to withdraw her revolver, but its talons tightened on the sleeve of her jacket and pulled her up into the air.

"WADE!" she cried out as she was carried higher and higher into the sky.

The Demon Gunner raised Thorn to shoot the monster, but a searing, sharp pain coursed through his back. He yelled in agony, realizing a flying Demon had gripped him with its claws.

WHOOSH!

The Demon then flapped its wings, and with a powerful gust of wind, they were airborne, leaving Quicksilver far below them. They rose higher and higher before they exited the fog and crashed through freezing clouds. Soon, they were hundreds of feet in the air, and wind and rain blasted Wade's face, causing his vision to blur.

And all at once, his stomach dropped. The Demon went into a nosedive, sailing back toward the ground. They broke through the clouds once more, and far below, Wade saw an enormous pit with hundreds of winged offspring, staring up, mouths open, ready to feast. Sarah was just a few yards in front of him—her arms pinned by the claws of the Demon, unable to draw her weapon.

But Wade's arms were *not* pinned. The claws were lodged in his back, leaving his hands free. He grabbed the chain of Thorn that dangled below and whipped it upward. The gun landed in his palm, and he thrust it above him, driving Thorn's blade into the Demon's soft, transparent wing. Then he fired, blowing a hole straight through it. The Demon screeched in pain and began to descend toward Sarah.

He had one chance—*one* move to save her.

Just as he was above the girl, he brought Thorn to the chin of the Demon and blew its head off. Its grip instantly loosened, freeing Wade and sending him into a freefall toward Sarah. He landed hard on the Demon's back and managed to grab hold of its wrinkled skin, nearly avoiding falling to his death.

He quickly steadied himself on its back before drawing Rose and shooting through both wings at the same time. The Demon screeched and began to rapidly lose altitude, sending them closer to the hungry offspring.

Wade then thrust Rose and Thorn's blades into the creature's back. It screeched again, and blood trickled from its wounds as Wade dug the right blade in deeper, steering the Demon toward the edge of the pit. They barely cleared it, and when they were close enough to the ground, Wade pulled the guns from the Demon's back, aimed at its head, and blew it clean off. Sarah dropped from its grip, and Wade jumped, crashing and tumbling across the snow covered ground. They both came to a halt a few feet away from each other, coughing and groaning in pain as the dead Demon crashed down next to them.

"Are you alright?" Wade asked, holding his shoulder in pain.

Sarah coughed hard, covered in snow. Her right pants leg was hiked up, revealing torn, bleeding skin, and on her left arm, a thin trickle of blood ran from the punctures in her jacket sleeve.

"I don't think we're even anymore, but I'm alright," she finally said. *"Thank you."*

Wade breathed a sigh of relief and looked at the barren and jagged landscape that surrounded them. Quicksilver was nowhere to be found, and they were now very high up, almost near the peak of one of the mountains that had flanked their trail. The only way back down looked incredibly steep and treacherous—nearly impossible to descend.

Fuck.

Wade remained seated for a moment, his elbows resting on his knees, attempting to catch his breath and collect his thoughts. He could now see that they were closer to the Rift, but there was no way Quicksilver could get to them, even if they called for her. They would have to once more travel on foot.

"Do you still have your guns?" Wade asked.

Sarah patted her rabbit skin holster and the sling that ran across her torso and said, "Still got 'em."

"Good, because I have a feeling we're going to need 'em."

• • •

Wade and Sarah carefully traveled across the rocky mountain ridge, watching their steps as they went. They followed a small path, perhaps cut out long ago by a herd of goats, but it looked as if it hadn't been traveled in years. Sarah's foot slipped, sending rocks tumbling down the steep slope and off a nearby cliff. Wade reached out and grabbed the back of her jacket, keeping her from further losing her balance.

The trail continued winding down the mountain, eventually leading to a skinny ledge with a hundred-foot drop below. They would have to traverse it sideways— certain death awaited them if they slipped.

"Just take it slow," Wade advised. "One step at a time."

He went first, placing his arms flat against the rock face and shimmying across it *very* slowly. He could feel the soles of his worn boots losing grip, sending small pieces of rock and dust falling off the edge to the drop below. He took a deep breath and attempted to stay calm, continuing across it and eventually making it to the other side.

"Alright, Sarah, your turn."

"I can do this," she whispered to herself while peering over the cliff.

"Don't look!" he shouted. "Just keep your eyes on the wall and the path ahead."

She gulped and made her way onto the narrow ledge. Her feet began to slide across it.

"That's it… easy does it."

Then, something behind them began to stir. Crawling down the trail on all fours was a Bone Eater. It snapped its teeth, black drool hanging from its mouth.

"A bit faster now, Sarah," Wade said, raising his gun in front of him.

The Demon inched closer, and Wade blasted it with Hellfire. The sound of the shot startled Sarah, causing her to flinch and nearly fall off the edge.

"Come on, you're almost there."

More Bone Eaters climbed over the rocks and inched toward them.

"Faster, Sarah, faster!" Wade yelled. Shots flew, and bodies dropped. "Come on!"

Sarah was nearly at the end of the ledge. She turned to face him as a Bone Eater lunged toward her.

"JUMP!" he yelled.

Sarah launched forward, and Wade extended a hand to grab her. Her own hand smacked his forearm, and her fingers slid down it before their palms interlinked and tightened around each other. He yanked upward, pulling her onto solid ground.

"Run."

They sprinted down the weathered trail as the Bone Eaters jumped over the gap and landed a few feet behind them. Sarah drew her revolver and fired at them with Wade, blasting them apart. More and more Bone Eaters were approaching, and Wade could hear their jaws snapping together. They ran as quickly as they could, slipping and sliding down the trail. One lunged forward, and Wade blew its head off before it could grab the girl. He swung open Thorn's empty cylinder and reloaded more rounds of Hellfire, before firing into the herd once more. Wade whistled as loud as he could—over and over again—one last desperate cry for help.

Then, the floor beneath them shook and broke open, and they plummeted into *darkness*.

DG

CHAPTER EIGHTEEN

THE CAVE DWELLERS

Sarah and Wade plunged through a dark tunnel, tumbling and flipping over each other until they were spat out the bottom of it. The cavernous room they now found themselves in was pitch black.

"Sarah?" Wade said, blinking rapidly, attempting to make out *anything* in the darkness.

"I'm right here," she responded, her voice echoing off the walls.

"Don't move, just stay right where you are."

Within Wade's hand, a small flame rose, illuminating the room. Dozens of tunnels leading in every direction suddenly revealed themselves. Sarah was laying on her back about ten feet from him, covered in dust. Behind her sat a tunnel with a wide mouth that descended into a dark void.

Wade forced himself up, wincing from the stabbing pain that radiated from his severely punished ribs. He then stumbled over to Sarah.

"Let's go, on your feet. We need to get moving," he said while helping her up.

"Thank you," she responded, dusting herself off and grabbing her hat from the floor. "Well, that was f–"

A deep rumble echoed from the tunnel they'd just fallen

through. Wade stepped in front of Sarah while slipping Thorn from its holster and raising it to the opening. Whatever the sound was, it was coming fast.

"Get ready to run, Sarah."

Suddenly, a Bone Eater emerged from the tunnel and launched toward them. Wade had his sight set between its eyes, but he *didn't* fire. Instead, he let the Demon get within inches of biting him before ramming Thorn into the Demon's face. It pierced through its skull, and its body immediately went limp, dangling from the knife. Wade flung it off his weapon and readied himself to face another, but something strange happened. No Demons came, but instead, loud *booms* reverberated from the surface, as if dynamite was exploding.

"What the hell was that?" Sarah asked.

"I don't know," Wade said, looking around at the shaking walls, and all at once, it stopped and the cave fell silent.

"Why didn't you shoot?" Sarah asked.

"We don't know what lurks down here. If I fired, we're as good as dead."

"Good call. You think that was the last of 'em?"

"I reckon it was. The others must not have followed that one down."

Sarah spun around, looking at all of the tunnels that surrounded them and said, "It looks like some type of system, and this is where they all converge."

"But the question is, who or *what* dug them?"

"The Bone Eaters?"

"No."

Wade brought the fire in his hand to the walls and inspected a deep set of claw marks embedded in the rock.

"These marks don't match up to theirs," the Demon

Gunner muttered. "I always had my suspicions, but this only further confirms it."

"Confirms what?"

"That the Demons have already begun terraforming our world and making it their own. Even if we somehow managed to close that rift, uprooting them from Rhodahn would be damn near impossible. It might even be too–"

"No, don't say it," Sarah interrupted. "Let's just look for a way out of here. Do you think we can climb back up the way we came?"

"No use," Wade said, kneeling down next to the Demon's corpse while removing his jacket. "That grade is far too steep, we'd never make it back up. Whoever lives down here uses their claws to traverse through these tunnels. We will have to find another way out."

Wade began to tear off the sleeves of his cotton, long sleeve shirt, revealing scarred but muscular arms.

"Going sleeveless?" Sarah asked.

"Making torches," Wade responded while wrapping the torn fabric over the blades of his guns.

He titled the weapons down and dipped them into the dark green blood that leaked out of the Demon's face. Then, he ignited the soaked, rolled fabric, creating two small torches that lit up the cave around them.

"I don't know what these fuckers are, but the one thing I do know is that they sure don't like fire." Wade scanned the tunnels and said, "Now, which way?"

"There is no right answer, so we've just gotta pick one," Sarah said, drawing a silver coin from her pocket. "How about we flip for it? Heads right, tails left."

Wade nodded and thought that flipping a coin was better than nothing.

May Nor guide us, whichever way this coin lands.

Sarah placed it on the nail of her thumb and flicked it upward. It flipped a few times in the air, and for a split second, Wade thought he saw its momentum momentarily change before it fell back into her palm. She flipped it over and slammed it down on top of her left hand.

Heads.

"Looks like we're going right then," Sarah said.

"Ready your weapon, but only use it if you *have* to."

Sarah nodded, and they stared at the entrance of a large tunnel that descended into darkness.

"How bad did the Demon get you earlier?" Wade asked.

"It was just a scratch, I'm alright."

"Good, then let's go."

And with that, the two set off into the unknown.

• • •

The tunnel they were now traveling down was not nearly as steep as the one they had fallen through, and as they walked, Wade pointed out the claw marks that littered the walls and ceiling. But what was most perplexing to the Demon Gunner was the existence of *smaller* marks that ran across the floor, as if they belonged to a separate creature fighting to free itself while being dragged further into the darkness.

But luckily, nothing had bothered them so far, and Wade suspected that they had been walking for at least thirty minutes now. The tunnel just seemed to descend endlessly, and the air grew colder with each step, causing their breath to fog. Sarah's teeth started to chatter next to him.

"Sorry," she muttered while holding her arms tightly. "I can't help it, it's just so cold."

"It's alright," Wade said. "Keep moving, and if you can't, I'll warm you."

The slope of the tunnel started to grow steeper before it veered even harder to the right. The walls began to expand, indicating that it was opening up to a *larger* cavern. But in the far distance, Wade thought he could see something glimmering–a faint green light emanating from a sunken place. Wade held out a hand in front of the girl, signaling for her to stop. He frantically extinguished the torches on Rose and Thorn by absorbing the fire back into his palm.

"Do you see that?" he whispered to Sarah. "Up ahead–the green light."

Sarah looked in the distance and noticed it too.

"I do. What do you think it is?"

"No idea, but we're about to find out," he said, signaling for her to slowly follow him.

They crept toward the source–the green light growing brighter and brighter. Finally, they approached a precipice, and down below were hundreds of Demons with bioluminescent lines and dots running across their bodies in strange, wave-like patterns. They had large, green eyes and incredibly long, slimy tongues that hung from their mouths and nearly touched the floor. They moved on all fours like Bone Eaters, but were bulkier, with three-toed feet tipped with razor-sharp claws. As Wade stared at them, he wondered if they might even belong to the same family.

Then, he heard a blood curdling scream from the opposite end of the cavern. They both looked for the source of the noise and saw a man being dragged by his legs. A Demon had its teeth buried deep into his calves and was pulling them apart, ripping off skin and muscle in the process.

"DEAR NOR! HELP ME! HELP ME!" he cried as he was dragged through the crowd of hungry Demons, until he came to a halt in front of a wall covered in thick webs and cocoons.

Sarah gasped, and Wade covered her mouth and pulled her back from the ledge, hoping that she hadn't been heard. He pressed her tight to his chest, expecting to be torn apart, but no Demons came for them. Wade slowly released her and looked back over the ledge once more, finally seeing what had caused Sarah to gasp. He had to stifle one himself as the sight before him was more gruesome than he could've ever imagined. Hanging from the walls of the cave were humans stuffed in cocoons. Their stomachs were grotesquely bloated, sagging, and rippling with glowing green veins that looked like they were going to burst at any moment.

Another scream echoed through the cave, and the man that had been dragged was now being lifted from the floor by his arms. The Demon looked into his fearful eyes, and he kicked and thrashed against its grip, but his attempts at escape were futile. The Demon held on tight and screeched as its mandible opened wide. A long, snake-like tentacle extended from its mouth and slithered toward the man's face.

"No…" the man pleaded as the tentacle ran across his skin, covering him with sticky saliva. "NO! NOR, NO! PLE–" The tentacle thrust into the man's mouth, cutting off his words.

He gagged and writhed in pain, thrashing violently

against the wall. Tears ran down his face, but his cries were muffled as it transferred an object through its tentacle and into the man's expanding mouth. The large object then traveled down his throat, stretching the skin of his neck like a water sack being filled, before it finally passed into his stomach. Once the insemination was complete, the man passed out, hanging his head. The Demon *smiled,* and its tentacle retracted from the man's throat and returned to its mouth before it spun him over and over again, covering him in webbing.

Wade felt sick to his stomach, and he fought back the urge to vomit. Even after everything he had seen on his journey, that had been the most haunting. They needed to get the fuck out of these tunnels and fast.

Then, he felt a hand gently touch his arm, as if not to startle him.

"Wade…" Sarah whispered.

He turned to his right and saw a Cave Dweller slowly crawling toward them. Before he could say anything, its tentacle shot from its mouth toward the girl. She screamed as it narrowly missed her face, but Wade managed to grab hold of it. He pulled with tremendous force and tore it from its mouth, sending blood spewing all around them. The Demon screeched and lunged forward at Wade, but it was blasted back by three shots from Sarah's repeater rifle. It collapsed onto the floor, and Sarah pumped one more round into its face for good measure.

They both gathered their composure and looked at each other, knowing what was coming next.

"Reload!" Wade demanded before turning back to the horde of Demons below them.

The Cave Dwellers were staring up at them, and they

screeched before charging forward and climbing up the wall of rock. Then, all at once, the humans on the walls began to wake up, screaming and shouting in agony before their stomachs exploded, spraying glowing green blood outward and spilling newborn Cave Dwellers onto the floor.

Wade looked to his right and saw another tunnel leading into the darkness. He pointed to it.

"Get to the tunnel!" Wade yelled, and above them, attached to the ceiling, glowing green eyes appeared.

Sarah didn't hesitate and took off toward the tunnel, but before Wade chased after her, he aimed at the ceiling and fired twelve rounds of Hellfire into the rock. It began to shake and crumble before crashing down onto the Demons below, crushing them.

Wade then got up and sprinted after the girl, frantically attempting to relight the fabric dangling from Rose and Thorn. With a flame from his finger tip, they finally ignited, revealing the tunnel's incline.

"Keep going!" Wade yelled as he reloaded and scrambled up it.

Behind them, scratching noises echoed through the tunnel. Wade flipped around and unloaded both revolvers into the Demons that were chasing after them. Their bodies exploded, sending them backward and taking out others along the way. But more were still closing in, and he could hear their screeching right behind them.

He kept firing, and Sarah attempted to do the same, but Wade yelled, "JUST RUN!"

Ahead of them, a faint light was starting to grow brighter and brighter, indicating that they were nearing the surface. They moved as fast as they could; the creatures only a few feet behind them now. Wade wanted to shoot the roof of the tunnel and crush them with rock, but it risked bringing the entire thing down on top of them. He had to wait for the perfect moment to do it.

But now, the walls of the tunnel were growing tighter.

"You're almost there!" Sarah yelled from the surface. "CRAWL, WADE, CRAWL!"

The tunnel kept narrowing until Wade was forced to his hands and knees, crawling as fast as he could. Behind him, the Demons snapped at his boots. The fresh air was so close now, and just as he freed himself from the tunnel, he felt a tentacle wrap around his ankle and tighten. Wade attempted to kick free, but it had him pinned. Above him, Sarah grabbed hold of his jacket, trying to pull him out, but the Cave Dweller was stronger, and Wade began to slip further and further back into the hole.

In one last act of desperation, Wade swung Thorn downward, slicing the tentacle in half and freeing himself from the Demon's grip. Sarah then pulled him as hard as she could, yanking him out of the hole and causing him to fall flat on his back. And just as he was grabbed by the Cave Dwellers once more, Wade shot at the entrance of the tunnel, causing it to collapse in on itself and crush the Demons beneath the rubble.

CHAPTER NINETEEN
THE WIZARD AND THE GIANT

Back on the surface, Wade and Sarah sat for a moment, catching their breath. Wade spotted a faint trail snaking off in both directions. He couldn't tell where it led, but it didn't matter. They would have to follow it regardless.

"Are you ready to keep moving?" Wade asked.

Sarah inhaled deeply once more and nodded. They started down the steep, loose trail, and it took them hours to reach the bottom of the mountain. Eventually, it converged with the wider path they had followed earlier, but now Wade noted a faint red hue bleeding into the sky, cast by the Blood Moon. Quicksilver was still nowhere to be found.

With the Consumption beginning, they needed to find shelter–*fast*. Wade slipped off the trail and ducked beneath a nearby boulder, spotting a narrow crevice hidden below. Luckily, no Demons lurked within it, and it looked just wide enough for the two of them. He waved Sarah over and guided her inside, then followed, squeezing tightly between her and the rock. Wade held his revolvers against his chest, and his stiff hands ached from the cold, but it did seem warmer within the crevice than on the surface, their bodies acting as miniature furnaces.

Then, the unmistakable sound of metal scraping across rock echoed down the trail, like a wounded knight dragging a sword behind him. They both rose slightly within the crevice and peered through a narrow gap, immediately spotting it: a large, gray skinned Demon walking upright, a greatsword laying across his scarred shoulder. Occasionally, the tip of the crudely made sword—its edges rough and uneven—scraped against the rock wall, producing the sound they had just heard.

As Wade stared at the Demon, he realized it was the first time he had seen one wielding a weapon of its *own*. They weren't all bloodthirsty monsters after all, no, they were more than that—something else entirely, something the Demon Gunner couldn't begin to understand.

The sword-wielding Demon continued onward and disappeared around a corner. Soon after, the clanking of bones followed. A skeleton with long, mangled hair and glowing green eyes stumbled down the trail, but just as it stepped in front of them, it stopped—its head craning toward them. Its jaw unhinged and snapped shut with a loud *crack*, like two wooden blocks slamming together. An ear-piercing screech followed.

Wade didn't hesitate, digging his hands into the snow and crawling out from the crevice. He yanked Sarah from it and spun around just as the skeleton leaped toward them. The blade of Thorn was drawn and thrust through the skeleton's brittle skull before it could reach them. Wade ripped it upward, splitting the skull in two and causing the rest of the bones to fall to the ground. From the pile rose a green spirit with no discernible shape. It hovered for a moment before taking off into the blood-red sky and vanishing from sight.

"What the hell was that?" Sarah asked.

Wade quickly grabbed the girl's hand before saying, "When I pull, we hide. When I run, you run."

He didn't wait for a response and took off down the trail.

He listened carefully, and every few feet, Wade pulled Sarah off of it, taking cover behind whatever they could find as Demons of all shapes and sizes sauntered past. Some had two legs, others four–or *many*–skittering across the ground like a millipede. Some even had none at all, merely floating through the air like the Soul Stealers they had encountered in the desert. A few resembled animals, others insects, and some defied all recognition. But they all shared a single, unmistakable trait: glowing green eyes and a mischievous look, as if they couldn't *wait* to explore this new world.

When the last of the Demons passed, Wade and Sarah continued on. The trail twisted and turned for several more miles before widening and sloping upward. At the crest of a small hill, they stopped, frozen by the sight ahead. Before them loomed the tallest mountain in the range, illuminated red by the Blood Moon above. It sat dead center at the end of a wide valley, and laying across the valley was a massive, decaying Demon corpse. Its horns jutted hundreds of feet into the air, and its gaping mouth hung open in a silent, eternal scream. It lay on its side, its massive body blocking the path to the mountain–only until *something* had carved a massive hole through its chest, exposing the land beyond. But what was most peculiar–perhaps most terrifying–was the rusted, chipped scythe still gripped in the Demon's hand, its blade buried deep into the side of a mountain.

"Do you see that?" Sarah asked, pointing in the distance.

"The giant?" Wade responded. "How could I not?"

"No, *that.*"

And then, Wade finally noticed that she was pointing *past* the giant's corpse. His eyes tracked upward, and he saw it for himself. Perched atop the mountain peak stood a monolithic, black, jagged castle. From its highest tower, a beam of light shot upward, piercing the Rift in the sky.

"Is that–"

"A castle," Wade responded, "and the source of the Rift. Sarah, it's right there. That is where we will find our answers."

• • •

They moved down into the valley, stealthily making their way onto the trail that led toward the giant's decomposing corpse. Every hundred feet, they ducked off the path, hiding from the Demons that passed by. But strangely enough, they didn't seem to notice them. Their minds were preoccupied with something else, as if they were on a mission.

But even with the Demons distracted, resting for the night was out of the question. They didn't have their tent, and Wade postulated that if they stayed in one spot for too long, they would eventually be sniffed out. He didn't want a repeat of the skeleton encounter, so, they would have to keep moving until they reached the castle.

If that were even possible.

As they hid and watched the Demons pass by, Wade began to notice a pattern: they moved in groups or *sets,* appearing every twenty minutes or so. When the pair resumed the trail, Wade kept time in his head, pulling Sarah off just before the twentieth minute. Like clockwork, the moment they hid, the next set would roll in. They held their breath, stayed silent, and let the Demons pass without incident.

The trail they were following led directly to the giant's decaying chest, with exposed muscle and bone protruding from it. The hole in the center of it was *massive*–at least thirty feet wide–and as Wade got a closer look at it, he couldn't tell if it had been carved out, stabbed, or shot by something. Regardless of what had done the damage, he struggled to comprehend the power required to deal such a blow.

Perhaps some Demon of unimaginable horror could've done it, but they never seemed to bother or fight each other. They just walked side by side, almost unaware of each other's presence. Some of them had no faces and were as tall as trees. They lumbered down the trail, as if they were in no rush to infect Wade's world. Others scurried past them with frightening speed, like goblins from tales of old. They even saw some with multiple heads, each one moving and blinking independently, twisted grins painting their faces.

And after a while, more Demons with weapons appeared–long swords, scythes, spears, dual sided blades, axes, crude knives–anything sharp and pointed, all looking for someone or something to shred and feast upon. But Wade never saw any guns or bows, so if they kept their distance, they would be safe.

Thank Nor.

Finally, they reached the passage through the Demon's

chest, and Wade realized they would have to climb onto the snath of the scythe to reach it.

Wade interlocked his fingers and created a step, and Sarah used it to climb up. He then withdrew Thorn, swung it by its chain in a circle over his head, and released it toward an exposed bone. The gun lodged itself behind it and secured firmly in place. Wade pulled himself up the chain, hand over hand, like a man scaling a cliff face, and eventually joined Sarah on the snath. They walked a few more feet across it and entered the hole. The inside was blackened and frozen—clearly burned. He now deduced that a projectile of some sort had passed *through* it, as it looked like a bullet wound, just on a massive scale.

"Come on," Sarah whispered, pulling on *his* hand now. "We don't want to stay here for too long."

Wade nodded and followed after her, exiting the hole onto the other side of the valley. What the giant's body once concealed was now laid bare: a sprawling, ominous forest stretching toward the mountains.

Great.

But then, Sarah stopped abruptly. Wade quickly scanned the forest for any threats, and sitting against a tree a few feet from them was a hooded figure, dressed in black robes. Wade's stomach dropped; it eerily resembled the figure he saw when they first entered the mountains. To its right lay a charred wooden staff, half buried in ice. Sarah and Wade looked at each other and then carefully inched toward the hooded figure. They were now nearly face to face with it, and Wade brought Thorn up from his side and placed the blade under the hood's lip and pulled, revealing a skull. He jumped back and aimed at it, but the skeleton *didn't* move. It just sat there—frozen—staring endlessly at the snow-covered ground. Wade could immediately recognize the skull's human features, and whoever it had been had died a *long* time ago. The person sure as hell wasn't coming back now, but then again, nothing would surprise the Demon Gunner at this point.

"Any idea who this could be?" Sarah asked, kneeling down next to the staff.

"If I were a betting man, I'd say some sort of wizard."

"Like the ones you were talking about?"

"Don't touch that." She withdrew her hand, inches from coming in contact with the staff's shaft. "We don't know what curses it holds."

"You're right," Sarah said, stepping back from the staff and joining Wade's side again. "How do you know he was a wizard?"

"Because… only wizards carry staffs and dress like *that.* But what do I know? I've never seen one before, just heard stories of them as a kid."

"While you were at the School?"

"Yes, *many.*"

Wade crouched down and got a closer look. The top half of the oak staff was charred and twisted like a wick, and the bottom half was smooth and polished. A glowing red gem sat in the center of it.

"What do you think happened to him?" Sarah asked.

Wade didn't know, but while looking back at the dead giant, he couldn't help but feel as if the two were connected.

"Let's keep moving."

And with that, they journeyed into the dark forest.

• • •

Sunlight began to pierce through the thick fog surrounding them, a silent herald that they had survived the night. Their legs throbbed with aching pains, their stomachs growled intensely, and their mouths were as dry as the desert they had come from. Yet, whether driven by necessity or hope, they pressed onward through the shadowed forest.

The Demons continued appearing right on schedule, never being absent for more than twenty minutes, and as they walked in their packs, Wade realized that *they* were the ones who had made the trail—all of the trails. They weren't walking on their own accord, no, instead, they were tethered to an invisible line, like trains on railroad tracks. Each pack, no matter who it consisted of, followed a nearly identical route, as if they were all communicating… or something was communicating with *them.*

But luckily, whatever the hell was going on kept the Demons at a distance, never noticing Sarah and Wade hiding off a few feet from the trail.

Back in the desert and forest, the Bone Eaters, Nightwalkers, Soul Stealers, and spider-like monsters were all able to *track* humans. Whether it be through scent or sound, they had an innate ability to hone in on their prey. But the Demons they now encountered had no such abilities. They almost entirely relied on their sight, and Wade wondered if that was the reason why the ones in the desert had ventured out so far from the Rift. They could smell the hordes of human flesh waiting for them out there in Rhodahn, ready to be devoured, and those Demons just couldn't help themselves, drawn to it like moths to a flame.

But as they walked, Wade was reminded of an absence,

an absence that could only be described as the longing one feels for a lost friend or family member. Quicksilver was still gone, and every so often, when the coast was clear, Wade would whistle as *loud* as he could in hopes of bringing his horse back to him.

But she never came.

Wade wondered how long they would be able to keep up this foolish pursuit without her. Sarah was growing more and more tired with each step, and he could tell from her irregular gate and slowing pace. It also didn't help that every time he looked in the distance at the castle, it seemed to grow further and further away, as if it were running from them.

Just a few more steps… Just a few more–

A large, jagged sword cut through the air, and Wade pushed backward off his heels, barely dodging it as it slammed into the ground and shook the trees around them. Wade's head shot up, immediately recognizing the Demon that towered over him. It had scarred gray skin and horns, with fangs jutting out from its bottom lip. It wore a loincloth, and a green glow radiated from its mad eyes. It looked *exactly* like the one they had seen earlier, as if they could be brothers.

"GUNNER!" the Demon yelled, before pulling the sword free from the snow and swinging it at Wade once more. *"DIE!"*

Wade dove to the side and tackled Sarah to the ground, barely avoiding the blade as it passed over their heads. He spun around and unholstered Rose and Thorn in one move, firing at the Demon. A few shots of Hellfire managed to pierce through its midsection before the Demon drove its sword into the ground and used the flat side of the blade as a shield to protect itself. Wade then rolled to the right, shooting at it quicker than it could reposition its sword, sending a bullet through its arm. It screeched and ripped its blade from the dirt, as Sarah scrambled to her feet again. With the flat side of the sword still facing outward, it charged at the girl, using the weapon like a ram. Wade and Sarah fired together, but the bullets ricocheted off the thick metal blade and lodged themselves in neighboring trees. Wade once again dove at Sarah and pushed her out of the way, just as he was struck by the blade and launched backward, tumbling across the snow and sliding to a halt.

His world spun, and his abused ribs screamed for his attention, but as he sat frozen on the ground, he heard a rush of wind growing over his shoulder. He immediately rolled to the side, *narrowly* dodging the sharp tip of the blade from skewering him. Wade attempted to get up, but the Demon punched him back down again with a meaty fist, knocking the wind from his lungs and breaking his arm. Wade gasped for air as the Demon pulled his sword from the snow and raised it over his head for the finishing...

BANG!

A bullet blasted through its heart, spraying green blood over Wade.

BANG! BANG BANG!

Three more bullets tore through its chest, causing the sword to drop from the Demon's grip and clatter to the ground next to Wade. Its knees buckled, and it fell to a kneeling position.

BANG!

A final shot tore through the back of its skull, exploding the Demon's face. Its body began to rock forward, and just before it fell, Wade crawled backward and spread his legs, barely escaping being crushed under its enormous weight. As he looked up, he saw Sarah standing there with a smoking repeater rifle in her grip. She extended a hand and helped Wade up off the ground. They both simultaneously readjusted their wide-brimmed hats.

"Come on," she said, slinging the weapon back over her shoulder and starting down the trail again. "We've got five minutes to make up lost ground before the next pack comes."

Wade didn't argue and limped after her, holding his broken arm in pain. They carried on.

• • •

The trail led down to a winding river that ran through the middle of the forest. Snow had started to fall more heavily now, and the air around them grew colder, causing Wade to pull up the collar of his jacket closer to his beard with his non-injured arm.

As they walked, Wade focused on his breathing while listening to the soothing sound of the rushing water next to them. With each deep breath, he stoked the fire inside him, and he could feel his bones healing. During this process, Wade thought about the Demon that had just attacked, but he wasn't thinking about the attack itself—that was just a natural part of their journey now—instead, he focused on what it had said.

Gunner.

Not only did it speak, but it *recognized* him—knew who he was—what he was, and it was angry about it. There was no explanation, and perhaps there never would be one.

"Wade?" Sarah asked.

"Yes?"

"You believe in Nor, right?"

Wade nodded and said, "Why do you ask?"

"I was just thinking about my parents, and… do you really think we will all go to the High Place after this?"

"I do believe so."

"Well I hope they're up there," she said, craning her head to the dense canopy above them. "Sometimes, I feel like *they're* the lucky ones–flying through the clouds, holding hands, sunshine on their skin… I imagine it's a little better than our current situation."

"Maybe, but maybe there's a reason Nor kept you here instead. Perhaps there's more for you to do here before you can go to the High Place too."

"But that sounds like a punishment?"

"You ever read The Evia?"

"I've heard bits and pieces from my momma."

"Well, it says that death does not come early, nor does it come late. It comes when the work our savior has laid out for us is completed. But he also seems to work in ways we can't fully understand. He is a god, after all, so it may be best not to think about it too much."

"But why do you think Nor let those people in the cave be tortured like that?" Sarah asked. "Was that just the fate he set for them?"

"Their work was done, Sarah. Their fate was no longer in his hands."

"Well I don't buy that."

"You don't need to, but I'd rather not dwell on it." But Wade wasn't speaking to the girl, he was speaking to himself.

The more he thought about Nor and the misfortunes

that took place on Rhodahn, the further his faith slipped. What he repeated to Sarah was what his mother used to tell him whenever he questioned his own beliefs as a child. Of course, his mother's words didn't help, and if anything, it made him dwell on it further.

"I know I said this before, but what if I died that day in the town? What if *this* is Hell? Have you thought about it since that conversation?"

"I have, and that up *there* is more likely to be Hell than where we're standing," Wade said, pointing to the Rift in the sky.

A splash echoed next to them. Wade and Sarah stopped in their tracks. Another splash, louder this time.

"Sarah..."

Glowing green eyes, belonging to a slimy, dark skinned serpent emerged from the black river, *staring* at them. Quicker than they could react, the serpent's body extended forward, grabbing Sarah by her jacket and lifting her into the air. Rose and Thorn were now in Wade's hands, and he shot the creature in the face. It recoiled and screeched, sending Sarah flying off into the distance.

"SARAH!" Wade yelled, but the serpent had *his* leg now and was pulling him toward the river bank.

His iron had dropped from his hands, and he scrambled to fetch the chains attached to them, but it was too late. Wade was already beneath the surface now, and the sound of rushing water filled his ears as the serpent dragged him along, smashing him back and forth against the rocks. He barely managed to break the surface for a quick gasp of air before being ripped back into the freezing water once more.

The serpent kept him underneath the surface, hoping to

drown him, and despite Wade's attempts to break free, he *couldn't.* The air in his lungs was depleting rapidly, and his mind screamed at him to surface at once. But the only thing he could do was pull on the chain of Thorn and attempt to grab it. His fingers wrapped around the metal links and he yanked, catching the gun with his right hand. With all of his might, he directed its blade into the monster's eye. An ear piercing screech echoed through the water, destroying Wade's eardrums before he was ripped from the river and thrown far into the distance.

On his descent, he crashed through multiple tree limbs before landing hard in the snow. His body screamed with pain, and his arm was surely broken again, but he stuck Thorn into the ground and used it as a crutch to help him get to his feet. He only had one thing on his mind: *Sarah.*

So, he set off further into the forest with a limp. Demons screeched all around him, as if they were taunting him, but he didn't give a fuck.

I must…. find… Sarah.

Wade trudged through the snow, as fast as he could physically move, but a creeping realization set in: Wade had no idea where the girl was. He had no tracks to follow, no direction to head in, no signs of where she might be– nothing.

"SARAH!" he yelled. "SARAH!!!!!"

There was no response, and Wade limped forward again. "SARAH!"

No response; he continued on.

"SARRRAAHHHHH!!" he shouted one last time before taking a step and collapsing to his knees.

Wade sat there, breathing heavily–*defeated.* At the same time, glowing green eyes appeared all around him.

He looked past them for the girl, but he found nothing–
only those piercing green eyes staring back. Through the
canopy above him, he could faintly make out the Rift and
the beam that was connected to it. There was only one
thing he could do, and Wade hoped he had trained the girl
well enough to survive on her own.

I will see you there, Gunner.

And with that, Wade set off toward the castle.

CHAPTER TWENTY

THE BLINDING LIGHT

Severe aches and pains coursed through Wade's body and made each step more difficult than the last. His vision was blurry, causing him to stumble back and forth through the snow like a drunkard leaving a tavern. His shirt and leather jacket, which had kept him warm and served him well until now, were torn and tattered, exposing his bare skin to the elements and allowing snow to fall into the deep cuts on his arms. It stung profusely, but the cuts *were* healing–albeit very slowly as the fire inside him worked overtime to warm him in the freezing cold.

He could only imagine what the poor girl was going through now.

Then, all at once, the green eyes that watched him grew *closer.* Wade's shaking hands made their way to his iron, but a terrible realization dawned: Rose and Thorn were waterlogged. If he wanted to fire them, he'd need to dissemble the guns and thoroughly dry them. Of course, that wasn't an option, which only left him with plan B.

The Demons had fully revealed themselves now, and they resembled a pack of Hellhounds, with decomposing skin and hollow ribs. Black drool spilled from their mouths as they bared razor sharp teeth and wrinkled their noses at Wade. One stepped forward from the pack, dragged a paw through the snow, and lunged at him. Just before it bit his face, Wade drew Thorn from its holster and thrust its blade into the Demon's throat. The Hellhound squealed and whimpered before attempting to try and eat Wade's face again. Wade gritted his teeth and slammed its body into the snow. With all his might, he drove the blade upward, slicing through its neck, head, and out the top of its skull, killing it instantly.

"COME ON!" Wade shouted to the others, but they didn't move. They just continued to watch him.

Without wasting a second more, Wade stepped over the corpse and continued on.

You're almost to the castle, Wade told himself. *Just a little further.*

But now, more Hellhounds stepped out from the shadows and surrounded him. Rose and Thorn's blades wouldn't be enough to fend them off. The only thing that could stop this horde would be *fire*–but he had none. If he tried to release what was left inside him, he would surely freeze to death. His legs were already numb and heavy, and he wondered if he could even keep moving. Sarah was lost; the castle sat atop an impassable mountain. He just wanted to drop to his knees and give up–another life consumed by the Darkness.

But a truly defenseless Gunner is not a Gunner at all, Ulysses said in his mind. *Isn't that right, Wade?*

That's right.

And what are you?

I'm a Gunner.

So, if this is the end, you better not go down without a fight.

The Hellhounds drew closer, snapping their jaws and laughing in a devilish way. Wade holstered Thorn and took a deep breath in. He focused on the small flame burning within him, and saw it sitting in a black, infinite void. The flame flickered while he called to it. Again, Wade sucked in air through his nose and released it out of his mouth. Suddenly, the flame started to rise. His adrenaline spiked, and blue flames appeared within his palms. He repeated this process while thinking of Sarah alone in the woods. If she were ever to find his body, at least she would find it beneath a horde of charred corpses.

WHOOSH!

Fire erupted from his eyes, and a wave of blue flames extended from his hands, igniting the Hellhounds. One by one, they exploded in green bursts of blood. They screeched, attempting to turn back, but the fire was too fast to outrun.

Burn, you sons of bitches. Burn.

More fire engulfed them, sending the trees around Wade up in flames. A smile grew on his face, watching the Demons writhe in pain. But suddenly, the flames from his hands started to sputter out.

"No…" Wade whispered.

He tried forcing more, but nothing came. The flame inside him had been extinguished, and he was suddenly aware of the freezing chill that surrounded him. His legs buckled, and he dropped to his knees.

The remaining Hellhounds had now circumnavigated the flames and drew closer to him, snarling. Wade let his head fall into the snow and accepted his fate. That was his final stand; the tricks were over. No longer was he a Gunner, no, now he was a dead man.

But then, a light started to glow in front of him, causing Wade's eyes to open with surprise. He attempted to look at it, but it was blinding. He raised a hand to shield his eyes and could just make out a log cabin, light pouring from its windows.

Had that been there before? No... It's not possible... It wasn't there... It wasn't...

Wade began to crawl, digging his frostbitten fingers into the snow and dragging his frozen body toward the light. Behind him, the Hellhounds took advantage of his weakness and attacked. Wade yelled in pain as they dug their teeth into the soft flesh of his legs and hips. They thrashed back and forth, sending blood across the snow while tearing the muscle from his bones.

Wade couldn't fight it, all he could do was look at the light in front of him and reach out toward it. And as he reached, a feeling of warmth and peace rushed over him like a hug from his mother. He saw Jess and his friends again, sitting in the field of flowers outside their school.

There was no pain now—no suffering—it was ethereal bliss. And just as he fully relinquished himself to it, he saw a cloaked figure walking toward him. Wade couldn't tell if the man was real or not, but he didn't care—it didn't matter now—*nothing* did.

Wade dropped his head into the snow and closed his eyes.

CHAPTER TWENTY ONE
AN UNLIKELY FRIEND

BOOM!

An explosion erupted beside Wade as he rode through the war-torn Southern Farlands. Rain poured down, turning the battlefield into a muddy swamp.

Wade's grip tightened on the soaked reins before he whipped them twice, sending Quicksilver into a full gallop, leaping over trenches and dodging corpses that lay face down in the mud. To his right, an army of traitors with iron on their hips, led by the Kutarian Knights, crested a hill, marching side by side. More explosions rang out as black powder cannons and mortars pounded the trenches, raining fire down on the Gunners. With each shell that struck, limbs, guns, and blood flew into the air.

"We need to push them back to the breach!" Wade shouted to what was left of his army.

Ahead stood the southern wall of the Farlands. A large section of it had been melted away and punched out, and with each passing second, more and more traitors and Knights poured through the breach. Wade turned to his left and saw Westin holding his rifle. Empty casings littered the mud where he sat.

"Wade," Westin said, defeated. "There's no use. It's too late."

A piercing screech rang out above them, and Wade

looked up to see a dragon swooping down to the battlefield. He pulled his horse to the right, narrowly avoiding a wave of fire that torched their trench. When the fire and smoke cleared, Westin and their fellow Gunners were *gone*.

Wade's ears rang violently, masking the sound of the chaos around him. He sat on his horse—frozen—unable to move. His best friend had been there moments ago; now he was gone.

Then, bullets whizzed past, barely missing Wade. He was immediately pulled out of the trance and directed his horse into a nearby trench to avoid the oncoming gunfire. He whipped the reins again, sending Quicksilver running through it. Mud kicked up from the horse's hooves, covering Wade's legs and holsters, and as he rounded a corner, Wade spotted Jess laying against the steep slope of the trench. She held her guns outstretched above her, her forearms pressed into the mud, waiting for the right moment to peak out.

"Jess!" Wade called out. "DON'T!"

BOOM!

Another explosion erupted next to Wade, sending him flying off the back of his horse. He barrel rolled multiple times across the mud before crashing hard against the wall of the trench. His world spun, and the air in his lungs was gone, but there was no time to focus on the pain as footsteps were quickly approaching. A battle cry followed, and Wade saw a Knight rushing forward with his sword raised above his head, clad in a full suit of gleaming silver armor. Wade aimed Thorn, and a bullet flew through the head of his attacker, piercing his helm and causing him to crumple into the mud.

Wade scrambled to his feet and took off, his boots

slipping and sliding as the heavy rain continued to pour down on top of them. Wade unholstered Rose and aimed both weapons down the line of the trench. More enemies charged forward, and the second their heads lined up with his sights, they were dead.

Where there is one, there are many, Ulysses said in his mind.

And he was right, as another battle cry came from behind him. Wade sidestepped, barely avoiding a sword that was stabbed into the wall next to him. He spun around, and the Knight stared at him with wide, frightful eyes through the slit in his silver helm, attempting to pull his sword free from the wall. Wade pumped three consecutive shots into his stomach, and with each shot, the man's body jolted. He tried to speak, but only a gurgle of blood came out before his lifeless body fell into the mud.

Wade continued on through the trench.

"Jess!" he yelled, scanning in every direction. "Where are you!"

Then, in front of him, he saw a traitor standing over a crumpled Gunner laying face down in the mud. A revolver was pointed at the Gunner's back, and the traitor's finger tensed on the trigger. Wade fired, but *two* shots rang out—one was not his. The traitor's body dropped into the mud, and Wade sprinted toward the collapsed Gunner. He slid down next to her and flipped her body over, immediately recognizing her beautiful face. She held her stomach where the bullet had exited, blood seeping through her fingers, only to be washed away by the rain.

"Wade..." Jess muttered, bringing her bloody hand to his face. "You fought... just... just like you said you would."

"Come on, Jess. We gotta get you up. We can still retreat to Arcenia. This is my fault, but we can still make it right."

And as he attempted to lift her, she cried out in anguish.

"*No.* This is the end, Wade. This is the end of the road we started on."

"Don't you say that–"

She held a finger to his lips.

"I see it, Wade... I see..."

Jess slumped to the side, light fading from her eyes, leaving only empty mirrors of brown and white staring endlessly into an unseen world.

"Jess?" Wade shook her lifeless body. "Jess, baby, you gotta get up. Come on, we can find you a medic."

But no medic could bring her back now. This was the end of the road; her final resting place, and Wade and Nor both knew this.

SINK!

A piercing pain coursed through Wade's back, and all at once, the explosions and gunfire around Wade stopped; the battlefield had become *silent.* Wade brought his hand to the source of the pain and saw blood gushing from his abdomen, a glinting sword stabbed straight through it.

The sword was then ripped out of him, and Wade stumbled for a moment; his legs felt like jelly–unstable, not responding to his commands–but his mind wasn't focused on that, no, it was focused on something else, a *different* sensation. A rushing, warm feeling was filling his body now, and the pain had already begun to dissipate.

"You call yourself a king?" the Knight chuckled, his voice muffled by his helm. "Well, here lies the king, dying in the dirt, while Gadriel falls."

Wade attempted to step forward, but he collapsed, catching himself on the wall of the trench. He rolled onto his back and slid down it. The Knight stood over him, sword raised high.

"The Order and your kingdom shall die with you, *Gunner*–"

Thorn fired one last shot, sending a bullet through the Knight's skull and killing him instantly.

The hands that held his iron loosened, dropping the guns into the mud. They vanished from sight, buried beneath it. Then, the world became bright–*very* bright, and silence filled his ears once more. Wade looked around, attempting to see the High Place–hoping to see Jess standing there with open arms–but there was *nothing*. He didn't see Nor or endless clouds and sunshine, no, he just saw the battlefield before him growing darker. His heart rate picked up, and a sinking feeling washed over him until he…

· · ·

Wade shot upright, breathing heavily. He brought his hand to his abdomen, but there was no bleeding wound, only a thick scar. Then, he noticed he was sitting in a bed– not one he had ever slept in before, and the room he found himself in was unfamiliar. The walls and floor were made of pine wood, but they didn't look weathered, worn, or cut, no, they looked like they had never even been walked on before. Next to him, there was a nightstand with a glowing orange candle resting on top of it. Its flame flickered and danced, lighting up the mysterious and unknown space. And when Wade finally looked down, he saw the bloody sheets he was draped in.

He jolted again and attempted to get up from the bed, but a searing pain immediately shot through his legs, causing him to yelp. He pulled the covers off and saw blood soaked bandages wrapped around them. His legs twitched as he attempted to move, but the pain doubled; his teeth gritted together.

"*Rest*," came a soothing voice from the doorway.

The cloaked man entered; his hands were interlinked in front of him, and his eyes were hidden under the brim of his hood. All Wade could see was a long, unkempt beard, as if the man had spent years alone in the wilderness and only just returned to civilization.

"That's close enough," Wade said, sliding his hands to his iron, but it wasn't there. His heart rate picked up. "Tell me who you are, *right now*."

"You ask this question, yet, the answer already lies within your mind."

Wade thought back to the war, but that *wasn't* what he had been saved from. That memory was from long ago—a world that no longer existed, a past life. So he thought harder, and the last thing he remembered was the forest, the Hellhounds… *the girl.* Wade lay his head back on his pillow, not wanting to picture the torture she could be enduring out there.

"You'll heal with time, you always do, don't you?"

"The Demons, where are they?"

"You won't have to worry about them here, just try and ease your racing mind. You're safe with me."

But how could he? Just moments ago, Wade was being eaten alive by Hellhounds. How could anyone living in this world say something like that?

Unless he wasn't living on Rhodahn?

"At least tell me your name."

The man stood at the door, holding onto the knob without speaking. His face remained low.

Finally, he said, "You already know who I am, Wade."

The door shut, and Wade found himself wishing for rest once more. As much as he wanted to press the man further, it was a mystery to be solved later. Sleep called to him like a cool, rushing river calls to a parched man lost in the desert. His heavy eyes closed, and he drifted to sleep.

• • •

When Wade finally woke again, he didn't know how much time had passed as the room had no windows. He also didn't dream during his slumber, which he deemed was for the better after the series of nightmares he had endured. His legs were now in a *much* better shape than when he'd last awoken, suggesting he'd been asleep longer than he realized. His body had healed—as it always did.

And, he was actually able to move when he tried, allowing him to swing his bandaged legs off his bed, touching his bare feet onto the cold floor. Scars now littered his legs, but he didn't care since he still had them.

Thank Nor.

A makeshift crutch leaned against the bed, fashioned from sturdy sticks bound together with string and a strip of cloth draped over the top for padding. Wade took it and jammed it under his armpit. He then placed his full weight onto it, stabilizing himself before heading across the room toward the door the cloaked man had left through.

And now Wade started to wonder if that man had even been real at all—if this *place* were even real, or perhaps it was just another mirage and the Darkness playing tricks on his mind.

He pulled the door open, revealing a modest room with

two rocking chairs and a small fire crackling in a hearth. The cloaked man sat in one of the chairs, facing him. Wade could still not see his eyes, though his body was illuminated by the flames.

"Take a seat."

Wade stared at the man, wondering if he should follow his orders, but he realized he didn't have much of a choice as his holsters sat empty. Besides, this man had saved his life, and he was best not to be fucked with. So, Wade hobbled over to the rocking chair opposite of the man and sat down.

"I've got something that will make you feel better," the man said, presenting a bowl of soup.

Wade didn't hesitate to take it. He hastily brought the bowl to his lips and gulped it down–the savory taste washing over him and warming him instantly. He stared at the soup in amazement, as he hadn't tasted something so delicious since his mother's last meal, many, *many* years ago.

"A drink?" he asked.

Wade wanted to decline his offer after what had happened at the fort, but he already drank the soup without thinking. It was too late, besides, Wade owed him his life.

He finally nodded, and the man slipped a silver flask from his sleeve, like a sleight of hand trick with a deck of cards. And embossed on the flask was a revolver–the unmistakeable insignia of the Order of the Gun.

Wade's eyes grew wide as he said, "Where did you–"

"Smoke?" the man interrupted, presenting a cigar.

But Wade didn't take it. Instead, he just continued to stare at him, dumbfounded, then, his gaze shifted to the flask and empty bowl of soup, before finally looking around at the barren room.

"What is this place?" Wade asked.

"Does it really matter, Wade? You remember the world out there, don't you?"

Indeed Wade did, and in that moment, he realized he had no rush to get back to it. His quest for the castle had been abandoned; he couldn't make it up the mountain in this state, hell, he couldn't even make it three feet through the snow to try and find Sarah. All he could do now was sit in this room with this strange man and take whatever he offered.

Finally, Wade reached forward and took the cigar, causing a soft smile to flash on the man's face.

"You've had a long journey," the man said conclusively, producing another cigar in his hand.

He held it up to Wade, as if asking him to light it. Wade squinted before extending his index finger, but he wondered if anything would even appear as the fire inside him had gone out. He then tried to summon it, but nothing happened.

"Take a deep breath," the man said reassuringly. "We've got all night."

Wade inhaled and exhaled, and a faint blue flame flickered on his finger tip, which he used to light *both* of their cigars. He then sat back, took a measured drag, and hung his head against the chair before finally blowing the smoke toward the ceiling.

"*A long journey?* Huh, I guess you could call it that," Wade said, the rocking chair creaking beneath him. He puffed on the cigar again.

"And the girl… I was sad to see her go."

Wade's eyes grew wide, and he quickly sat up.

"What did you just say?"

"*Sarah*–I hope she is alright."

"How do you know her name? How do you know *my* name?"

"The less questions you ask now, the better. All will be answered soon enough, Wade. Now is the time for rest."

And with those soothing words, Wade's anxious grip on the flask loosened. He didn't know what the hell was going on, but he didn't care. So, he took a long sip, draining the flask of its contents, and before he knew it, it was *full* again. Wade smiled and shook his head before hanging it back once more. And for the first time in Wade's life, he let *go*.

DG

CHAPTER TWENTY TWO

THE SMILING DEMON

S arah flew through the air, arms waving frantically in front of her. The forest below was rapidly approaching, and she screamed as she smashed through thin tree limbs before bursting into a clearing. There was nothing left to slow her fall, and she crashed *hard* into the ground.

• • •

Melted snow ran down Sarah's back as her eyes fluttered open. She immediately gasped for air, drawing in a deep, painful breath. Above her, the Blood Moon hung high, glaring down like a king upon a disloyal apostate. Her arms wriggled by her side, until she finally broke free from the snow that trapped her. Sarah sat up and found herself in a deep snowbank in the middle of a clearing of trees, the *one* place she could've landed that didn't guarantee death. Her body ached grievously, but she was alive.

She pushed against the snow and clambered to her feet. Her hat lay a few feet away, and she scooped it up and placed it atop her head again, but something was missing. She felt for the rifle strap across her chest, but it was gone. Her fingers jammed back into the snow like a shovel, and she began digging around in the bank until she found the gun, pulled it out, and brushed it off before slinging it back over her. The rabbit skin holster still held her revolver.

Thank Nor.

And the only thing that now seemed to be missing was *Wade*. She looked around for him, spinning in circles, but only found Darkness.

A tree limb snapped to her right, and she shot a glance toward the sound. Then, she saw it: a deformed, gray-skinned Demon creeping out from the Darkness, walking crookedly on two legs. Long, ebony claws curled from its fingertips, while an unsettling grin stretched ear to ear, with black ichor dripping from razor-sharp teeth. It had no eyes.

Sarah's revolver was already in her hand, and six shots followed—three missed, and three pissed it off. The Demon screeched and charged forward, and she ran in the opposite direction. Behind her, trees exploded as the Demon effortlessly tore through them. Sarah attempted to reload while running, pulling rounds out of her pockets, but her cold and stiff fingers fumbled and dropped them into the snow, only to be trampled by the Demon. But, by Nor's grace, she finally managed to get one bullet into the cylinder before spinning and firing. The bullet missed by a mile, and the Demon charged on.

Sarah knew she wasn't aiming with her heart. She was aiming with her eyes and paying the price for it. She needed Wade; she couldn't do this alone, she...

The Demon leaped forward and swatted at her, sending her skidding across the snow and tossing her revolver aside. When she looked up, she saw the Demon pouncing down. She rolled to the side, narrowly avoiding a claw as it stabbed into the snow.

In front of her, she saw a small tree burrow–her only chance at survival. She scrambled toward it, fingers digging into the snow, pulling herself along. And just as she ducked into it, the bark above her was slashed apart, cutting the tree in half. She dropped deeper into the burrow, reaching the pit of it as the Demon clawed at the stump, trying to reach the tasty snack that hid inside.

But Sarah wasn't going to die like this; Wade wouldn't allow it, and neither would she. She pulled her repeater rifle from her back and took it into her hands. She flipped the lever down, chambered a round, and pulled the trigger.

BANG!

It struck the Demon square in the face. Again, she loaded more rounds, cocked it, and fired.

BANG!

Another shot rang out, and another hole appeared in its face, but it didn't die. It just continued to smile.

BANG!

CHICK!

She swung the lever down with incredible speed.

BANG!

CHICK!

BANG!

CHICK!

BANG

CLICK!

The gun was empty, but the Demon's attacks had slowed to a halt. It collapsed forward, spilling green blood onto the snow which ran down into the pit where she lay. It was dead, but its twisted smile still remained.

Sarah sat for a moment, breathing heavily while checking herself for wounds. Her back burned slightly, but she didn't think the Demon's claws had cut too deep when it raked across her. But there was no more time to waste. Now she needed to get moving and find Wade.

She attempted to crawl out of the burrow, but the Demon's bleeding corpse blocked her exit, and the second she attempted to move it, another screech echoed out into the night.

What would Wade do? What would Wade do! she thought to herself.

Sarah pressed her head back into the stump, trying to rack her brain, but it spun wildly, and in that moment, she realized there was nothing she could do. But then it dawned on her. That was exactly what Wade *would* do.

Nothing.

The Blood Moon was up, and there would be no traveling toward the castle now. She would need to sit and wait it out until the sun rose again. Then she would start looking for Wade in the morning, yes, that was what she would do.

But she felt an itchy, hairy, tingling sensation running up her arm and across her neck, tickling her. And then she felt that same sensation all over her body. There were small, spindly legs skittering across it, and she looked down and saw black spiders crawling all over her. She wanted to scream and dig her way out of the burrow, but the screeches outside picked up again, so, there was only one thing left that she could try. She brought her fingers to her lips and whistled as loud as she could multiple times in a row. She froze as she felt something tickling her bottom lip–a spider crawled across her mouth, over her eye, and up her forehead.

Sarah tried to remain still and not scream by breathing

in through her nose and out through her mouth as more spiders continued to dance across her skin and through her hair. She was out of options, and so for the rest of the night, she sat there as motionless as possible, thinking about a world filled with light, hoping they wouldn't attack.

• • •

And they didn't.

Thank Nor.

But there was no sleep for Sarah that night, and by the time a faint glow of light peeked through the opening to the burrow, she was ready to bolt. After reloading her repeater rifle, she figured that the only way she could escape the tomb she was trapped in was by *cutting* her way out.

She drew the pocket knife Wade had given her from the sheath at her waist and gripped it tightly in her right hand. Then, she leaned forward and stabbed into the Demon's body, piercing through its thick, leather-like skin. She gritted her teeth and pulled hard, ripping the knife back out again. She raised it once more and brought it down with force.

SINK!

She punctured an artery, and green blood squirted past her. She pulled the knife out again.

SINK!

The Demon's body was now flayed, and the path to freedom became visible, but there was still more work to be done. She raised the knife again.

SINK!

SINK!
SINK!
SINK!

She screamed as she stabbed into it and pulled the knife out again, over and over, tearing apart the Demon's flesh and gouging out its face, covering her in blood, until its corpse was nothing more than an unrecognizable pile of guts. She jammed her arm into the slimy mush, felt the cold soil behind it, and pulled herself through, as if being reborn into the demonic world again. Finally, she yanked her legs free from the pit and escaped.

She collapsed flat on her back, staring up at the gray sky while breathing heavily. Her first instinct was to scream and cry, but at this moment, she just felt *numb*. She wanted to get back to Wade, and that wasn't going to happen laying in the snow. She found her revolver, brushed it off, and placed it back into her rabbit skin holster before turning away and setting off into the forest again.

• • •

Sarah walked toward the sound of the roaring river and eventually found it, but she made sure to stay a safe distance away in fear of the river monster lurking below the surface. Every few minutes, she'd call out for Wade, but heard no response. He was nowhere to be found, and after hours of walking down the river, she started to feel increasingly hopeless about ever seeing him again. She tried whistling too, but the thundering of Quicksilver's hooves never came. Her hunger was also impossible to ignore now, since her growling stomach seemed to remind her with pain every few steps.

Even though she was determined to carry on and reach the castle, she couldn't deny how awful she felt, as her body was failing her. She dropped to her knees and stared forward, and to her surprise, she saw steam rising between the trees. She reluctantly forced herself to her feet again and told herself to keep going, just a little further, to the source of the steam, *then* she could die.

So, Sarah set off again, cresting a hill, and lo and behold, sitting in a small gulley below was a hot spring. Bubbles boiled to the surface, bursting with steam, and she could almost *feel* the warmth from where she stood. She limped toward it, removing her clothes as she approached. She didn't care if a monster lurked below the surface; she needed warmth, even if it meant she'd end up in the belly of a Demon.

The second she stepped in and her freezing cold skin hit the warm water, a feeling of euphoria washed over her. She was back in her home–back when the light of the world was still there. She could see her friends and family, and they were all having a big feast at a long table in a field of flowers. It was *beautiful.*

Her mother came around the side of the table and hugged her.

I missed you, Sarah darling.

I missed you too, Momma.

Sarah slowly lowered herself into the water, dipping her head below the surface and sitting underneath it. She couldn't recall the last time she had felt this warm since starting the journey, and she had no intention of ever leaving the hot spring. She surfaced again and hung her head back on a rock before closing her eyes and drifting to sleep.

• • •

By the time she finally awoke, the sun had dipped below the trees again. She had slept the whole day, and now wondered what the point of leaving even was—it seemed like a fine place to die. But then, Sarah spotted a faint set of glowing eyes on the edge of the hot spring. She tensed as they stepped out from the trees, becoming brighter and brighter, revealing a blue hue to them. Sarah looked across the water and saw her guns resting on a rock. She quickly swam toward them, but whatever was approaching her was much too fast. Then, a decaying horse emerged, and Sarah sighed in relief. Quicksilver stood on the edge of the bank in all her glory.

"Quicksilver!" she cried out. "You came back for me, girl!"

Quicksilver neighed, and Sarah swam toward her.

"You really came back for me." Tears ran down the girl's face, falling into the water. "We gotta find W—"

But before she could finish, Quicksilver neighed again, this time louder and more aggressively. The horse seemed to almost look *past* Sarah, causing her to spin around, and standing behind her iron was a man, dressed in a torn and bloody trench coat. A wide-brimmed hat sat atop his head, and for a moment, she thought it was Wade coming to save her. But he wasn't right; his rotten flesh hung from his bones like ill-fitted clothes, and he hobbled toward her, growling and gurgling as black drool dripped from his mouth.

A Nightwalker.

Without hesitating, Sarah charged out of the water and

toward her guns, but the Nightwalker did the same. She dove to the ground and grabbed her revolver, and just as she brought it up to fire, the Nightwalker's teeth sunk *deep* into her forearm. She screamed in pain as it tore at her flesh and ripped off a chunk. With her last bit of strength, she angled the gun upward and pulled the trigger.

BANG!

An explosion of dark brain matter and blood erupted out the back of the Nightwalker's head before it collapsed into the snow. Quicksilver raced toward the girl and trampled the Nightwalker's corpse, but it was already too late.

Sarah breathed heavily, sitting frozen in the snow. Her ears rang; her heart rate picked up. She slowly raised her arm and stared in horror at the pronounced bite mark embedded in her forearm. Black veins had already started to spread out from the wound, and she could see putrescent fluid bubbling and oozing within it.

"No, no, no..." Sarah muttered, quickly putting her clothes back on and covering up the wound with her jacket sleeve before gathering her repeater rifle and running toward Quicksilver. She jumped onto the horse's back and whipped the reins twice.

"Find Wade," she yelled to the horse. "Please find Wade!"

And with that, Quicksilver took off into the forest, leaving the melting corpse of the Nightwalker–its purpose fulfilled–laying in the snow behind them.

DG

CHAPTER TWENTY THREE

THE WHISPERS OF THE FLOWERS

Wade and the cloaked man sat in the cabin for hours—or was it days? The truth was, Wade did not know how much time had passed. The only thing he knew for certain was that the flask in his hand was now empty again, and the hooded man continued to watch him, not speaking.

"Well? Are you going to say anything," Wade finally asked, "or are we going to just sit here and stare at each other?"

"Yes, but not here, not now."

"What? Then why the hell am I here?"

"Because you *needed* to be. Now, your guns are waiting for you under the cloth on the table—dried, cleaned, and reassembled." The hooded man got up from his chair. "Good luck on your journey to the castle, Wade. We will be seeing each other again, *very* soon."

The man swung open the door of the cabin, and Wade could see heavy snowfall outside.

"Hey, wait!" Wade shouted, shooting up from his chair and scrambling to the door with a limp. "Who the hell are you!"

The man stepped into the snow and looked over his shoulder, revealing an old, weathered face, his eyes glowing white. A chill coursed through Wade's body.

Nor.

The man smirked before disappearing into the snowfall.

Wade turned to his right and saw a cloth resting on a table. He pinched the edge of it and flipped it over, revealing his freshly cleaned iron underneath. The two revolvers sat side by side, each pointing in different directions—as was tradition with Gunners when setting iron down. The candle's light glistened off the polished silver and gold surface and made the weapons glow. Wade swept them up before hobbling out into the snow storm and chasing after Nor.

"WAIT!" Wade yelled into the Darkness, but there was no response. When he glanced back at the cabin, it was *gone,* as if it had fallen apart and dissolved into nothingness. There was no going back now, so, Wade picked up his pace as best he could and attempted to follow the god's footprints in the snow. "Nor! Come back! Please!"

But then, in front of him, he saw glowing blue eyes approaching. A small silhouette sat atop the horse, shrouded in darkness.

It can't be.

As they drew closer, Wade could make out a wide-brimmed hat and long, blonde hair beneath it. Sarah's pain stricken face finally came into view.

"Sarah…" Wade mumbled.

Sarah began to dismount Quicksilver, and when her feet touched the ground, she ran as fast as she could toward the Demon Gunner.

"Wade!" she yelled, stomping through the deep snow.

Wade sprinted toward her, and they collided, wrapping their arms around each other.

"How?" Wade said, gripping her tightly. "How did you find me?"

"I didn't, *she* did," Sarah responded, signaling to the horse with small blue flames curling from her nostrils.

"Are you alright? What happened to you?"

Sarah looked up at Wade and said, "I'm alright." But there was slight hesitation in her voice.

"You were thrown away? Where'd you end up?"

"I landed in a snowbank… only after hitting a few branches on the way down, hence the limp."

Wade smiled and hugged her again.

"Thank Nor," Wade whispered.

"Thank Nor."

They released, and Wade placed a hand on her shoulder, making her tense slightly.

"Sarah, look at me. Are you sure you're alright?" She nodded. "When was the last time you ate?"

"I found jerky and water in the saddlebags, I'll be alright for a while."

Wade stared at her intently, just as Nor had, and he could tell something was *wrong*. She wouldn't meet his eyes, and an unspoken pain lingered on her face, pulling her thoughts to a distant place that which he could not see.

"Sarah…"

"I'm fine, okay? Can we please just get going to the castle? *Please?"*

Wade nodded, removed his hand from her shoulder, and turned to Quicksilver.

"On you go then," he said, hoisting her up.

Wade mounted the horse after her and looked where the cabin should've been. Falling snow began to fill the patch of dirt where the cabin had once stood.

If that were really Nor, why would he have visited me? How did he know who I am—what I am? It doesn't make sense, but then again, when has anything in this world?

He snapped the reins twice, sending them off into a void of snow, trees, and Darkness—toward the castle on the mountain.

• • •

Wade kept Quicksilver at a slow trot to avoid alerting any Demons that might lurk in the shadows. They were now out of the forest and on a direct path to the castle, ascending a rocky and steep trail with the Blood Moon hanging directly above them.

"What happened to *you* after we were attacked?" Sarah asked as they rode.

"I fell into the water, and I was swept away by the current."

"What about the serpent?"

"I managed to fend it off and was thrown out of the water and deeper into the forest. I looked for you, Sarah, but I couldn't find you… then the Hellhounds attacked."

"Did you shoot them?"

"I did."

"And did they bite you?"

Wade hesitated—how could he even begin to explain what had happened? There was no point, as he didn't even fully understand it himself.

"How'd you get those bandages on your legs," she asked

again, and before he could respond, she asked another question, "And where did your limp come from?"

"They bit me, but I fought 'em off too and have since healed from the attack."

"Well that was quick–" Then, Sarah coughed aggressively behind Wade.

"Sarah?"

She cleared her throat. "I'm fine," she assured. "Were you just wandering through the woods after that?"

"*Yes*. What about you? Were you attacked by the same Demons?"

"Only... Only one thing attacked. I don't even know how to describe it. It was skinny and crooked–and long talons hung from its fingers, and it even walked upright. Have you ever seen something like that before?"

"Maybe something similar."

"But it had this big smile on its face. No eyes, just a creepy smile, as if it were *happy* to have found me."

"How'd you manage to escape it?"

"I climbed into a tree burrow and shot it–shot the son of a bitch to death."

"Like a true Gunner."

• • •

Many hours had passed, and they were now nearly to the peak, which provided an incredible view of the surrounding mountain range. Wade even thought he could see the desert again. And as they rode, conversation between the two was sparse–as it often is when a journey nears its end. Nothing had attacked them on the trail, which should've been a relief, but it seemed to worry the

Demon Gunner greatly. It was *too* quiet, and he hated the silence that was only broken by Sarah's coughing.

"Are you ready to see the castle?" Sarah finally asked behind him.

"Yes."

Sarah coughed violently now, swallowed, and said, "Me… Me too. I'm ready."

"Where'd that cough come from?"

"It's just the cold."

Wade shook his head and continued to steer Quicksilver along the trail, beginning the final ascent toward the peak.

"When did you find Quicksilver?" Wade asked.

"A little while after I crawled out of the burrow. I was whistling for her, and she found me. Then we rode to you."

"Well thank you for bringing my horse back to me."

He felt Sarah's head rest against his back.

"Sarah?" he said. There was no response. "Sarah, are you alright?"

"Wade… I had a long night. I just need a second… to rest."

"Alright, I'll tell you when we can see the castle."

But she was already asleep; they rode on.

• • •

Quicksilver had managed to navigate the rocky trail well. A benefit of an undead horse was that they do not have the intrinsic fear of dying, so by virtue, she had no fear of heights. But as they continued to climb and the loose rocks rolled under the horse's hooves, Wade realized they wouldn't be able to travel much further on her back. She was struggling to gain traction in the snow, and their progress had now slowed to a halt. They would have to travel the rest of the way on foot.

Luckily, they were nearly at the peak. Forests, mountains, and valleys stretched endlessly in every direction they looked. Tall trees below appeared as small shrubs, and great, intimidating mountains looked like easily-traversable hills. The wind had also started to pick up, and the air was noticeably thinner. Wade could hear the girl wheezing and struggling to breathe behind him.

Wade finally dropped Quicksilver's reins and said, "This is as far as she can go. We have to walk the rest of the way to the castle."

"A...Alright," Sarah said, sliding off the back of the horse before Wade could turn around to help her. She immediately took off up the trail, coughing as she walked. But Wade could now see that something was wrong–*very* wrong. She tried to hurry, but she swayed back and forth, struggling to keep on a straight line.

"Hey, Sarah, wait up!" Wade shouted, diving into the saddlebags and bringing out a handful of rations.

He then chased after the girl, but she was moving fast and stumbling with each step.

"Sarah, just stop for a second," he said, finally reaching out an arm and grabbing her shoulder.

She spun around and revealed a horrific sight. Black tears streamed down her face, which was riddled with dark, thick veins that writhed beneath her skin like worms desperate to escape. Green blood and puss ran down her forearm and dripped into the snow.

"I can't stop, Wade. I *can't*."

"Sarah–"

"If I stop, I don't think I'll ever be able to get goin' again."

"What happened to you back there? Tell me the truth, *now.*"

"Please, Wade. We need to just keep–"

Wade grabbed her bleeding arm and pulled back the cuff of her sleeve, revealing a deep, black and green, oozing wound in her forearm. Maggots squirmed in the blood and buried themselves deeper into her flesh. For her sake, Wade didn't react to the repulsive sight. But as he stared at it, he knew exactly what it was: a bite from a Nightwalker.

Wade looked back up at her and saw more black tears running down her face.

"I'm sorry, Wade. I'm so, so sorry I let this happen."

"No, don't you say that. It's going to be alright. Let's just get you to the castle. There might be someone inside that could help. Now, come on."

Wade grabbed her hand and tried pulling the girl along, but she only made it a few steps before her legs gave out and she collapsed into the snow.

"Just hang on, Sarah!"

Wade released her hand and ran a few yards up the trail and around a bend, and standing before him, in all of its glory, was the obsidian, jagged castle sitting atop the mountain's highest point. The Blood Moon shined down upon it, calling them toward it.

"We're almost there!" Wade called out. "It's right here! Come on, Sarah, just a little bit further!"

He ran back down and kneeled next to her.

"We're right there, Sarah. We can do it–*you* can do it."

"Wade…" she coughed violently, expelling green blood from her lungs. "I told you… if I stopped, I couldn't get up again."

Wade put an arm around her and forced her to her feet.

"And I'm tellin' you that I don't give a damn. Now come on, I'm going to get you some help. Please, just keep moving, Sarah. I promise, I'm going to help you."

She tried to take another step but fell back down again. The black veins that traveled across her skin were shaking violently now; the maggots were eating her from the inside out.

"We both know what's about to happen," she said, staring up at him, her eyes almost solid black now. Then, she ran her small hand down to Thorn and firmly gripped the iron. "You know what to do, Wade. You've always known what to do."

"Sarah... *no*. I can't... I can't do that."

She nodded and said, "Yes you can. You can do it, *for me*."

Wade gritted his teeth in anguish as Sarah knelt before him, gazing out over the endless, beautiful view of Rhodahn.

"Wade? Can... Can you tell me... a story?"

Wade's fingers trembled, making their way down to Thorn.

"Sure, Sarah, I can tell ya' a story."

Sarah gripped her stomach and cried in pain; her eyes darkened until they became nothing more than empty, black voids floating on an innocent girl's face. Thorn was slowly being slid from its holster now, and Wade opened the cylinder and saw six shots sitting within.

"There once was a field outside the School," the Demon Gunner started. "It was filled with colorful roses, sunflowers, and tulips... The most beautiful–" Tears fell from his face and landed on Thorn's gold engravings. His voice was cracking now, and he fought hard to speak again.

"The most beautiful place in the world, and the only place I've ever felt safe. I used to go there when I was struggling, and I would lay out in those flowers until the sun set." He raised the gun behind her head; his hand trembled. "It would ease my racing mind and replace my fears with peace. The flowers would whisper that everything was going to be alright. Do you see them now, Sarah? Do you see the flowers? Do you hear them whispering?"

"I do, Wade, I really do. *They're beautiful.*"

His finger shook violently.

"I love you, Sarah."

"I love you too, Wade."

He pulled the trigger.

PART FOUR
THE
CASTLE

D⅁

CHAPTER TWENTY FOUR

THE CASTLE OF DARKNESS

Wade covered her body with rocks, her iron buried with her. He stood over the grave; wind rustled his jacket and the few strands of hair that hung below his hat. The girl was gone, and there was no bringing her back now. Everything she once was and stood for was now eternally resting beneath the snow. All of her thoughts, feelings, emotions, and memories reduced to *nothing*. The only thing left for the Demon Gunner now was his quest.

"Goodbye, Sarah," Wade said, before turning his back on her. "Don't wait for me, I'll see you up there."

Wade started back down the rocky path toward the castle and came around the bend once more. And there it stood, towering over him, an ancient, dark monolith of stone, with weathered walls that were as black as coal and tall spires that looked as if they were reaching out to the High Place itself. The turrets and archways were crumbling, and truthfully, it looked abandoned—as if no one had stepped foot in it in a millenia. It stood alone at the top of the mountain, and there was a singular winding path that led to it, cut through a field of dead, frozen flowers.

The castle called to Wade, much like the Soul Stealers,

begging him to enter. This time, he did not block out its song. But the second Wade stepped onto the path, Bone Eaters revealed themselves, coming out from their hiding places behind rocks and under the snow. Rose and Thorn effortlessly slipped from their holsters and hung down by his side. He pressed on toward the castle.

The Bone Eaters snapped their sharp teeth and charged him. Without breaking stride, Wade aimed his guns and lined up their faces with his beads. Both guns fired at the same time, striking their targets square between the eyes. He kept moving, firing more shots into the Bone Eaters. Above him, large towers loomed, and a massive wooden door with a heraldic, brass knocker shaped like a staff sat in the center of it.

But Wade couldn't focus on the castle any longer as the Bone Eaters continued to descend upon him. He walked toward them, unfazed, dropping them into the snow before reloading to start killing again. More bullets were fired; more Demons died.

The path before him was now clear, and Wade broke out into a full sprint. But to his left and right, more Bone Eaters appeared, crawling up the sides of the mountain and tearing through the dead field of flowers with great speed. He didn't even look behind him; he just kept firing ahead–firing and reloading, firing and reloading. He needed to make it to the castle.

A final Bone Eater leaped at him, and he jammed the blade of Thorn into its mouth before slamming it into the ground and blasting its head off. He bounded over the corpse and sprinted toward the castle again. He heard the growing horde of Bone Eaters behind him, like railcars thundering after a runaway locomotive. But the great door to the castle was now directly in front of him, and he could see the letters, *W* and *C,* embossed into the wood. He was so close now, he could almost touch them, and within them held *all* of his answers.

His guns swung wildly by his side as he ran, pumping with his arms. The door was right there, and he reached out to grab the worn, brass knocker that hung idly from it. But instead of touching it, his hand folded into an invisible barrier, followed by his body, rebounding him backward and sending him flying into the snow.

What the hell?

Wade looked behind him and saw that he was almost out of time. He spun around and fired a few rounds into the horde, causing explosions to erupt within it, before clambering to his feet and charging forward again. Wade jumped this time and collided hard with the invisible barrier, hoping to break through it, but instead, it *caught* him, rebounding him like an uncoiled spring. His body flipped to the side before slamming hard onto the ground once more.

Rose and Thorn were thrown from his hands and scattered a few feet from him. Wade quickly grabbed their chains and yanked them back, catching the iron. He again fired into the horde, but there were too many of them. He couldn't fight them all; he *had* to get through the barrier or this would be his final stand. He was so close to the castle–his answers were right there, and only the Bone Eaters stood in his way. If he were to fall, Sarah would have died for nothing.

No, I shall not fall.

Wade flipped back around and ran toward the barrier once more, but instead of jumping, he firmly pushed his shoulder into it. The barrier started to flex like melting glass, but it still didn't break or crack. He pushed even harder, boots slipping and digging into the snow, but again, it would not budge. He frantically looked around for something–*anything* to aid him in this moment.

I gave you those damn guns for a reason, boy! Ulysses shouted in his mind.

Wade looked at the blades attached to his iron. Perhaps, he could *cut* his way through. With all his might, he thrust the blades into the barrier. They sparked and hissed like hot metal being placed into a bucket of water, and slowly but surely, the blades began to pierce it, creating a small gap. Wade pushed harder, gritting his teeth while pulling the barrier apart. It began to spread open, gold sparks flying wildly past his face. But the barrier was now fighting him again, forcing itself closed.

You can do it, Sarah said to him in his mind.

Wade yelled and channeled all of his rage, pushing as hard as he possibly could, forcing the barrier back apart. Ripples of energy and light cascaded up it, and his guns started to glow bright red from the heat, like the blade of a great sword pulled from a forge.

For me, Wade. Do it for me.

In a flash, Wade launched himself forward and slipped through the gap in the barrier. It snapped shut behind him like a bear trap, singeing the edges of his hat and jacket. The spur of his boot was also caught in it, slicing it clean in half.

Mere seconds later, the Bone Eaters crashed hard into the barrier behind him and were sent flying backward, colliding with each other. Wade then collapsed face first into the dirt, as no snow had fallen there, before flipping over and staring back at the Demons. They bit and chomped at him madly but were unable to break through. They finally stumbled backward, defeated, burned, and terrified of the barrier that sat between them.

Wade breathed heavily, watching this play out before getting back to his feet and placing Rose and Thorn in their rightful homes. He spun on his heels and faced the obsidian castle once more. It had impressive, stained glass windows that faced the field of flowers, and above it, a steady beam of light shot up through the roof toward the Rift.

Wade had never been this close to it before, nor had he ever seen anything like it in all of his life. Demons endlessly poured from the Rift, and he could now see that it *wasn't* a black void, no, it was a window into an incomprehensible world of unknown horrors. He thought he saw a ring of mountains within it, but they were upside down, their peaks pointing to him. His very mind felt cold and twisted in knots just by staring at it.

Wade focused again on the castle and the large door that stood in front of him, and he wondered if getting through it would prove as difficult a challenge as the invisible barrier. But as he stepped toward it, it immediately groaned and shuddered. Wade stopped, raising his guns before him. The middle of the door split apart and began to push inward, opening itself into the castle. Wade peered in and saw that it was as dark and ominous as the exterior. He felt a cold draft of wind blow past, like a tomb of a lost king being opened for the first time in a century. Wade took a deep breath and entered the castle. He started down a long stone hallway with dusty archways overhead.

Booooom.

The doors behind him sealed shut, and Wade pressed on further, each footstep echoing throughout the immense and seemingly empty castle. It was cold and gloomy, and Wade now found himself entering a great hall with a massive arched ceiling. Portraits of hooded men and women, dressed in black robes and holding staffs of twisted oak, hung on the walls, *watching* the Demon Gunner with following eyes.

In front of him, dual staircases rose behind a silhouette of a foreboding statue. Wade approached it and lit a fire within his hand, revealing an old, bearded man holding a staff. Below a hood, Wade saw thoughtful eyes made of striking white marble, and he recognized the face instantly.

"Nor..." he whispered.

Wade then stepped closer to the statue, running his index finger across the smooth limestone, causing a thick layer of dust to accumulate on his finger tip. A terrifying thought began to fester in his mind: no one had been here in years.

Bullshit, he thought to himself.

Someone *had* to be here. He came too far to only gaze upon dusty statues and paintings of lost souls. The answers he was looking for were somewhere within these walls–all of the signs pointed to this place–and Wade would find them if it were the last thing he'd do.

But as time passed, and Wade continued to search through the castle, his fears only seemed to grow. *All* of the halls and rooms sat empty and shrouded in darkness. Wade found kitchens, dining halls, and bedrooms, all barren and desolate–not a single lit candle or corpse within them. Wade even discovered a vast and grand room filled to the brim with treasure. It held impressive weaponry, such as swords, bows, axes, and guns, along with decorative shields, gilded and ceremonial armor sets, piles of gold and jewels, ancient pottery, resplendent paintings from far away lands, and a seemingly endless wall of twisted staffs, all left abandoned and unguarded. But this sight still didn't discourage the Demon Gunner, and he continued on, up past the statue of Nor, and to the second floor of the castle.

Carefully, he crept down a long hallway with stained glass windows on either side of him. Beams of red light were refracted into the hall, casting a beautiful mosaic across the floor. Through one of the windows, he could see down to the path cut through the flower field. It seemed now that the Bone Eaters had all but dispersed from the area in search of another victim, no doubt dissatisfied that they hadn't been able to devour Wade.

Wade then kept searching, ducking into various rooms—some containing tables with unknown maps and books, and others holding jars and cauldrons of strange liquids and dead Demons, as if they were the past subjects of twisted experiments. But no matter what he found, it all looked deserted and forgotten about.

He gripped the handle of another door and pushed, but it would not budge. *Something* was blocking it from the other side. He leaned harder against it this time, digging his shoulder into it, and the object behind the door began to scrape across the ground as it was pushed backward. Wade finally burst through the door and stared face to face with a skeleton, draped in a tattered robe. Wade jumped back, aiming his weapon at it, but the skeleton didn't move. The only thing that did were the spiders that crawled within its empty eye sockets. The part of the robe that covered its stomach was torn open, as if something had *bursted* through it.

Wade looked up and saw a hole dug out through the ceiling. He then noticed that it was a bookshelf that had blocked the door, realizing that this person had barricaded themselves in the room, attempting to prevent anything or anyone from getting in or out. He shook his head and continued down the hall, but then he saw *another* robed figure laying sprawled out across the floor. He approached it and knelt down next to it, flipping the corpse over with the tip of Thorn's blade. The skeleton seemed to be missing its lower jaw, and its spine was shattered and reduced to a pile of dust. Its former staff also lay a few feet away, snapped in half. A gaping hole was punched through the ceiling above the skeleton, with broken planks of wood scattered below it.

Wade continued on and found a locked, red door at the end of the hallway. He stepped back, aimed Thorn, and shot through its lock. Wade raised a leg and kicked it open, revealing a room with a massive domed ceiling and a glass sky light that beamed down red light. A large, circular wooden table sat in the center, surrounded on all sides by dozens of chairs. Then, Wade saw the skeletons that were scattered throughout the room. Some lay bent over the table, others still sitting in their chairs with their heads hung over the backs. A few were collapsed face down on the floor, and another hung by a rope from a chandelier above a grand fireplace.

The Demon Gunner stared in disbelief at the gruesome sight that lay before him, and then he spotted a single piece of paper sitting on the edge of the table. He inched toward it and picked it up before reading:

To any who may find this,

The light of the world has gone out, and Rhodahn will soon be consumed. We cannot stop the Darkness now, nor can we watch what is coming next. Perhaps we shall see the light again in the next life.

Ashan Davar, Convictionist of the First Rank

Wade inspected the note before flipping it over, but he found nothing written on the back. He read it again and again, hoping there was *something* that he had missed within it, but saw only the three lines of despair. And that was it–there was nothing else–no answers left behind. The light was gone, and Rhodahn would be consumed, and as was said in the note, whoever had once sat around this table took the easy way out, as they could not bear to see what was coming next–whatever that was.

We cannot stop the Darkness now.

Wade had traveled this far–brought *the girl* this far, only to find nothing. This journey was for nothing, the pain was for nothing, and her death was for *nothing*. An immense feeling of rage washed over him. He yelled as he brought both flame covered fists down onto the table, sending a crack through the middle of it. With a loud groan, it split in two and crashed to the floor. He breathed heavily, staring at the destruction before him.

What was there to do now?

"I quite liked that table," a voice called out from behind him. "It was no easy feat getting it up this mountain, you know?"

Wade spun around and fired Rose and Thorn. The

Hellfire struck its target with perfect accuracy, only to bounce off an invisible barrier and ricochet into the stone walls. Standing before him was an old man, draped in the same robes that all the other skeletons in the room wore. He had a long gray beard–longer than Nor's–and it nearly reached his feet. His back was severely hunched, and his skin was as wrinkled as a well-worn leather saddle. His eyes also shared the same eerie whiteness as Nor's, but they did not glow.

"Do you Gunners always shoot those who try to talk to you?" the robed figure asked with a chuckle.

"Who the hell are you?"

The man smiled and said, "How about we have a chat?"

CHAPTER TWENTY FIVE
THE WIZARD'S TRUTH

This way," the man said nonchalantly, starting across the room and passing in front of Wade without even a glance in his direction.

An oak staff, twisted around itself like a withered vine, was gripped in his left hand, aiding his hobbled gait. Wade stood there, unmoving, watching this painful sight. Finally, the old, robed man reached a stone wall on the opposite end of the room. He tapped the wall with his staff and pushed inward, creating one sunken stone among the others. The wall shuddered and began to slide sideways, sending a loud scraping noise echoing throughout the room. A small doorway had now appeared in the wall, and the man looked back at Wade with surprise, as if wondering why he wasn't following.

"Are you not coming?" the man asked. "If you seek answers, then this is where you shall find them."

Wade didn't know if the man was planning to kill him, or actually give him knowledge, but at this point, he didn't care. Wade had nothing to lose, and it was a risk he was willing to take. Wade slid his revolvers into their holsters and started off toward the doorway. The man smiled and directed him through it by pointing with the end of his staff. Once inside the wall, Wade saw a spiral staircase ascending up the middle of a tall stone tower.

Wade looked back at the man who bowed and said, "After you. As you can see, it will take me a minute."

Wade started up the staircase; the spurs of his boots echoing throughout the tower with each step. The staircase was incredibly long, and Wade's mind raced, wondering what he'd find at the top of it, and when he looked down the middle of the spiral, his stomach turned.

Below him, he heard the distant hobbling of the old man, grunting, panting, and even humming a tune as he went. Wade made sure to stay leaned to his right, running his hand along the wall until he finally reached the last step, which led into a small, circular room lined with tall bookshelves. And to Wade's horror, he saw that the roof had been blown open, leading directly to the outside world, where a multicolored beam of light blasted straight into the Rift.

Wade looked back down and noticed two windows and a door leading to a balcony that divided the shelves into three distinct sections. In the center of the room sat two leather chairs with tall backs, and next to them were two wide-bowl wine glasses and a bottle of an unknown liquid.

Then, Wade saw *it:* a perfectly round glass orb that glowed and flashed, as if lightning and thunder were contained within it. Wade stepped closer, bringing his face right up to the smooth surface of the transparent orb. His hand rose from his side, fingertips almost touching it…

"I wouldn't do that if I were you," the man said from behind him, struggling to catch his breath after finally clearing the last step, "unless you want to see the death, destruction, and suffering of thousands of Rhodahnians across this land."

Wade looked at the man with confusion; his hand slowly lowering to his side again. Then, the robed man stumbled toward one of the chairs and plopped himself down in it. A great sigh of relief followed.

"It never gets easier, those damn stairs," he said, looking up at Wade before flashing his eyes downward toward the other chair. "Please, take a seat... Wally? Wilson? W—"

"*Wade*," he interrupted.

"I knew it was something with a *W!* And I would've gotten there eventually without your help, thank you very much. My memory might not be what it once was, but I'm still kicking." He reached for the bottle next to him. "Wine? I know you've traveled far."

"How do you know me?"

"Nevermind that," the man said while pouring himself a glass. "That's the easy part." He then went to fill Wade's, but Wade held up a hand, refusing it. "Not a drinker? That's surprising for a cowboy like you."

Wade stared at the old man with acute interest. If the wine was poisoned, he would not be getting out of this alive, but then again, why did he care to?

Wade finally lowered his hand and nodded, signaling for a glass of his own.

"Ah, you know, I almost forgot about what happened earlier. I'm sorry that you had to go through that, but don't worry, this *isn't* laced. If I wanted you dead, you would already be."

He finished pouring Wade a glass before setting down the bottle and sweeping his own up into his hand. He raised the glass, as if inviting Wade to clink his.

"Cheers," the old man said. "To a long, and *hopefully,* worthwhile journey."

Wade brought his glass forward and cheered the man before taking a long sip, drinking more than half of it in one gulp.

"Good, isn't it?" he said. "It has been aging in the cellar under this castle for over one hundred years. I just needed a special occasion to finally bring it out, so *thank you.*"

Wade wiped his mouth on the sleeve of his jacket and brought the glass back down to the table.

"Now, I know why you're here: you want answers. Huh, don't we all? So, Wade, where would you like to start first?"

He mulled over all of the questions in his mind. He had been waiting for this moment since his quest began long ago, and now that it was here, he didn't even know where to begin. He focused, trying to think of the best way to approach this, while the man before him stared at him inquisitively.

"Thinking things over, are you?" he said with a smile. "Fret not, for there is no wrong question to ask—only the first."

"How about we start with who the hell you are?"

The old man smiled.

"Good question, good question…" He brought his fingertips together in the shape of a triangle. "My name is Theus."

"Theus?"

He nodded and said, "I am a Convictionist, or a *wizard*— as some might say—but I suspect you already know that. Much as you come from the way of the gun and bullets, I come from the way of the staff and Conviction. The others you saw down there were my brothers and sisters, Convictionists of the First Rank. They looked up to me… They *trusted* me…"

"How did you know I'm a Gunner?"

"With that beautiful iron that sits on your waist, it was easy to guess. And let me tell you, I've never seen anything quite like it before," the wizard said, before pointing toward the smooth ball of lightning. "But besides that obvious clue, *this* has shown me many things about you while on your journey."

"What is it?"

"It is what we call a focal point—the same thing as the staffs we carry to channel our Conviction. We found it in a cave off the coast of Candor, covered in mud, nearly lost to time. While on a quest of our own, we had detected its high magical presence, but we could have never predicted what it was going to give us."

"And what was that?"

"*Insight*–knowledge, Wade. That little ball right there allows us to see the lives of every living person in Rhodahn."

"And that's how you know me? You watched me through that thing?"

"Precisely. I have listened to your conversations, heard your stories, and seen your most precious moments leading up to this one. And here we finally are, sitting *face to face*."

"So you knew I was coming here."

Theus signaled to Wade's glass of wine and said, "That was waiting for you, wasn't it?"

"Then you know *why* I'm here."

The wizard nodded and said, "No wonder you made it this far. You're smart, unlike the others."

"There were others?"

"*Many,* all in the same trivial pursuit as you."

"What happened to them?"

"They all died on their journey here. I watched it happen.

Most never even leave the desert."

"Gunners?"

Theus nodded and said, "Some—at least what is left of them—and they were *bad* ones at that. Others were knights from far away lands, perhaps a few rogue and pathetic wizards as well. 'Heroes' as I like to call them, all thinking they would be the one to save the world, only to die in the sand at the hands of the Demons. But it wasn't until *you* were selected that things changed. I know not how, but I could tell you were special. Whoever he was, he did a mighty fine job of choosing you to carry the fire."

"I... was *selected?* What in the hell are you talking about?"

Mid gulp of wine, Theus stopped and looked at Wade with confusion.

"Oh, you don't know, do you?"

"Know what?" Wade said, gripping tighter on the leather banisters that hugged his thighs.

"Have you ever looked at your right arm?"

Wade glanced down at his arm and rolled up his sleeve, revealing the letters *DG* branded onto his skin.

"I've had this my whole life."

"Have you now? Then what does it mean?"

"It's..." Wade stared at the branding once more, sure he had the answer to the wizard's question, but the longer he looked, he realized his mind was blank. He didn't know what it stood for—not even a guess.

"They've all had that—every last one of them. *Demon Gunners,* chosen for some grand mission, one which I cannot see. It's easy to find them, wandering alone across a cold and desolate desert. Their goal—the coveted castle on the mountain where they shall finally find their answers!" Theus said with a deep laugh while shaking his head.

"I don't know who is responsible for this, but it's pathetic, desperate, and uncalculated, like firing off shots in the dark. Now, why do these oafs try to come here? I do not know, nor do I really care. But you're here now, right? You made it! *Terrific,* but I hate to tell you that you're nothing special. You're just a cog in a wheel that someone else is spinning. So tell me, Demon Gunner, why *did* you come here?"

"Answers…"

"And when did you first have that thought?"

"In the desert. That is why I started this quest."

"Did you ever have that thought *before* the desert? How did you even know to travel this way?"

"The Veil, I went in the direction it grew from."

"Perhaps that is what you told yourself, but you always knew, didn't you? How did you even get to the desert from Gadriel? That is quite a perilous journey to do alone, if you ask me. Now, on your quest, if someone had pointed you in another direction, would you have listened to them? No, of course not. Your conviction was stronger than anything and anyone—no one could've swayed you, not even those you loved. You *had* to complete your mission. And the mission… What a funny little thing that is. Your mission, your goal—it was planted inside your mind like a seed, Wade. You were a tool—a *pawn* in someone else's game, you just didn't know it."

"You're lying," Wade said, gripping his seat even tighter.

"Am I? Think, Wade! For the first time in your life, use your brain and think! Where were you before the desert?"

"I…" Wade stared dumbfounded, as thoughts and memories began to flood his mind. His last nightmare in the trenches—the war against the Kutarian Knights—the fall of Gadriel—wasn't just any memory, it was his *last.* Wade reached down and felt the scar on his abdomen. "I was stabbed."

The wizard smiled and said, "Aha! Now you're thinking!" He guzzled his wine and hastily poured another glass. "I'm learning things here too. I always wondered where you were selected from, and I have finally figured it out. You were selected from the grave, Wade, and the best part is, you're not even alive right now."

Wade shot up from his seat, drawing his guns.

"Sit back down and put those away!" Theus demanded with a look of disgust. "Is that your first instinct every god damn time? You came here for answers, and now you want to kill the man who is giving them to you? *Pitiful.* I thought you were better than this, Wade, since you're the only one who has ever made it this far, but now I see why you were chosen. You're just another grunt with a gun, designed for one thing…"

"Shut the hell up."

"How dare you speak to me in such a way. If I wanted it, I could turn your skin inside out while I sodomize you. I could pull your eyeballs from their sockets and dip them in boiling water while you looked through them. I could submit you to every conceivable and painful torture method that has ever existed without even lifting a finger, and you say something like that to me? For the first time in your pathetic life, Wade, I am telling you the truth!"

The guns in Wade's hands shook violently.

"Now, sit back down, you undead swine, unless you are finished with your questions, and if that is the case, then I will have no choice but to erase you from existence as your work here is *done.*"

Wade's guns slowly lowered. His bullets would be

ineffective, but what was the point of killing the man? He *was* getting his answers, just as he always wanted. Finally, Wade holstered his iron and sat back down in his seat.

"That's better," the wizard said, smiling.

"I'm… *dead?*"

"It would appear so."

"How… How is this possible?"

The wizard extended his staff toward Wade, as if pointing at his heart.

"I can feel it–something *powerful* sits inside of you, but I know not what. Its very existence defies our reality, and its power is one that is not from this world, such that only a god could deliver."

Wade looked up at him with wide eyes.

"Nor…" Wade said, causing the wizard to burst out laughing.

"Nor?" the wizard responded. "Do you really believe Nor exists?"

"Of course, I met him."

"Don't be so daft, Wade. While you were dead and buried six feet underground, tell me, what do you remember? Darkness? Was it cold? Or were you in the High Place, flying through the clouds dressed in white robes with wings on your back, living in harmony with all the people you hated during your pitiful existence that was spent fighting in meaningless wars? Tell me, what did you see when you died?"

Wade thought back to the time before the desert–the war, when he was stabbed. He saw *nothing.*

"I can see it on your face, and you know it to be the truth. There's *nothing* after this. There has always been nothing and there will always be nothing beyond this world. Just as it was before you were born, when millions of years passed without your knowledge, it will be that same way after you die again. This present moment–sitting here, drinking this wine and talking–*this* is all we have. No gods will save us, Wade, we must save ourselves! My brothers and sisters who sit dead below us must've only realized that after they foolishly took their own lives. Or maybe they never did, which makes their deaths even more vain. Their thoughts, feelings, memories–their very *existence* has now vanished into nothingness, and that is precisely why I haven't joined them before I'm forced to. Because what is the rush? Nothing awaits us after this, so why race toward the darkness? I don't know how long you'll be kept alive for, but I know that you cannot live forever. No one can. Whatever is inside you that is keeping you alive– that little blue flame–it *will* burn out and fade away, just like everything else. I assume whatever it is and where it came from, is connected to your quest in some way, even if you don't know it yet. Which brings me to your biggest question of them all–"

"*The Rift.*"

"Yes," the wizard said, tapping the side of his head with his finger. "I like that name. The Rift... The Rift... The Rift... It was actually my doing, believe it or not."

Wade sat frozen, staring at the man.

"What did you just say?" Wade asked.

"Yes, *I* brought the Darkness upon this world, and I will be the first to admit it."

Wade sat speechless, unable to muster a single word. His nails dug into the leather, and his knuckles turned white from pressure.

"*You...* You did this? Why?"

"It was an accident, really. Just as you and whoever you serve search for answers, I searched for my own. I was aware from an early age of the nothingness that awaits us after this. It haunted me–kept me up at night and terrorized me all my life. The thought of disappearing from this existence for eternity was perhaps the scariest thought of all. It was actually what originally got me on the path of Dark Conviction, as some would call it. My thirst for immortality was insatiable, leading me to form the sacred Coven of Convictionists. It was all we studied–focused on–channeling our collective knowledge, power, and abilities to find a way to live forever. We read every book and every scroll in our vast library, scoured the world for every magical item we could find, tried every spell, every jinx, every curse… we tried *everything*, and guess what it all led to?"

"Nothing…"

"NOTHING!" the wizard shouted, slamming down his fist on the leather bannister. "WE FOUND NOTHING, WADE! We could prolong it, but not without destroying ourselves or going mad in the process. We could extend our days momentarily, tricking our bodies into thinking we were healthier than we actually were, but nothing ever worked that truly allowed us to live forever and beat death. We could turn water into wine, cure illness, heal wounds, fly through the sky, and make gold from dirt, but to live forever–the answer to avoiding the *nothingness* that awaited us, that was the one thing that Conviction could never solve. The problem couldn't be cracked, as death seemed unavoidable and came for us all the same. That was *until* we found something deep within a sealed, underground tomb. It was a cave littered with corpses of those who had tried to access what it protected.

"In the center of the tomb sat a circle and star with candles on every point. Within it held our answer: the *key* to immortality. It was a dusty, old book, but not from this world. How it got here, we do not know, but it talked about a realm much different than ours–a realm of magical items and beings of unfathomable power that was right in front of us at all times, unable to be seen or accessed, divided by realities. The book talked of immortality and how to achieve it, and all we needed to do was get to that realm. I convinced the others of the Coven to help me tear through our reality and enter a new one, promising them eternal life. Through Dark Conviction, we opened the Rift."

The wizard raised his staff and pointed to the blown open ceiling with the beam of light shooting straight through it. And for a moment, he just stared, looking into the demonic world with bright but fearful eyes.

"And there it was, another realm that had been locked away and hidden from this world. And for good reason, as we thought it contained the power we so desperately sought, but instead, it brought into Rhodahn vile and terrifying Demons–designed to kill, torture, and *consume* other forms of life at all costs. You see, Wade, the book didn't hold the key to immortality like we thought, no, it delivered death upon this world instead, punishing us for attempting to beat fate. And perhaps it was a vengeful god who did it, teaching us a lesson for messing with things we didn't understand. Or, perhaps it was death himself who wrote the book and prevented us from ending his true purpose. And let me tell you, Wade, *no one* wants to live without purpose, not even the Grim Reaper himself. Regardless, we walked right into a trap and opened the

Rift, and the light and life of this world was sucked out, our hopes and dreams with it. In our attempt to live forever, we assured an early death for Rhodahn and all of those who lived within it."

"Alright, I've heard enough. You opened the Rift, great, so tell me, how do we now close it? How do we stop it from consuming anymore of Rhodahn before it's too late?" Wade asked, sitting forward anxiously in his seat.

The wizard stared at him, as if he were about to utter something profound—give him the answer he so desperately seeked—but then, his quizzical look changed to a devilish smile. Theus started to laugh, slowly at first, then growing louder and louder until it was filling the room and making the Demon Gunner incredibly uncomfortable.

"Close it?" The wizard shouted. "As if it were a door? Grab the knob and swing it shut? HA! Of course not! What's done is done, Wade! There is no closing it now!"

"HOW DO YOU KNOW!"

"BECAUSE I TRIED!" the wizard yelled, leaning forward.

Wade wanted to yell back, but stopped himself, retreating further into his chair.

"Just as we tried everything to open it, we tried everything to *close* it! Just look beneath your feet."

The wizard's staff began to glow, and the carpet beneath them shuddered and slid away, slamming against the wall and revealing a burn mark shaped like a book, seared into the floorboards.

"We destroyed it, but the beam and the Rift remain, as if something or someone *else* is keeping it open. The bell cannot be unrung, Wade. The Demons that have entered this world are here to stay, and there is nothing you, nor me, nor anyone else can do to stop it! This world is now theirs, and that is why my brothers and sisters left me here alone. They knew what was coming, so, they saw no point in carrying on with the guilt of knowing they destroyed Rhodahn forever. Some even tried to fight back—you saw one of my fallen brothers in the valley on your journey here—but they all lost their lives and changed nothing. I hope their sacrifice gave them peace in their final moments, but for the rest... they just couldn't bear the weight any longer. Poison made that pain go away. And I commend them, as it must not have been easy, but *I* on the other hand share no such guilt."

"What? You don't feel anything for what you did?"

"*No.* In our pursuit of what we want the most lies the very thing that can destroy us. Our greatest fear hides in the shadow of our greatest dream. It waits to reveal itself for the moment that can cause the most pain—the most suffering. The path of salvation and damnation looks the same to the determined man, as he cannot see which is which. I—of course—was tricked, set up, and punished *greatly* for it. Who got the best of me? I do not know." He grabbed the bottle of wine and began to pour the last drops from it. "Lesson—" The bottle was now fully upright. "*Learned.*"

Wade felt rage building inside of him; his hands began to warm, slightly burning the leather.

"That's one of my favorite chairs, you know? Please don't—"

"Lesson *learned?*" Wade interrupted, staring at the shadow of the cursed book on the floor. "That's all you have to say?"

But now the wizard wasn't listening, instead, he was

solely focused on downing his glass of wine. When he finished, he wiped his lips, tossed the glass behind him, and faced Wade once more.

"Now, is there anything else you wish to know? If not, then that means your quest has come to an unfortunate end and it is time for me to rest for the evening. I am awfully tired and–"

"Rhodahn is being consumed... Everything I've ever known and loved will soon be destroyed, and that is all you have to say to me?"

"What else is there to say, Wade? I already told you, there is no turning back the clock now. All we can do is wait for the inevitable to befall us. Now, are you going to finish your wine or may I drink it? I would rather not let it go to waste."

"Go ahead, enjoy it."

The wizard swept it up and began to drink it, as Wade's hand slowly slid down to his side, unseen.

"Sarah, you knew her, right?"

"Oh, that annoying, whining girl? She got closer than I expected, but, thank Nor–as you say–that she didn't make it here. We would've never gotten her to shut up! Could you imagine all of the questions she would've pestered me with? We would've been here all night!"

Wade gritted his teeth, nearly cracking them.

"*I loved her*... and she died trying to get here–trying to fix the world you destroyed."

"Well sometimes in life we don't always get what we want, do we!" the wizard yelled, throwing the glass and shattering it on the floor. "Sometimes we have to live with the consequences of our actions when things don't go our way! I was trying to save the world from an eternity of NOTHING!" He shot up, sending his chair flying backward and slamming the foot of his staff onto the ground before pointing the glowing tip at Wade. "If anything, you should be thanking me for my efforts! But now that I think about it, I was wrong from the beginning. This world is full of lost, misguided, and delusional fools like yourself, that cannot see the good that those with power are attempting to deliver! Maybe we needed this cleanse–a fresh start to rid the world of ungrateful, sinful heathens like YOU! Maybe I am the Devil, and maybe I have told you what you truly needed to hear, not what you wanted! MAYBE THIS WORLD DESERVED TO BURN IN–"

BANG!

"He–" Theus muttered, as blood slowly started to drip from his mouth. "*Hell...*"

Wade stood with Thorn outstretched before him, the tip of its blade pierced through the wizard's transparent shield. The barrel of the gun smoked, and Theus looked down and saw a gaping hole in his stomach that gushed blood onto his black robes.

"That was for the girl," Wade whispered. "You don't deserve to live while she lays buried in the snow. Now, enjoy nothing."

Wade pumped two more shots into him, before pulling the gun back out of the shield.

The wizard, with his mouth hanging open, blinked twice and said, "I see... *nothing.*"

His staff dropped, his shield fell, and smoke rose to the ceiling, before he collapsed face first onto the seared outline of the book. A pool of blood slowly formed around him. Wade stood over his corpse, holding his smoking gun in his right hand. His mind raced, and his body felt numb. He looked at Thorn and then at the *DG* branded on his forearm, before stumbling backward slightly. He barely managed to keep himself from falling over by grabbing the back of the chair and steadying himself.

Where am I? The castle on the mountain. But why am I here? The mission… The quest... Yes, I remember it now. It is time to close the Rift. There had to be an answer somewhere in this room. Why else would the wizard bring me here?

Wade would find the answer, close the Rift, and bring the light back. That was what he would do. Perhaps the answer sat behind the door in front of him?

He stepped over the wizard's bleeding corpse and grabbed the brass knob of the door. He then pulled it open, and a powerful gust of wind blew past him, nearly sending his hat flying off his head. Wade secured it and stepped onto a balcony overlooking an endless valley of mountains covered in the Darkness. Wade then followed the beam of light upward toward the Rift, and watched as it endlessly poured Demons into his world. He looked back over his shoulder at the body on the floor, and in that moment, he realized he was truly alone.

His journey, his quest–it had all led to *nothing*. He was now no closer than he had been in the desert to finding the answers he needed to seal the Rift. Sarah's death, everything they had been through, the torture he subjected her to–it was all for *nothing*. Wade dropped Thorn in defeat and let the iron dangle pathetically by its chain. He placed his back against a cold, stone wall and slid down onto the ground.

The Blood Moon shone down upon him like a judgemental eye in the sky–the only witness to his failure– and Wade watched as the Darkness grew further.

THE END

DG

AFTERWORD

And that concludes my first ever horror novel, *The Demon Gunner: The Darkness Grows Within.* I really enjoyed writing this, and I hope you enjoyed reading it.

After publishing the first book in The Gidorian Saga in June of 2024, I received lots of helpful feedback. It seemed that the graphic and gory scenes, along with the vivid imagery and action, really resonated with a lot of readers. One of them told me that I should try and write a horror novel next. I had never stepped into that world before, and truthfully, I am only a fan of a few great horror movies such as Hereditary, The Thing, and Alien, but nevertheless, I decided to go for it and give it my best effort. Twenty four days later, I had my first horror novel.

When I first started writing this book, I really had no idea where it was going or where it would end. Almost all of the ideas for this came to me while I was creating it, and the story began to reveal itself in ways I had never even imagined. At times, I reached points where I felt like I wouldn't be able to continue and that I should just give up, but I always make a promise to myself that if I start a book, I *will* finish it. So, through some way or another, I kept finding ways to keep pushing forward with this story. And all in all, I'm very happy I finished it, as I have fallen in love with it and can't wait to explore more of Rhodahn and the characters and monsters within it. This was easily the most fun I've ever had while writing a book.

But believe it or not, the initial conception for this story was very strange and unexpected. I've always been intrigued with gunslingers, cowboys, and westerns, and after reading *The Gunslinger* and *Blood Meridian,* which are two of my favorite novels, I knew that I wanted to write a western next, I just didn't have the idea yet. Then, a few days after publishing *The Golden Academy,* it finally came to me when I visited my best friend Foster in New York City. We went to the Met museum, and within a glass case sat these beautiful revolvers adorned in gold and silver. While staring at them, the first idea for this novel appeared in my imagination. I saw a gunslinger receiving those very same revolvers in some type of ritual, before being sent out alone across an unknown world. That original idea then blossomed into a much bigger one that involved darkness, demons, and *a lot* of blood, which ultimately created my first horror novel.

A lot of the ideas for this book were fleshed out during my first and second rewrites, and I'm very happy with where this story went and how it ultimately ended. I think there is a lot of room for future novels in this universe. I'm sorry if that was not the ending you were expecting or hoping for, but it *is* a tragic, nihilistic horror novel after all. But the good news is, this story is *not* over yet, so stay tuned.

I will say that writing in the horror genre was very difficult, and I definitely learned a lot along the way, but I still have much more to learn, and I hope to expand my horror knowledge in the future. I will be reading and watching more horror to continue immersing myself in this wonderful and thought provoking genre. I can promise that this will not be my last horror novel that I write, and I hope the wait for the next installment of *The Demon Gunner* series isn't too long.

Luckily, while editing this, new ideas have already begun racing through my mind. The second and third books are slowly coming to me piece by piece, and yes, I already have the ending planned out. I even wrote down the final sentence, but of course, I can't show you that yet. Do I have the *entire* story perfectly plotted already? No, but when is that ever the case with my novels? To me, that is the ultimate joy of writing: discovering the story along the way. All it will take is for me to sit down and start the next book, and the rest will come, just as it *always* has.

If this book can be anything, I want it to stand as proof that the "sit down and write" philosophy that I preach can work for you too. Sometimes, all you need to do is sit down and write, and the rest will come together eventually.

Now it's time for me to get back to work on what is coming next. Thank you all for joining me on this journey so far, and I will see you wherever the winds of creativity take us, whether it be on Gidoria or Rhodahn, more stories are sure to come if you just stick around.

—Eric Bowden,
AUGUST 20TH, 2025

THE DARKNESS GROWS WITHIN

www.ingramcontent.com/pod-product-compliance
Lightning Source LLC
Chambersburg PA
CBHW020942260626
47169CB00006B/1785